Things to Make and Mend

Ruth Thomas is an acclaimed short-story writer. Her first collection, *Sea Monster Tattoo*, was shortlisted for the John Llewelyn Rhys Award and the Saltire First Book Award in 1998. *The Dance Settee* won a Scottish Arts Council Award in 2000. Her stories have been read on Radio 3 and 4 and she is a regular guest at the Edinburgh Book Festival.

Further praise for *Things to Make and Mend*:

'Skilled, subtle and shaded . . . [with] characterisation so quietly complete that the reader can easily imagine Rowena and Sally at all stages of their lives from young schoolgirls to middle-aged mothers.' *Scotsman*

'Rich and brilliantly funny.' *In Style UK*

'An unpretentious tale whose power lies in the author's empathy, observation and painstaking artistry.' *TLS*

'Alive with the details and disappointments of life.' *Scotland on Sunday*

'A delicate yet sturdy tale of trapped adolescence, nostalgia and acceptance.' *Guardian*

RUTH THOMAS

Things to Make and Mend

ff

faber and faber

First published in 2007
by Faber and Faber Limited
3 Queen Square London WC1N 3AU
This paperback edition first published in 2008

Typeset by Faber and Faber Limited
Printed in the UK by CPI Bookmarque, Croydon, CR0 4TD

A CIP record for this book
is available from the British Library

ISBN 978-0-571-23060-0

2 4 6 8 10 9 7 5 3 1

For my sister Ann

. . . and then, while she threaded her darning-needle with
the right worsted,
she would fish about in her memory for a tale to fit the hole.

Eleanor Farjeon, *The Old Nurse's Stocking Basket*

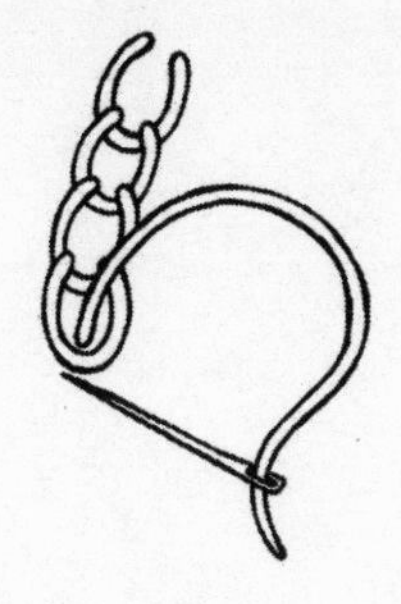

Here are some of the things you might make:

Tray cloth
Handkerchief
Curtains for a puppet theatre
Belt
Hairband

It is best to use:

Firm material
Largish needles
Embroidery silk or cotton

The Brownie Guide Handbook, 1968

Hem

Sally Tuttle loves haberdashery departments.

Sometimes she will walk into one just to gaze at its beauty: at the ribbons and feathers, the broderie anglaise, the stacked rainbows of silk and cotton. It is like admiring a mountain or a still lake. Sally stands and regards the rows of threads, the baby wools, the beads, the sequins, the poppers, the cloth-covered buttons. She is soothed by the stiff, wicker dummies modelling their cardigans; the wide strips of satin, the magazines with their racy titles (*Creative Cloth! Stitching Today! Cross-Stitch!*). She even admires the word *Haberdashery*, printed on the swinging sign above her head. *Haberdashery*, with its hints of the Middle East and of the village hall.

There is also the fact that you hardly ever see a man in there. Haberdashery departments are havens; convents dedicated to the Patron Saint of Quiet Women. She walks into them to kneel at the altar of stranded cottons.

Most nights at the moment Sally has a curious dream about haberdashery. Her latest one involved a vicar sitting on a three-legged stool, eating peanut-butter sandwiches and stitching together a patchwork quilt. When Sally – her hovering dream-self – looked more closely at the pieces of cloth, she realised they were all her old school badges. The vicar had a huge pile of them beside his sandwiches: grey flannel badges bearing the picture of an owl and the motto *patione et consilis*. Patience and judgement. *What was that all about?* Sally wondered when she woke up.

She once went to see a counsellor who talked about the value of dream analysis.

'Dreaming about water, for instance,' said the counsellor, 'can signify something to do with your relationship with your children.'

'Not something like dodgy plumbing?' Sally asked. 'Or a burst water main outside your house?'

(This had in fact been the case at the time – their street had been awash for two whole days, like a fast-flowing river. At night the rippling sound was calming, taking her mind off things.)

The counsellor looked at Sally. She had big, eye-magnifying glasses.

'No,' she said sternly. 'It is often nothing to do with actual' – she paused – 'watery events. How are you getting on with your daughter?'

'Fine.'

'And your parents?'

'Fine.'

'How about, erm . . .' She looked at her notes.

'Yes, fine thanks,' Sally said.

Dream analysis has always seemed a bit airy-fairy to Sally. As does counselling. She has no patience with it. She only saw the counsellor (a Mrs Bonniface) three times before saying, 'I'm sorry, I just don't think this is for me.' Looking relieved, Mrs Bonniface said, 'You have to be ready, Sally. You are obviously not ready.'

'No,' Sally replied, picking up her bag, the one with far too many straps and buckles, and heading for the liberating rectangle of the doorway. 'But thank you very much,' she said. She felt as if she had failed an exam.

She wishes she could be one of those people who embrace things. But even though she likes the floating styles and pensive music of the Seventies, even though she is, she hopes, a gentle child of the Sixties, she is impatient with anything New-Agey, crystallish, alternative. It must be her upbringing – her practical, pragmatic parents with their routines and their slippers and their slices of sponge cake. She was picked up from that life, though, and dropped into another. That is the problem. It causes confusion. So she puts her trust in tangible things, material things, things that connect to other things. She likes her cat-shaped keyring fob, her lined curtains, her folksy wooden bookends, her crocheted, beaded doilies. They make her feel safe. In any case, her own vagueness, her 'gossamer-light hold on reality' (to which one of the men in her life once alluded) does not need further encouragement. Maybe that is why she became a needlewoman. There is nothing more tangible than threads sewn through cloth. She is happiest with something that is stitched down, not given the chance to slip or unravel or change.

The clothing-alterations shop where she works is called *In Stitches*. She has been there for eleven years. On difficult days it is a solace, requiring just enough concentration to take her mind off things, but leaving her daydreaming space. At other times it can be tedious, tedious, as she sits at her work-table surrounded by boxes of pins and name-tapes to sew into the collars of some unknown schoolchild.

Occasionally it is a source of amusement to others. ('*In Stitches* as in *had me in stitches*?' asked Graham, a man Sally was seeing recently – an estate agent from Hither Green. 'Can I have you in stitches?' he had asked clumsily – they were sitting in a dark cinema at the time, on their second date. 'No,' Sally hissed back, failing to achieve an intended tone of high spirits, clenching her ticket in her right hand. Neither of them had been any good at innuendo.)

Most people would have left In Stitches straight away if, like Sally, they'd suddenly been awarded a large amount of money.

But Sally hasn't. Sewing is a job she can do. It will still be there when she has spent the money. She is in fact a little scared of leaving. In Stitches is a comfort in her life, despite being a poky little shop located down a side street in East Grinstead, between a car-display showroom and a dog-grooming parlour. ('A thorn between roses,' Sally's mother calls it.) It is owned by a man called Clive Brayne, who is hardly ever there, and is worked in by three women, Sue, Linda and Sally, who seem to be there all the time. Over the years they have developed their own *specialities*: Sue works on trouser legs, Linda takes in side seams and Sally re-stitches broken hemlines. The shop is busiest at lunchtimes, just when they are tiring and need a break themselves. The over-locker invariably locks. It is always too hot, 'Evil Edna' the steam-iron creating a kind of jungly atmosphere which they try to counter by wedging the front door open with a needle case, allowing the cold winds of East Grinstead to blow in. By one-thirty they find themselves confronting a pile of broken-down clothes, their stitches burst and buttons lost. And Sue, Linda and Sally have to mend them within an hour. The shop has established itself upon its one-hour alterations service. They stitch against the clock, the silence broken every so often by the swearing that accompanies a stabbed finger. Sue and Linda and Sally. They have become friends in the detached but intense way of put-upon work colleagues. They love each other in a sense, and also know that any day one of them could leave and never return. *I'm out of here, girls*, and away one of them will go, into her future. But who is it to be? Meanwhile, they share each other's submarine rolls and talk about their husbands, exes, children, parents. They would never dream of inviting each other home. They went carol-singing together once, for charity: they called themselves The Needlepoint Sisters and traipsed around in the snow outside other people's homes. They had all had a hard autumn and early winter, culminating in this: three grown women shuffling around in the cold, ringing doorbells, singing 'We Three Kings', 'Good King Wenceslas' and 'Ding Dong Merrily on High'. Sally shook the collection box, Linda held the torch, Sue started off the singing. They harangued the suburbs. Sometimes, people's living-room lights would be on but no one would come to the door.

'Isn't it funny,' Sally said to Sue the other day, 'the way you suddenly realise you're not twenty-eight any more?'

Sue looked at her. 'I realised I wasn't twenty-eight a long time ago.'

'Yes,' Sally said, 'but you don't notice it catching up on you, do you? Age. You just think you're in your late twenties for years, and then suddenly you're not. You're in your forties. And the father of your child's nearly fifty! And people start calling you madam. And you never get whistled at by builders any more . . .'

Sue stilled her work – a floral skirt – in her lap.

' . . . and you think,' Sally continued, 'why have I got these lines on my forehead? And where have all these white hairs come from? I didn't know I had all these white hairs.'

'Sally's having a midlife crisis,' Sue yelled to Linda, who was taking in an enormous pair of trousers at the back of the shop.

'Been there, done that, got the postcard,' Linda shouted back, pins in her mouth. 'Except people never call me madam.'

'And you're halfway down the ages in those tick-the-box questionnaires,' Sally said. But now she was thinking, *Stop it, stop it, stop talking*. She really had been worried, lately, about her life. She laughed, rearranging her position on her locked swivel chair. 'It's just funny,' she said.

And she shut up.

Sue hung on to her hemming. Then she leaned forward to pat Sally on the knee. She smiled, her lips warm and lipsticked. She said 'You've still got to get on with it though, haven't you?'

She is a sensible woman, Sue. Sage, owlish. She is heavily built and wears a lot of floating chiffon to counter-balance her girth. Despite this concession to impracticality she always washes up everyone's mugs at the end of the day.

'Why can't I be as wise as you?' Sally asked her.

Back

St Hilary's, the school Sally attended in the Seventies, had a peculiar preoccupation with *the gentle arts*. Arts for girls. Cooking and needlework. Quiches spilled out from the ovens, haberdashery from the cupboards. St Hilary's itself was hidden behind skeins of conspiratorial rhododendron bushes. Several grey, unalluring Portakabins adorned the grounds, plonked down beside the high-windowed classrooms. There was the Arts Block and the Science Block. There was a 'playground' where the girls slouched and whispered. There was a netball pitch, a hockey pitch and an outdoor long-jump, to which girls were sent out in midwinter in tiny shorts, their thighs mottled with cold. Sally will never forget the desolate wail of a sports-whistle across mud-whorled playing fields, or the pointless thud of hockey ball against stick.

She hated needlework then. Every Thursday morning, from ten to eleven thirty, the girls were supposed to sit in the Arts Block (classroom H) to improve their skills with needle and thread. And most Thursday mornings they did: they sat there, dutifully sewing. But they all destested it. Why bother making a '*young woman's skirt / jupe pour une jeune femme*' when you could go to Miss Selfridge and buy one? Their teacher's name was Miss Button, as if she had been destined all her life to do this: to instruct teenage girls on the importance of neat fastenings. She was as unyielding as a newly-sewn button, too. She appeared at school, taut and disconcerting, the term Sally began her fourth year. Sally and her best friend Rowena Cresswell had been sitting in a Chemistry lesson at the time, trying to analyse the properties of carbon dioxide (*Method: First we removed the oxygen from the gas jar by holding it underwater. Then we placed the gas jar over the . . .*). They had turned their safety-goggled gaze to the window to observe a young woman dressed in shades of brown and tan, disembarking from a Spider car. She looked very neat. She glanced up, registered Sally and Rowena and then looked away.

The girls discovered, after Miss Button's arrival, that Needlework was not a peaceful occupation, not a pleasant hobby with which to while away the afternoons. Miss Button possessed a ruthlessness that was alarming.

'Karen Worthing, do you honestly believe this hemming is adequate?'

'Rowena Cresswell, you have pinned the pattern on upside down.'

'Sally Tuttle, this is a part of the trouser leg, it is *not* the pocket.'

She possessed something called a 'Kwik-unpick': a cruel-looking metal instrument with two prongs, one sharp and one blunt. It was very efficient at dismantling bad sewing. Miss Button loved her Kwik-unpick and was always very quick to use it.

When her mood was light she would sometimes issue photocopied sheets of 'traditional sewing songs' that she wanted the class to sing. This constituted the 'fun' part of the class. They *would*, she informed them, have fun.

'Today,' Sally recalls her saying one autumn afternoon as she returned magnificently to her desk, 'we are going to sing "Wee Weaver".'

And Sally and Rowena Cresswell had sat up straighter and looked at their photocopied sheets.

I am a wee weaver confined to my loom,
My love she is fair as the red rose in June,

She's loved by all young men and that does grieve me,
My heart's in the bosom of lovely Mary . . .

Confined. Sally knew exactly how that person had felt.

'Wee Weaver?' she mumbled to Rowena Cresswell.

'Bosom?' Rowena mumbled back, and they both began to snigger. Sally placed a Black Jack in her mouth and offered one to Rowena. Black Jacks were good at stifling sniggers; it was not a good idea to undermine Miss Button's appreciation of Needlework. Because Needlework was extremely important. The term Miss Button arrived, she had arranged for the class to go on a French exchange *specifically* to stay in a village close to Bayeux and its tapestry. Sally can't remember the name of the village now, but it had had dozens of road signs pointing the way to Bayeux, a café called *La Bataille* and a small gift shop that sold mini-tapestry gift-sets. It had been very rural apart from that, with old cars rattling down white dust-tracks, fields full of sunflowers, dead chickens hanging from their ankles in the market. At school the girls had sat with their penfriends and marvelled at the relaxed maturity of the class. Where were the serried ranks of desks? Where were the uniforms? They still, however, had to sing traditional songs, just as they did in Needlework classes back in England. And their French Literature teacher still issued photocopied sheets.

Le coeur de ma mie est petit, tout petit,
J'en ai l'âme ravie, mon amour le remplit.
Si le coeur de ma mie n'était pas si petit,
Il y aurait de la place pour plus d'un ami;
Mais le coeur de ma mie est petit, tout petit,
J'en ai l'âme ravie, mon amour le remplit . . .

'I dunneven know what "ma mie" means,' Sally remembers whispering to Rowena.

'I presume it means "mon amie",' Rowena hissed back, 'I presume it's one of those thingummies.'

'What – a corruption?'

'Yeah. Is that the word? A corruption. Or a declension or something.'

Rowena and Sally had both gone to look at the famous tapestry of course; they had both located poor Harold with the arrow in his eye and all the fallen soldiers in their chain mail. They had admired the satin-stitch and the intricacy of it all. Rowena had got *l'autobus* to Bayeux with Miss Button and a motley assortment of girls. Sally had been taken there in a car by her exchange family, *la famille Duval*, who had been genuinely keen for her to appreciate their region's celebrated artwork. They were a very cultured family, Sally recalls, although she picked up all kinds of swear words from her elegant penfriend. She learned to speak with a freedom she never acquired at school. French words tumbled out of her mouth. *Les idiomes, les colloquialisms, les bons mots.*

'You speak French absolutely,' said Madame Duval, holding Sally's face between her warm palms and squashing her cheeks slightly, as if she was still a small child. She smiled. 'You have an ear.'

Sally loved that family, that fortnight, that trip. That was when she thought she would go on to study French at university. Ha ha ha.

Rowena had had a less successful 'placing', she recalls, with a policeman's family on the outskirts of the village. Her penfriend Laurence was surly and uninterested – she would not even go to look at the tapestry with the other girls; there was a deranged Alsatian called Bertrand, and they ate undercooked steak all the time. They never went out in the evenings. *En famille*, they stayed in and watched football in their small, overheated *salle à manger*. Eventually, Rowena came out in a rash – a stress-induced rash which itched and bled and turned out, when she had it diagnosed back in England, to be impetigo.

'What a bloody nightmare,' she used to joke sometimes, when they reminisced about it.

Oddly, on their final day in France, Rowena's 'family' had taken her on a sudden excursion to Rouen Cathedral and proceeded to shower her with gifts: boxes full of chocolates, a pair of fashionable shorts, a broderie anglaise tablecloth for her mother. 'Pour notre petite écolière anglaise,' Madame had written on the tag. 'Guilt gifts,' Rowena said, marvelling at that unexpected sight of the cathedral, and the possession of a hand-embroidered *nappe pour table*. She had shown the *nappe* to Miss Button on the ferry back to Folkestone. Miss Button had fingered the cloth. 'Sad,' she said, 'how banal modern embroidery can be.'

Spider's Web

She was never an intellectual girl, Sally. More of a *plodder*. Quite common too. Quite working-class. Within three years of arriving at St Hilary's she had given up the following subjects: Latin, Social Studies, History, Geography, Art, German, Physics.

She persisted with Needlework.

Most girls, including Rowena, were studying eight subjects for their O-levels. Some were doing as many as ten. Francesca Ball, a kind of prodigy, was studying eleven O-levels and two AO-levels. But Sally Tuttle was studying five, one of which was Needlework. Needlework, said with a sneer. Neeeeedlewuuurk!

On Thursdays, Sally and Rowena were together all day. Conspiratorially they endured:

Maths
Needlework
Needlework
Chemistry
LUNCH (highlighted in glorious, happy pink)
French
French
French

Thursdays were bad. But they were lightened by each other's presence. They were Sally'n'Rowena, Rowena'n'Sally: a natural phenomenon, like twin rocks in the sea. If one of them was spotted alone at school, people would be surprised. 'Where's Sally?' they would ask. 'Where's Rowena? Is she ill?'

In every class, they shared a desk. Rowena was left-handed

and so their writing hands clashed. It did not occur to them to sit the other way around until this was suggested one day by Miss Button.

'Sit on Rowena's right, Sally, for pity's sake,' she said, 'and you won't keep bashing into each other.'

Rowena and Sally looked at each other, giggled, got up, swapped seats and sat down again.

'Wonder of wonders,' said Miss Button.

After that, the only time Rowena intruded on Sally's writing space was when, head almost in her arms at the end of a lesson, she would twirl her hair around the fingers of her right hand.

Be careful always to follow the correct size-lines.

Do not attempt to begin tacking until all the tailor's tacks are in place.

NEVER cut into a notch.

'Look at Miss Button,' Sally whispered to Rowena that autumn afternoon, the afternoon of the 'Wee Weaver'. Because Miss Button had started to sing, launching herself into the lyrics with a handful of girls sitting in the front row. How many more traditional songs were there?, Sally wondered. The week before it had been 'Wind the Bobbin Up' and the week before that, 'Greensleeves' (. . . *Thy smock of silk, both fair and white, with gold embroidered gorgeously;/ Thy petticoat of sendal white,/ And these I bought thee gladly . . .*)

'Look at her go,' Rowena whispered.

Miss Button was singing boisterously, a smile on her face, amber jewellery sparkling at her neck.

'Why was the weaver confined to his loom?' Sally wrote in her rough-book, sliding it across to Rowena.

Rowena considered, silently.

'Maybe he wove his beard into it,' she wrote, pushing the book back to Sally.

Some of their classmates were singing the words quite enthusiastically now – the voices of Christine Pringle and Susan Temple, dismissed long ago as the class goody-goodies, could be heard quite clearly above the drone. And Sally felt a little sad not to be joining in. She would have sung – she secretly enjoyed singing – but with Rowena she had appearances to keep up. So after a moment she stopped, sighed and started to doodle in her rough-book. A biroed heart, its circumference gone over and over in blue so that it left an impression over several more pages.

('*She's loved by all young men and that does grieve me*,' warbled Christine and Susan . . .)

An emphatic blue heart, through which she drew an arrow.

They were in the middle of the second verse –

As Willie and Mary rode by yon shady bough
Where Willie and Mary spent many the happy hour . . .

– when there was a sudden rap on the door, then the jack-in-the-box appearance of St Hilary's deputy headmistress: a large, exasperated person. She walked, fast but solemn, across the room towards Miss Button. The two women stood close, teacherish, and whispered. Then Miss Button nodded her head, raised her hand and shushed the singing girls.

'Sally Tuttle. Miss Gordon would like a word with you outside please.'

Sally felt her face become pale. She glanced at Rowena and Rowena glanced back. *They know. Someone has told them.*

And she was on her feet, the faces of her classmates looming up at her like lilies in a swamp.

'You OK? Shall I come with you?' Rowena whispered. This was not about embroidery. Rowena was the only person who knew what this was about.

Sally looked away.

'Wish me luck,' she croaked, and she felt Rowena touch her sleeve as she brushed past to the end of the row of chairs and across to Miss Gordon.

'OK. Drama over. Let us resume,' she heard Miss Button instruct the class. 'Where Willie and Mary spent many the happy hour . . .' she pronounced, clapping her hands together. The warbling resumed.

The green-upholstered Resource Area was meant for the sixth-formers to sit in during breaks, but nobody ever did. It was always as deserted as the *Marie Celeste*, all the sixth-formers preferring a broken-down brick wall behind the Assembly Hall.

Sally walked behind Miss Gordon. She looked down at her feet: at her oversized shoes moving her on, one step after another. She thought of Mary, Queen of Scots climbing the scaffold.

'We'll sit here,' Miss Gordon proclaimed, swinging her substantial weight into one of the little chairs. She looked at Sally. 'You've gone very pale,' she said, noticing finally. 'This is nothing to get alarmed about, Sally. You look quite . . . unwell.'

'Do I?'

'Yes,' said Miss Gordon. She frowned, paused, drew in her breath and then pulled an envelope out of her pocket. Sally was reminded of the conjuring tricks she had seen once, years before, at a children's party.

'It's just a phone message from your father,' Miss Gordon said.

Sally's heart thumped on.

'The secretary kindly made a note of what he said and said she would pass it on. So here I am,' said Miss Gordon, 'passing it on. Aren't I the lucky one?'

'Right.'

Sally took the note from the amused Miss Gordon. It had been sealed in the envelope, but someone, *someone*, had unsealed it.

MESSAGE FOR SALLY TUTTLE (4F) FROM HER DAD. REMEMBER TO LEAVE AT TWO THIRTY FOR DENTAL APPOINTMENT.

'OK?' Miss Gordon said, the small smile struggling not to appear on her face.

Miss Gordon had, Sally felt, always thought that she was slightly ridiculous – not really worth the generous bursary bestowed upon her – and here was the proof. *A father who sends messages about dental appointments! And what does the father do? The father is a postman!* Most of the girls who went to Sally's school had parents with proper jobs. Solicitors. Doctors. Dentists. Accountants, like Rowena Cresswell's dad. Diplomats: there was even a diplomat! Miss Gordon looked at Sally, her eyes small and twinkling and mud-coloured behind her glasses. She had a large, upholstered bosom behind a stiff grey jacket. Sally was aware of the pulse inside her head, of her heartbeat, of her ten fingers clutched into cold fists in her lap.

It was not her father who had phoned to leave that message. That message was a ruse. And now she had nowhere to place her fear of discovery. She felt as if she might be sick.

'Not earth-shattering then?' Miss Gordon asked.

'No.'

Miss Gordon composed herself and continued. 'You still look terribly guilty about something, though, Sally Tuttle. Any dark secrets we should know about?'

'No. None at all.'

'That's all right, then,' said Miss Gordon.

Couching

When you're fifteen, of course, you don't quite believe that things will change, alter, end. You can't imagine that you might not always go *down town* on Friday nights; that you might not one day possess cheap dangling earrings as heavy as gobstoppers, or silver-blue eyeliner, or a pair of woven-soled espadrilles. You can't foresee this. Sally, for instance, did not know that she would one day be the mother of her own fifteen-year-old girl. And that she would be a Needlewoman. *Needlewoman*, homelier sister of Wonderwoman. An award-winning Needlewoman, even. Who'd have thought it?

Sally and Rowena had first met him, this boy, this young man who had sent the message about the dentist, at Razzles nightclub. His name was Colin Rafferty. It was a Friday evening, August 1979.

Razzles was a dank, Italianate establishment near East Grinstead station. Long-since closed and turned into a garden centre with sofas, fibreglass gnomes and scented candles. But at the time it was the place to be on Friday nights. Rowena and Sally used to go with unquestioning resolve. They slunk nonchalantly past the bouncer who knew – but overlooked – their age. They hurried to the dismally yellow cloakroom, hung up their coats and checked their reflections in the wonky mirror. Then they wove their way back to the main room, to the edge of the dance floor and spent the rest of the evening rooted to the spot, clutching glasses of Fanta – the only drink the bartender would allow them. They listened to the records the DJ put on the turntable. 'Boogie Wonderland', 'My Sharona', 'Bright Eyes'. They both held their heads at a slight angle, their long hair mysteriously flicked to one side, and regarded the boys from beneath it. Bands of coloured light zoomed and flickered around the room and when it brushed across their faces they were convinced that it made them look intriguing – mysterious, knowing, slightly *triste*. They wore baggy tops, swishing skirts and suede pixie boots. The music was always too loud, and Sally was always shouting 'What? What?' into Rowena's ear.

Rowena had been the first one to spot Colin Rafferty, under the strobe lighting. It was Rowena who, beneath the over-amplified words of 'When You're in Love with a Beautiful Woman', had moved her hand up to her ear and shouted the words *dishy* and *he fancies you*.

Sally did not believe her. She did not picture herself as a girl who was fancied by men in nightclubs.

'Look,' Rowena yelled. 'He's coming over.' And Sally turned and felt her heart blanch. She noticed the way the boy walked beneath the light-scattering mirror-balls: a kind of off-kilter but determined walk, accompanied by a sweetly intense gaze. He smiled, and when he got closer she noticed his amused eyes, his neat chin, the charming creases at the edges of his mouth.

'I hate this song,' he opined, leaning one arm casually against a silvery pillar.

Colin Rafferty. It was Sally he wanted. Sally, not Rowena. She was so shocked she could hardly breathe.

Quarter Cross

In a couple of days Sally Tuttle will be giving a talk in Edinburgh, entitled (rather pompously, she fears now) 'The Secret Art of Embroidery'. But what to say, when talking about embroidery stitches? About moss stitch and Pekin knot? And how to say it? How to seem? How to *be*? Embroidery has always been something she just *does*, and the idea of talking about it frightens her.

Preparation is all, she reminds herself. Like a properly pinned-down dress pattern, all the tailor's tacks in place.

She is not a particularly tidy person but she does keep her workroom neat. She has a pine shelving unit containing all the things she needs. It is labelled, ordered, organised. There has to be a little area in everyone's life that is organised. On the top shelf she has two baskets of cotton reels and three of embroidery threads, stranded cottons, wools, tapisserie silks. On the bottom shelf she has her old hand-operated sewing machine, her new foot-operated sewing machine, her goffering iron and her patterns. In the middle she keeps a small red filing-cabinet which has six drawers. These drawers contain, in descending order:

Needles and needle cases
Pins and pincushions
Buttons, poppers, fastenings
Sequins and ribbons
Canvases and squares of felt
Scissors, unpickers and pinking shears

In other areas of her life she is not tidy. She often leaves washing-up until the next day, and does not reprimand her daughter for leaving dirty plates and schoolbooks lying around the living-room floor. Embroidery, though, needlework, requires neatness. Cleanliness. Respect. Her trays and drawers at work are neat too. If they became a mess – a knot of threads, loose buttons, hooks and eyes – she feels she might as well call it a day.

Her elderly mother comes to visit her at In Stitches occasionally, stoically, often bringing something to eat – an individual muffin wrapped in cellophane, a slice of carrot cake. 'Something to keep you going, darling,' she says, glancing around the shop. It is not the career she hoped for her.

Sometimes after school her daughter Pearl comes to see her too but seems to have no comprehension of what her job involves: the careful measuring and pinning, the necessary ironing, the patient tacking and hemming. Careful work, Sally finds herself thinking, is lost on her daughter's generation. Then she remembers Miss Button's admonishments and sessions with the Kwik-unpick. She remembers how careless she was at Pearl's age.

'Good day at school, sweetheart?'

'Hmm,' Pearl replies, looking down and pressing the tiny silver buttons on her mobile phone. The buttons are so small that she has to use her fingernail.

'Did you . . .?'

'Yeah, hang on, Mum,' Pearl says, bringing the phone up to her ear.

Since Sally left school, disastrously, at the age of fifteen-and-a-half, her career has been a series of nine-to-five jobs.

The first job she ever had was as a waitress in a café called The Country Kitchen. There was a uniform: a brown nylon dress with short puffed sleeves, a white, ineffectively small apron and, most mortifying of all, a nylon mob cap. She was supposed to look like a country wench; a pretty serving girl. Looking back, she thinks perhaps she did look pretty: she certainly got leers and comments from the middle-aged men who came into the café at lunchtimes. Or perhaps it was just that she was young. Youth was all that was necessary to attract middle-aged men. *Hello there, Maid Marion,* they used to say. Or: *It's Nell Gwynne.* Or: *I'll have a bowl of porridge, Goldilocks.*

They were supposed to serve wholesome things. Wholesome, late-Seventies style. Lumpy lentil soup. Big dry brown rolls. Hard-boiled eggs and tomatoes cut into water lilies. And Sally was supposed to smile, to giggle and sigh over the steaming soup bowls in a pretty, girlish way. She did not manage the giggling often, though, because her life had recently collapsed around her. So she stomped about in her big shoes, sweeping crumbs off the tables into people's laps, scalding herself against the stainless-steel serving dishes, dropping boxes of loose tea and having to clatter around the too-small kitchen, sweeping up with a plastic dustpan and brush.

She put on weight and her apron became too tight. She dropped a tray, breaking five smoked-glass ashtrays, three cups and a soup bowl. She swore at one of the middle-aged men, telling him, in a not very Goldilocks way, to 'get out of my face'. She was not having a very good time. She had become coarse and jaded.

The next job she got was in the accounts department of a plumber's merchants. She sat in an open-plan office full of smoke, investigating the company's dozens of unpaid bills, which appeared as tiny account numbers on a microfiche. She sat opposite a woman called Brenda Bright who always wore red and smoked one high-tar cigarette after another, pausing only to take swigs of ink-black Maxwell House from a mug that said 'I'm a Mug'.

'Get out while you bloody well can,' Brenda Bright used to advise her, as if she was Andromeda chained to the rocks.

The accounts office of the plumber's yard was a terrible shock after her school's wholesome classrooms – *which I left willingly*, Sally began to realise, *of my own free will.* Now she remembered St Hilary's School for Girls with something approaching grief. She even thought of Miss Button with a kind of fondness. *I was supposed to do A-levels! I was supposed to go to university and study French!* And then catastrophe had intervened and she had done the only thing she could think of doing. She legged it. She ran.

She used to run from the plumber's yard in the evenings, on to the wet, sparrow-chirping pavements, and not be able to make out the numbers of the buses home. 'Three?' she wondered, squinting, as they hove into view at the top of the hill. 'Or eight?' She can trace her short sight from her month-and-a-half at Capel's Plumbers.

Now, peering at her hemming in the back of the shop she sometimes has a fleeting vision of that desk at the plumber's yard, and that mug and that smoke, and Brenda Bright in the most enormous pair of glasses. What a vision, that vision of Brenda Bright.

Wise people are in the minority, she has found, over the years. Despite the owl on her school badge, she herself has not made wise decisions. Practicality has little to do with wisdom.

Knotted

Take care, when threading the needle, not to use too long a thread because it will be inclined to knot. There is no need to knot the end of the thread. An unknotted thread makes for a neater finish.

Sally used to write quickly, heedlessly, her ink-pen pressing a groove into her finger.

'Put your sewing away neatly now, girls, and tidy up,' Miss Button would shout after fifteen minutes' dictation and an hour's hopeless *practical*. And there would follow a desolate scraping of chairs, a flinging of material scraps into the scraps bucket, a lobbing of cotton reels into the haberdashery cupboard. At the back of the cupboard lurked the sequin box, which had been there for years and was hardly ever brought out. It was pretty, like a tiny treasure chest. Sally used to like that sequin box. But there was never time to apply sequins to things.

All the girls in her class that year had worn long, floating scarves. Rowena's was turquoise and green and had a badge pinned to it that Sally had given her. It said, in tiny letters, 'What are you staring at?' Sally's was blue. They used to wear them all day, even though scarves were disapproved of by the teachers. Memos had been passed around the staffroom.

'Remove that unbecoming item now please, Rowena Cresswell,' Miss Button would say as she strode past their table of gloomy pattern-cutters. And Rowena would begin to pull the scarf slowly from her neck. But then, when Miss Button had moved on, she would stop. Style, *allure*, was important, particularly at the end of the day when encountering boys from the school up the road. You would take your scarf off and put it back on again when the teachers were not looking. Sitting at your desk, you would wrap it several times around your neck, put your hands up to your round, moon-like face (your nails varnished apple green, your hair long and sweeping), and sigh. Sometimes you would put a Black Jack in your mouth and chew. Black Jacks were *ironic*. Eating Black Jacks (while sewing and wearing floating scarfs) was *ironic*. This was the tail-end of the dreamy Seventies. The punk look had begun to clash with that of the skulking hippy. Rowena and Sally still dressed somewhat feyly, like medieval ladies-in-waiting. They would peer at Miss Button through their long fringes and tap their green-varnished fingernails against their cheeks. Sally kept her packet of Black Jacks on her lap or behind the big Bernini sewing machine, and would take it out to share with Rowena when Miss Button was not looking. By eleven-fifteen the packet would be empty and they would feel slightly sick, mainly with themselves. Their needlework was not progressing. They had both been working on the same blouson for months. Sally had not even got as far as sewing on the neck interfacing.

'Hey, Ro.'

'What?'

'Do you think Miss Button's got new eyeliner? A blue one? Not her usual lovely mud shade . . .'

'Mm-hmm. I think it's one of those glittery ones. You know, like those ones we looked at in Boots.'

'Do you think she's going out on a date?'

'Well, who could resist? With that eyeliner on?'

'I think she's . . .'

'Sally Tuttle,' Miss Button's voice snapped, interrupting her own dictation. 'Are you with us? What was that last sentence about?'

'It was about knots.'

'It was not,' Miss Button said. 'It was not "abaht" knots. The knots sentence was two sentences back. Stop nattering and keep up.'

Sally looked at Miss Button, sitting behind her de-luxe teacher's sewing machine, wearing fluffy red earmuffs, like a helicopter pilot at the controls. Miss Button the rebel. As well as eyeliner and foundation, she was fond of lacy bras which she wore beneath slightly see-through cheesecloth blouses: her underwear was clearly visible in the summertime.

'Say *how*,' Sally,' Miss Button said with that flattening, teacherish attempt at humour. '*How now brown cow*.'

'Haah naah braahn caah,' Sally said.

Miss Button sighed and contemplated the top of her head for a moment.

Sally did use to try very, very hard, like Liza Doolittle, but her vowels *would* slip. And sometimes she wondered if her status as 'fortunate girl' was slipping too. Maybe she would have her grant rescinded, or be thrown out of school before she got a chance to do her exams. Perhaps the teachers would write reports on her. *Fundamentally too common for St Hilary's and will amount to nothing*. But she didn't really care that much. Because of her secret life, secret from everyone except Rowena.

First life: schoolgirl.

Second life: girlfriend.

And she used to think about the 'half life' of carbon dating that they had discussed in History. The older something was, the less of a half-life it had. It was infinitesimally reduced. Or increased. Or something. Actually Sally was rather baffled by carbon dating. Half lives. Half a life. Second lives. A lot of people seemed to lead them though.

*

She has had to tell Sue and Linda about winning the award. There was no way to avoid it: it was all over the newspapers. *I am the local woman made good*, she thinks, the blood rushing to her face. *I am the needleworker plucked from obscurity.*

'Good on you,' says Sue. 'I'm bloody jealous. I could do with nine thousand squid.'

'So I suppose you're going to leave us now?' Linda asks, going to the overlocker to rattle up a seam.

'No,' Sally replies, like someone who has just won *Who Wants to be a Millionaire?* 'My life is going to go on as normal.'

'Pull the other one,' says Sue. 'Just go, girl, while the going's good.'

'I'm quite happy here really. I'd miss it, actually.'

'You've become institutionalised,' says Linda. 'Like those prisoners who can't face leaving prison.'

'No I haven't. I probably will hand my notice in.'

'Hark at her. Lady Muck.'

And Sally laughs, slightly thrown by the mixture of praise and envy. The push and pull of their affection.

'You're always going on about how hot it is,' Linda points out, 'and the customers being rude.'

'And you're always getting burned by Evil Edna.'

'You should set up an embroidery business,' Sue suggests, leaning back in her chair, licking a tiny bead of blood from her finger.

'Come off it,' Sally mumbles. 'People don't need embroiderers like you need . . . plumbers. Or dentists.'

'Who needs dentists?' Linda says. 'I just had a filling which lasted two days. Cracked on a walnut. Had to get it done all over again.'

'Who needs plumbers?' says Sue, and their conversation drifts from embroidery to U-bends.

Sally sits and thinks about the clunky headlines in the national and, even worse, local papers.

SALLY TUTTLE'S HIDDEN GEMS

FITTING A CAMEL THROUGH THE EYE OF A NEEDLE

'IT'S A STITCH-UP' FOR LOCAL WOMAN

A STITCH IN TIME MAKES NINE THOUSAND POUNDS

What is the reason for this stitching of pictures, people ask, this pulling of wools through cloth? Sally's embroideries have grown over the years – in number and scale. Now they fill up the small house she shares with Pearl like exotic, slightly frightening plants. They lean in their frames against the walls, the threads on the unworked side like mad, multicoloured spaghetti. Picture after picture. It is a compulsion. And she has been doing it for years. Her daughter has grown up thinking it is totally normal.

What does your mummy do?
My mummy sews pictures.
What is she working on at the moment?
A peacock, a tower block and a big grey elephant.

Her embroidered figures have the sort of faces that an arts magazine recently described as 'Tuttle faces'.

'Tuttle faces,' pontificated the writer – someone with a double-barrelled name, Anthony Blahdy-Blah – 'have a charming naivety, a childishness, with, of course, their ever-present trademark sequins . . .'

Trademark sequins? Ever-present trademark sequins?

She wonders how she became the sort of person about whose hobby the word 'trademark' could be applied. Or the sort of person who sits at home in the evenings, embroidering characters from the New Testament.

'I probably will leave,' she says to her In Stitches colleagues, 'when I've got my head round it'.

Sue breaks off from her plumbing anecdote. She picks up the broken waistband of somebody's trousers.

'Who wouldn't leave?' she says.

French Knot

I was knocked down by a taxi a couple of years ago – a small, quite insignificant knock – and for a few days I suffered short-term memory loss. For a week or so I forgot various aspects of my life. I forgot to turn up to two French tutorials, prompting wailing, overbearing emails from my eighteen-year-old students (*re: where are you??!*). I spent £103 at Sainsbury's and left half my shopping bags in the car park. I left my new, small and stylish mobile phone on top of a parking meter. I forgot that my parents-in-law had come to stay and locked them out of the house (I discovered them when I got home, sitting like gnomes on a pile of rocks in the front garden).

'It's OK,' my seventy-eight-year-old mother-in-law said, heaving herself up from the rocks. They had come all the way from Canada to stay with us. Nice people, civilised.

I have always forgotten appointments. Coffee dates. Dental check-ups. I mislay my glasses and my keys. But this was something new. These were disconcerting gaps in my memory. 'My name is Rowena Cresswell,' I said in Accident and Emergency, a couple of hours after the accident. I had, distressingly, forgotten my married name.

Fortunately the important facts of my life returned quickly – I remembered that I have a job as a French lecturer and translator; that I have a new Canadian husband and a quite old English son. That I live in North London, walk every day beneath the pretty shadows cast by London plane trees; that I spend a lot of time at either Stansted or Heathrow airports. But there were still occasions when I would completely overlook something. It was as if there was a tiny gap in my brain, caused by the accident, down which pieces of information got lost. It was, I said, describing my condition to Wilma McHale, the departmental secretary, like losing things down the back of a sofa. Little, valuable things that you might not even know were missing. And then, when you were in the middle of looking for something else, they would suddenly surface.

'I've gone blank. What's the French for needle?' I asked my husband the other evening, hunched, too late at night, over a translation. I had to be up at six to catch a plane, and I was trying to finish an essay on the nineteenth-century manufacture of Persian carpets. Camels were involved – in the context of their urine being used to bleach the wool. *Le blanchissage du tapis à l'urine de chameau* . . . and tapped my pen against my bottom lip. I thought of the quote from the Bible about camels and eyes of needles. I thought of needles in haystacks.

'A needle . . . ,' Kenneth mused, not looking up from the fiercely spot-lit book he was reading. 'L'aiguille,' he said after a moment. 'Masculine.'

'Oh yes. I was thinking it was "clou" for some reason.'

'That's a nail.'

'I know.'

'You couldn't get much sewing done with a nail.'

'I know.'

I looked back at the page I was working on: . . . *and the intricacy with which the brightly-threaded needle was used* . . .

I worry about my forgetfulness a little. But I know it's probably just due to tiredness and that little knock I had. I remember most things eventually. Important things, like words, phrases, turns of phrase. I love words; have always had a fear of misinterpretation. Which, I suppose, being a translator, is just as well.

Long-legged Cross

Sally Tuttle walks to East Grinstead station carrying her handbag, a plastic bag from Harrods and a floral umbrella. The sky is a brightish grey. She is a *professional woman*, her heart calm, her mind uncluttered.

She gets on an ancient, door-slamming train to Victoria. It is early afternoon but the train is busy. She sits beside a woman who glances up, smiles, then returns her attention to her magazine. She is filling in a word puzzle, slowly circling around words that she has located in the jumble of letters. She works horizontally, vertically, diagonally. The words, Sally notices, are all to do with medicine. STETHOSCOPE. ASPIRIN. WAITING ROOM. The woman is gripped, as if there is nothing more important in the world than to locate the word SCAPULA. Sally sits beside her, her plastic bag on her knee.

She has come up to London to visit haberdashery departments. She likes to empty her mind at times of stress by gazing at the ranks of colours.

In John Lewis people are collapsing their umbrellas, folding their raincoats over their arms, walking purposefully towards their prospective acquisitions. It is three o'clock on a slow, pale afternoon, but there is nothing like a large department store to make you feel there is a purpose to life. You just have to glance at the Storage Solutions to know there is an answer to everything. Bras in a muddle? There are bra organisers! Cat hair on your coat? There are pet-hair de-fluffers!

In Sally's plastic bag are a large number of unwanted clothes. She has it with her simply because, this morning, she opened her wardrobe and decided to have a clear-out. She was in a purging mood, sifting through her ranks of swinging clothes: a collection of blues and greys. *That has to go, that has to go.* Her daughter has often commented upon her less successful garments ('Mum, what is *this*?'). And so she had cast things off ruthlessly, sticking yellow Post-it notes to all the things she no longer wears:

two linen jackets with shoulder-pads donated by Sue
one grey tunic with a snag in the hem
one turquoise blouse with strange épaulettes that she used to wear during an unfortunate, structured phase
three pairs of stonewashed jeans
one blue woven hat with plastic fruit attached to the brim.

(God knows why I bought that hat: a wedding? I have no recollection of ever wearing that hat.)

And then there was the dress, her green silk dress, with its sequins and tassles. With its sweetheart neckline. With all its haberdashery. She loved it once, that dress – it was given to her, in fact, by Rowena Cresswell – but now it was much too small for her. And much too girlish. It was already old, a hippy thing, in 1979. What was the point, Sally wondered, in hanging on to that?

Brightness: she had this vision of brightness. Bright, good-quality clothes that would reveal a new, cheerful professionalism.

So this morning, quickly, she had stuffed all her old, half-liked or inherited clothes into the large Harrods bag (chosen for its connotations of grandeur although it actually came from Oxfam), and left the house. She had walked, in her green home-made coat and her summer-sale boots, up the street to the main road and then on to a shop called *A Second Glance*. A dress agency. It was the only dress agency, probably, within a twenty-mile radius of their house, located in a tiny row of boutiques and gift shops, all struggling to pretend they were not in East Grinstead at all but somewhere fashionable, like Brighton or Chelsea.

A small bell tinkled as she stepped inside. Playing on an overhead speaker was some indeterminate piece of classical music: something noble and slightly tragic, with a lot of violins harmonising in thirds.

She stood on the soft carpet with the plastic bag. The interior of A Second Glance was warm and painted a sombre olive-green. There were lone twigs jutting out of vases at strategic points. A floral curtain concealed a small dressing room.

For a moment she couldn't locate the shop assistant, and then she spotted her, sitting on a low chair by the till, reading the *Daily Telegraph*. She was camouflaged, wearing olive-green: a polo-neck jumper and matching woollen skirt. Over her jumper she wore a string of large green stones. They looked like gobstoppers. Sally advanced and the woman looked up. She glanced down at Sally's bag: a *second glance*? She did not say hello.

'Hello,' Sally said, the word falling out of her mouth and clanging around the shop.

The woman lowered her newspaper, smiled and then lowered her eyelids.

'I was wondering if you might be interested in looking at these,' Sally said. Something, some restrained, stomach-plunging atmosphere about the shop, reminded her of her old school. Her politeness, her deference bounced off the walls, making her feel belligerently humble, like a knife grinder or someone going round the houses selling dusters and polish.

The shop woman carried on smiling, her eyes still closed. Then she opened them. 'We're not really taking things at the moment. But I'll have a look. Seeing as you've brought them.'

'Right.'

And Sally put the bag on to the floor beside the counter. She wondered if she should do some sort of sales-pitch. Was that what you were supposed to do in dress agencies?

'This is linen,' she began, pulling out one of the jackets, 'It's . . .'

'No,' said the woman.

'Oh,' Sally said. 'OK.' And she put the jacket to one side and pulled out the next linen jacket.

'How about this one?'

'That looks almost identical.'

Sally didn't reply. She put the second linen jacket on top of the first and dragged out the grey top.

The woman put on a pair of half-moon glasses. She advanced a maroon-nailed hand and fingered the sleeve. 'No,' she said.

Please take your hands off my blouse, Sally thought. She was suddenly feeling very defensive about these clothes, very protective. They were a part of her history. *What do you know about these clothes? You wouldn't know good clothes if they slapped you.*

'OK. Are you interested in hats?'

'We don't usually take hats,' said the woman, smiling. 'Particularly if they don't arrive in a hat box.'

Sally glared at her. She felt like doing something melodramatic: taking out an enormous pair of scissors and slicing her way through all the shop's dreary, self-satisfied clothes.

'The only thing I have left,' she snapped, 'is this.'

And then she dragged out her green dress: the one she was given by Rowena Cresswell just before they never spoke to each other again; the one Sally nevertheless could not quite bear to part with, and used to wear when she was newly slim after her daughter's birth. She wore it for years and years when she went out in the evenings on various unsuccessful dates after she had split up with Pearl's father, and her mother would come to babysit. (Her daughter was a toddler by then and would sit on her lap before she left and pull at the tassles – 'You looks pretty,' she used to say . . .)

The woman hesitated, brushed the silk between thumb and forefinger, looked at the label. 'I'll take that one,' she said.

'Sure?' Sally asked, feeling suddenly sad. (*I am changing,* she reminded herself, *I am moving on.*)

'Yes. It's vintage,' the woman said breezily. 'So it has some value. Do you know the system? Have you sold with us before?'

'The system? No.'

The woman turned to her desk and wrote something very quickly in a notepad, tore the page out and handed it to Sally.

'This is your receipt. You can phone in a month or so to see if it's sold. If it hasn't sold in about six months we'll give it back.'

'OK,' Sally said. *Thanks a bunch, dear*, she thought. She took the receipt from the woman and looked at it. She did not want it now. She felt she had done something heartless, given away something she could not retrieve.

'So I don't . . .'

'No,' smiled the woman. 'You don't get money up front.' She looked at Sally. 'That's not the way we do it.'

'OK.'

Sally paused, aware of the practical, working clothes she was wearing, in the midst of so much feminine, floating attire. 'How much do you think you'll get for it?'

'Thirty pounds, perhaps? We take forty per cent commission. So you'd get' – swiftly, she made a calculation on a clonky, infantile-buttoned calculator – 'eighteen pounds.'

'Eighteen pounds,' Sally croaked.

She looked up at her dress – *her dress* – which somehow was already hanging up on a rail like a trophy pinched by a magpie. There was even a label on it: '70s dress, green silk, good condition'. *How did she do that so quickly?*

Eighteen pounds was not enough. But she was suddenly very aware of their continuing lack of security, hers and her daughter's; of the constant need to keep the wolf from the door. Loved ones, she reminded herself, are more significant than clothes.

'I'll phone in a month then,' she said, and she left the shop with her unwanted wares.

The bag of clothes has since been an encumbrance. It has sat on her lap, on the train, beside the word-puzzling woman, all the way to Charing Cross. It has squashed into the Tube train with her. It has bounced and bumped down Oxford Street and been wedged into lifts. Sally has not found a single charity shop in which to discard it.

In John Lewis's Fashions, she wanders nervously past rows of impractical chiffon blouses and too-tight jeans – *not for me, not for me* – then takes the lift back to the haberdashery department. A little girl, about three years old, stares unblinkingly at her as they glide downwards. Sally looks back at her and smiles. The girl reminds her of her daughter at that age; she has the same seriousness and long, bright hair. The child, her eyes wide and brown, does not smile. Just as the doors are opening, she turns to her mother.

'Mummy,' she says, 'is that lady cross?'

'Shh, shh, shh,' replies her mother, stroking the top of her daughter's head with her flattened palm and directing her towards the bed-linen department. ('Look!' the child exclaims. 'Bob the Builder duvets!')

'Cross?' Sally wonders, leaving the lift and striding quickly through the departments (she has long legs and has been told by two significant men in her life that she looks like Big Bird from Sesame Street). As she approaches haberdashery, with all its ribbons and poppers and comforting skeins of embroidery silks, she glances at her reflection in one of the store's mirrored pillars. She had thought she was looking calm, dignified, full of renewed purpose and optimism. But now she sees that the little girl was right. She does not look *cross*, exactly, but harrassed. She has that spaced-out, overworked look. She looks like a woman in her forties in a panic. Her hair is coming adrift. Her collar is half up and half down. Her skin is pallid after an early and continuing winter. She is carrying a plastic bag which looks creased and distorted, even though it originated in Harrods. And she has that anxious expression that she knows she has had since she was a teenager: that small, preoccupied frown that could be misinterpreted for anger.

Scottish

We are, at the moment, in Edinburgh. It's cold, much colder than London, the dampness fingering its way beneath our coats. The sky is huge and white as a bowl of milk. We're staying in the Royal Burgh Hotel, a place wrapped in miles of green tartan. But it is warm, with kind staff and a bowl of mints at the reception desk.

I suppose we are the sort of people this hotel thinks of as its target customers. Well-heeled, educated, forty-something. Madam is English, quite posh. Sir is Canadian, somewhat furrowed, academic type. He has suede shoes. She has leather gloves. Both smile wearily as they emerge from the lift into the lobby.

We are here so we can visit my son. And every time I think of this, something happens to my heart, something rises, expands and hurts. Because after we have seen him, he will be leaving. He has just split up with his girlfriend and is leaving Edinburgh – Scotland – the UK – for a new job in America.

'Good evening, sir, madam,' say the hotel reception staff.

'Good evening.'

'Nice evening lined up?' the staff enquire, perhaps imagining a concert, a play, a dinner.

'Yes, thank you.'

In reality we are a lot less sure of ourselves. We are not sure about the evening ahead of us. Maybe it will be nice and maybe it won't. I grab a mint from the bowl at reception. Kenneth hands in the key.

It is cosy in the hotel. But as soon as you step outdoors, you are whirled into a kind of discreet melancholy which hangs over the

High Street and tries to nose its way under the doors of all the tourist boutiques and overpriced cafés. A kind of gloom beneath the cheery early-evening lights. Or maybe it is just me. At the bottom of the hill there are bright boxes of Edinburgh rock and fudge and tablet illuminated in the shop windows. Sweetshops full of gobstoppers, sherbet dips, lollipops, chocolate bears, Love Hearts, Flying Saucers, peardrops. I can't remember the last time I saw so many sweets *en masse.* It makes me think about the two childhoods in my life: my son's and my own. Kenneth and I are walking past a sparkling window display when I suddenly remember the craze we once had at school for Black Jacks. *Black Jacks!* We were obsessed with them. My mother couldn't stand them: the way they blackened your teeth.

'Did you used to eat Black Jacks?' I ask Kenneth.

'Fralingers taffy was my favourite,' he replies promptly, making me wish I had known him then, when he was a schoolboy in Ontario eating too many candies.

My son is a man in his twenties, not even his early twenties, and he has his own life. It is nine years since he left home. But I still can't imagine how much I will miss him, even *how* I will miss him when he is in a different country. It will be a different quality of missing. Mothers and their children are not meant to be this far apart.

'It's cold,' I say.

'We're in the frozen North.'

A vast seagull lands abruptly on the pavement in front of us and regards us with its reptilian eye. It plucks a chip from a discarded wrapper and takes off again. A young woman with a toddler in a buggy swears and dodges around an overflowing rubbish bin.

We decide it will take too long to walk all the way in this temperature, so we get on a bus and trundle down the streets, across North Bridge, over the lights and around a roundabout. It is dark. A large hill looms to our right. Beneath it, a café displays exhausted-looking doughnuts, éclairs, cream puffs. We get off the bus at the top of London Road and begin to walk again. I notice that Edinburgh gets a little less salubrious, a little less 'Festival City', the nearer we get to my son's flat.

Kenneth is still impressed though. 'Fine proportions,' he is saying – he has, for the last few minutes, been in a kind of reverie about Scottish architecture. He can be like that. Wondering. Awed. But I am not in the mood. I am nervous and sad, in anticipation of saying goodbye to my boy.

'I've always thought the Scots –'

'Yes. Here we are,' I say, halting outside a battered black door situated between a video rental shop and a launderette. 'Number eighty-three. And it's' – I consult my piece of paper – 'buzzer six.' I sound like a game-show host.

Standing on the worn stone step, I press the buzzer.

'Hi, Mum,' Joe's voice says through a little steel grille. 'Come up.' There is a distant buzzing sound. I lean my shoulder against the door and push it open, into the unlit stairwell.

'Hi, Mum,' Joe says again at his doorway two floors up. 'Hi, Kenneth. Good to see you.'

He steps forward and gives me a kiss on the cheek. He does that these days. I forget sometimes how old my son is. He even has faint lines on his forehead which I want to rub away, the way I used to wipe jam off his face.

'So how was the flight?'

'Short. There was hardly time to look down.'

'Yes. That's the thing with . . .' Joe says, trailing off. He looks rather pained that we have to see the place where he lives. It is not, I feel, what he wants us to see.

'This is a lovely flat,' I say, looking up at the high yellowish ceiling in the hallway; at the line of my son's underpants hanging from the pulley. It reminds me of the apartment we stayed in in

Paris once, my son rattling around the hot streets on his too-small, plasticky tricycle. And all the women smiling and saying 'Ah, qu'il est mignon!' I remember the oddly grey quality of the light. The jars of honey in the markets. The height of the buildings. The sense of other, more exotic lives going on around us.

The light in my son's hall does not appear to work. I squint and smile at him.

'Come and have a cup of tea,' Joe says, and I want to hug him; I want to say, *Don't go, don't go, don't go*. But I just walk politely behind him.

In the kitchen there is a stack of unwashed dishes and a damp dishcloth, left in a ball on the draining board. He has not wrung it out and hung it neatly over the taps to dry, as I would have done. As I suspect his girlfriend might have done. And now it smells stagnant. It has probably been like that for a couple of days. While he is searching for a box of teabags, I pick up the cloth between the tips of my fingers, walk quickly over to the bin in the corner of the room and drop it in. I glance at my son and freeze: he has observed me.

'Old habits.'

Joe raises his eyebrows and smiles.

'Mothers,' he says to Kenneth. He is so mature, so worldly; my mothering, I suppose, is no longer a concern.

'Milk in your tea?'

'Please, Joe.'

He opens the fridge. The fridge seems to be full of half-finished jars of gherkins. Sprigs of yellowing dill float in the brine, preserved, suspended, reminiscent of something in my old school science lab.

'So,' Joe says into the fridge, 'would you like a biscuit? I expect you're hungry.'

And he closes the fridge door, goes to a cupboard and takes out a new packet of chocolate bourbons.

'Or we have digestives,' he says. 'I mean . . .'

My son has never been very good at hiding things. Girlfriends. Lost girlfriends. Once, when I went to visit him in a flat he was living in in Newcastle, I bumped into a girl of about twenty varnishing her nails in the bathroom. Burgundy varnish. She had apparently been living with Joe, in his flat, for six weeks.

'Hi, I'm Constanza,' the girl had said, looking up and giving me a big, delightful smile. She was olive-skinned and pretty. She sounded Spanish. 'And are you Joe's . . .?' she began, baffled.

'I'm his mother.'

'His mother? You are too young.'

'Yes, well, I had Joe pretty young. I expect he told you.'

'No, no, he didn't tell me.'

Even now, at forty-three, I am still thrown by people's astonishment. *You have a son of twenty-seven? No! How is that possible?* Often, I am mistaken for his older sister.

'I was a teenage mum,' I used to say a few years ago, when I wanted to shock people at dull departmental dinner parties, or at conference 'jollies'.

'How unexpected,' one man joked, flapping his damask napkin. 'You seem so cultured.'

'How . . . French,' said another man.

'I am cultured. I am not French,' I said, irritated.

'Yes, but you act as if you are. French, that is.'

'Do I really? How do French people act?'

'Bossy.'

'Bossy?' I repeated, feeling a rush of irritation. 'Bossy? Well. Ha! Maybe I have reason to be bossy. Maybe I've had to put up with a lot of comments like that over the years. Maybe I –'

'Calm down,' the napkin-flapper said, slightly alarmed. 'I was joking.'

'It is so nice to meet you,' Constanza the pretty Spanish girl said when I left my son's flat in Newcastle. 'I look forward to meet you again.'

But we never did meet again. My son's girlfriends come and go, come and go. One day they are in his bathroom, polishing their nails, and the next, they are gone.

While the kettle is boiling, I go to the bathroom. It is long and thin and in need of repainting. There is a tall window at the far end, above the lavatory. The view is of other tenements and the distant, dark North Sea. I look at the things he has in his bathroom: a modest collection of cheap shampoos and shaving gel. There is still some evidence of his former girlfriend's life here: a blue glass bottle on the window sill, a small whale-shaped mirror stuck to the wall, a half-empty box of cotton buds on the bath ledge.

'He is packing to leave,' I think. 'And I am here to help him.'

'Mum?' Joe calls from the kitchen. 'Tea. We're in the living room.'

'OK,' I reply, walking back into the hallway, and wondering for a moment where the living room is.

Buttonhole

Sally does not go out much in the evenings. She likes home. But she did recently go to a party with Sue from work. It was an hour's drive away and she thought, well, she should. Sue drove – efficient, motherish – peering through the rainy windscreen at the dark, hedge-narrowed roads.

The party was full of middle-aged women, babies, husbands and wheezing, unwashed dogs. Sally sat next to a woman introduced to her as Veronica Beard. Veronica and Sally crouched on couches beside a low, pale table (Ikea, probably), and attempted to prong olives on to cocktail sticks.

'So. What do you do?' Veronica asked.

'I work for a clothing alterations company in East Grinstead,' Sally began shiftily. 'I also do a bit of emb–'

'Really? How interesting. And how long have you worked there?'

'At In Stitches? Pretty much all my life.'

'Ha ha,' tinkled Veronica. 'And you live there, too? You live in East Grinstead?'

'Yes.'

'You don't go in for exotic locations, then?'

Sally was about to say something about a place being what you made it – which she is not quite sure she believes herself – when Veronica Beard snorted, put another olive in her mouth and said, 'Anyway, maybe you can take the girl out of East Grinstead but can you take East Grinstead out of the girl?'

'What's wrong with East Grinstead?' Sally asked. It isn't chic, it isn't metropolitan, but you could do worse. She hasn't ever left, for instance, which is proof enough. Then there are the floral displays. There is the proximity to London. There is the nearby miniature steam railway, which her parents used to take her to, and which she also used to visit with Pearl when she was little. Clattering around the tracks, Pearl in her flowery pinafore dress, asking all those unanswerable questions.

'Mummy, why is smoke coming out of the train?'

'It's not smoke, sweetness, it's steam. It's how the train moves along.'

'Why?'

'Because steam is what pushes it. The fire heats up the water and the water turns into steam.'

'Why? Why does the water turn into steam?'

'It's . . . a kind of chemical reaction, Poppet.'

'Why?'

'I don't know, Pearl. Y'know, not every question has an answer.'

'Wh–'

'Oh look, there's a rabbit out there. Running along.'

There were very few towns which had their own steam railway, Sally reminded Veronica Beard. And not all towns have won the South-East in Bloom award.

She discovered later that Veronica Beard lived in Southend-on-Sea. *Hardly Saint Tropez either, eh?* she should have said. She wished she had swept up to her at the tail-end of the party and said something shocking, betraying her working-class origins; something about Essex Girls or end-of-the-pier jokes. But she never says things like that to people she dislikes. She is not good at withering comments. Sometimes, in the presence of such people, her confidence fizzles, is trampled upon. She is Sally Tuttle, grant-aided girl; Sally Tuttle, who did not stay at school long enough to learn the subjunctive, or the reasons behind the Boer War.

*

She has never liked social gatherings in any case. She turns into a bit of a hermit-crab, arriving early to hide in the shell of a big leather sofa and scuttling out occasionally to refill her wine glass or grab a handful of pretzels. She also has, she knows, a pincer-like way of conversing; of throwing startling statements into the middle of a sober discussion on interest rates or school catchment areas. 'I saw someone in a chicken suit today,' she said at a rather solemn fortieth birthday party a few weeks earlier, 'and they were crossing the road!' The little group she was with stopped talking and looked at her.

'A chicken suit?' said a woman.

Before she speaks, she always trusts there will be someone in the assembled gathering who is on her wavelength, who will appreciate a different kind of conversation. She is often wrong. There is often a silence, a look of bewilderment. Where have they gone, she wonders, the people who used to appreciate comments like that?

Maybe I am too childish.

Maybe I am immature.

Maybe I am regressing.

Or progressing the wrong way.

And she remembers the way she used to laugh with Rowena Cresswell at school: those gasps for breath over things that were not even funny. Except they were, they *were*. Certain sights. Sounds. The way their Geography teacher's briefcase used to snap importantly shut, and then flop open again, half an hour later. The way Miss Button used to strut, peacock-like, around the Portakabin. The vision of a distant, struggling line of cross-country runners wearing numbered sports-tunics. And words. The word 'sports-tunic' had once made Sally Tuttle and Rowena Cresswell laugh, hysterically, for days.

East Grinstead has changed a lot since then. Changed, altered, developed. Rowena Cresswell's house, for instance, brand new in 1974, has acquired an established look. It has softened, gained a kind of bloom; it has ivy and honeysuckle growing up the wall and a front gate that doesn't sit properly in its frame. (A young family lives there now: a resilient young couple with three wild little boys who are always swinging on the gate.) After the death, nearly twenty years ago, of Mrs Cresswell, and Mr Cresswell's subsequent death four months later (heartbroken, apparently), the Willows was renamed. It is now the Gables. And when she thinks of it, she can recall gables, and baby birds nesting in them, beneath Rowena's window.

On her way home from work, she still walks past their garden. She walks past the yellow roses and the crazy-paving and the cherry tree and remembers Mrs Cresswell planting it, clad in apron and spotty-palmed gardening gloves. Now, on early summer evenings, the tree is often completely covered with little birds. Sparrows, singing in the pale light . . .

'Did you actually do Needlework at school?' Pearl asked her the other day.

'I did.'

'So your school wasn't very emancipated, then?'

'Well,' Sally replied, feeling somewhat crushed. She thought of St Hilary's, now a housing estate with selected Victorian *features*. 'Considering we survive on my sewing abilities, sweetheart, I think . . .'

But she trailed off. She knew what her daughter meant. Needlework lessons had not been emancipated. Even in 1979 they were archaic. They might as well have been doing *needlepoint* or *crewelwork*. They might as well have sat in an inglenook with their tapestry frames, sipping mead from pewter goblets while the pallid sunshine seeped in through the Portakabin's high, metal-framed windows.

*Select pattern pieces needed. With right sides together, pin sleeve into armhole, matching symbols and large * to shoulder seam.*
(* *indicates Bust Point and Hipline*)

But everything, it seemed then, could be made to fit. There was an armhole for each sleeve, an adjustment line for each non-standard waist.

'Bust point and hipline,' Rowena whispered, and they would both begin to laugh.

('What do you get out of embroidery?' Graham the estate agent asked Sally on the last occasion she went out with him. 'I mean,' he said, 'you don't strike me as someone who'd be into fussy little stitching.'

Fussy little stitching. Sally looked at him.

'I enjoy it,' she said. 'I like the feel of the cloth. I like getting a load of different-coloured threads and turning them into a picture. You know, what do *you* get,' she added, 'out of writing "this delightful room boasts a dado rail" God knows how many times a week?'

This was when she and Graham had begun, slightly, to hate each other.)

She is currently working on a commission she received after winning the award. She is going to talk about it at the conference in Edinburgh. It depicts Mary and Martha, of Biblical fame. Large frame, satin stitch, straightforward in style, apart from the fact that she is sewing on hundreds of sequins. A fiddly, laborious task. But there is something irresistibly cheerful about sequins, like the sparkle of neon lights.

Her Mary and Martha are possibly a little too bejewelled for religious figures, so she has toned them down by giving them very plain dresses. Mary, the most daring sister, wears a maroon A-line thing while poor put-upon Martha must be content with a kind of smock in *taupe*. She has tried to give them different expressions, but has in fact managed to make them look very similar – they both have beige, satin-stitched faces, slightly wonky eyebrows and scarlet lips. They both have brown hair parted in the middle. As she stitches, Sally wonders what people will write about them. *A wonderfully naive take on the embroiderer's art*, the judge of her winning entry pronounced last year, *with a delightful enthusiasm for sequins*; and she had felt slightly insulted at his assessment of her skills. She was not trying to be naive. But she supposes her embroidered figures do look a little childish; even the worldly Mary looks disingenuous, cartoonish, a bit simple. The two sisters have round faces, big ears, trusting eyes.

Innocent. Gullible. No doubt about it. It is never intentional, but there it is.

She was commissioned to do this embroidery in March by the Ecclesiastical Arts Foundation, a group of vicars who spend most of their time in Southwark Cathedral. Reverends Avery, Beanie and Hope. When she got the commission she had to travel up to London to meet them. She had never really had a *career* as such; she had never had a business meeting in her life. And now she was going to have one with members of the clergy. *Typical*, her daughter's father would say – *How typically perverse of you, Sally.*

The journey was actually more straightforward than she had imagined; there had been no need to lie awake the night before, staring at the luminous stars on her ceiling. In the morning she got up at seven, whispered goodbye to her sleeping daughter, got the 8.30 train up to London, took another train from Victoria, got on to two Tube trains and a bus, then walked up three roads, through a gateway, along a path and beneath the slapping wet boughs of a willow tree. She could feel her heart thudding. She looked around the Ecclesiastical Arts Foundation's garden: at its cotton-yellow jasmine, its seagull-grey chippings, its battlement-black gate, and her mind went through a possible choice of stitches for the scene. *Cloud filling? Fern? Knotted satin?* She walked past a wooden board stuck into the lawn bearing the words 'The Ecclesiastical Arts Foundation' and resisted an impulse to turn and run. She stepped through a low doorway into a small lobby, where she sat surrounded by piles of green hardback copies of the Common Prayer Book. There was a smell of dust and mildew and a sign on the wall which said 'Please D'ont Leave Your Cups Here'. She sat and looked at that apostrophe until Reverend Beanie called her name.

She was the only person in the room without a dog-collar. She had chosen something demure for the occasion, though: her home-made green coat and her nice, swishing, below-the-knee skirt. A skirt that was really intended for the admiration of less lofty men. She smiled and cleared her throat. Then the Board and she sat down around a large mahogany table, upon which were arranged a teapot, pretty Indian Tree cups and saucers, side plates and a dish of custard creams. The oddly louche scent of coffee and cigar smoke hovered in the air.

'Well, Mrs Tuttle,' smiled the Reverend Avery, 'Your work is charming, absolutely charming. That peacock for instance, that peacock is quite inspired.'

Sally wriggled in her seat. She wasn't sure she liked the word 'charming': it was the sort of word an estate agent might use to describe a house that was too small.

'Your use of sequins –' began the Reverend Beanie vaguely, pouring tea into her cup.

'What we're looking for,' interrupted the Reverend Avery, 'despite the fact that this will be an award from the Ecclesiastical Arts Foundation' – and he suddenly stopped talking, put his clenched fist up to his mouth and coughed; then he continued – 'is something quite homely. Something that reflects a more everyday take on Christianity.'

Sally looked at him. She thought of her old RE teacher, a short, bald man who used to breathe 'We break this bread' melodramatically into the school microphone at assemblies; she also thought of her embroidery of *Jacob Wrestling with the Angel,* sited in her parents' living room above their occasional table.

'In fact I often . . . ' she began.

'Hmm?' said the Reverend Avery.

'I often choose Biblical images for my work.'

'Well, that's most interesting. Why do you think that is?'

She pondered for a second.

'Because they seem so colourful, I suppose. You know, there always seem to be a lot of vibrant animals and birds and . . . angels. Angelic figures,' she added, fearing that she had begun to make no sense. She had seen Reverend Avery raise one eyebrow quizzically when she mentioned the vibrant animals. *Why did I say that?* Maybe it was because an image of Noah's Ark had suddenly flashed across her mind, with its myriad honking and growling occupants. Lions, bears, chameleons. Sally picked up her teacup and took a quick sip. 'And,' she continued, trying to adopt a more educated tone, 'it is, as we all know, a kind of embroidery tradition – an almost innate tradition. Think of all those Victorian samplers. And medieval religious tapestries.'

'Ah yes,' Reverend Beanie smiled knowledgeably. 'The marvellous Apocalypse of St John.'

'Yes,' Sally replied. She had never heard of the Apocalypse of St John. The only famous tapestries she had heard of were the Bayeux Tapestry and *The Lady with the Unicorn*. She was suddenly horribly aware of her ignorance, her curtailed education.

'I'm not in fact religious myself,' she said.

'It's not a requirement, regrettable though that may be,' the Reverend Hope replied, allowing himself a series of small, perfectly spaced laughs. Then he carried on. 'We're simply keen to project a more welcoming image of the Church. And at the same time we want to embrace modern art. We want to embrace modern, practising artists.'

Sally was quite touched to know that the Church wanted to embrace her. She couldn't think what to say. The term 'practising artist' made her feel proud and shy.

'So you want me to embroider a particular scene?' she asked.

'No, it's entirely up to you,' Reverend Avery said, helping himself to another biscuit. Beneath the table, a black labrador sighed and thumped his tail in his sleep. It was the first time Sally had been aware of a dog beneath the table. She thought of her comment about vibrant animals, and clutched the edges of her portfolio.

'So I can do anything?'

'Anything. As long as it's Biblical. As long as it inspires contemplative thought,' said the Reverends.

On the train home, she looked out at the greyness of Network South-East's junctions and halts. She looked down at her green coat and her nice below-the-knee skirt. Her heart was full, bulging with ambition. She thought, *I am an artist. I am wanted.* A tiny flame of happiness flickered and grew. And that was when she decided to embroider the picture of Mary and Martha. She had been thinking a lot, that spring, about the role of women. Women's lot in life. And here were two interesting examples: those two difficult sisters. Mary going glamorously out into the world and Martha staying at home, crashing around the kitchen, doing the washing-up. Or was it the other way round? She couldn't be sure.

Mirrored

There's a small hole in the pane of my son's living-room window. It's letting in a thin stream of air. No wonder the flat is so cold. Somebody, some previous tenant, has drawn a thick black line from the window-frame to the surround, and written 'De-luxe flat, fully air-conditioned'. It's not Joe's writing.

I have been thinking about all the people I've known in my life. Speculating on the number. There must be thousands now – from the little girl at primary school who once let me hold her gold star earrings, to Mrs Stanley, my ballet teacher, who used to open her mouth wide and shout 'Remember your arms!' above the clank of the ill-tuned piano. There were ephemeral acquaintances like my Needlework teacher Miss Button, about whom I knew little but conjectured much. And others, like my friend Sally Tuttle, whom I thought I would always know.

I once heard two women talking in a Chinese restaurant, late at night, on either side of a flower-vase. 'She had a string of lovers,' one of the women said, confidentially but loudly, to her friend. 'Really?' her friend replied. The first woman folded her arms across her plump breast, sending her pearl necklace scuttling down her cleavage. 'An absolute string,' she said. 'I shudder to think . . .'

I never found out what the woman shuddered to think, but since that night, the phrase has always made me think of a necklace. Lovers like beads on a string. My particular string of lovers is a rather short one. Before Kenneth there was:

Peter ('88–'98), my 'fiancé' of ten years. I left him when he hit Joe during an argument.

Julien ('85–'87), a sweet French man, unemployed, blue-eyed guitarist and poet, ultimately scared off by the fact that I had a young son.

Matthew, ('82–'84), a very tactile engineering student who had also become fed up with the constant presence in my life of noisy toys, bedtime *routines*, morning *routines*, strewn pieces of Lego, unreliable babysitters, curtailed arrangements.

And one other – my earliest dalliance ('79–'79), whom I can hardly count as a lover. Not really. Except that he was Joe's father.

My son is almost twice the age I was when he was conceived. The age I was, that autumn. It does not seem possible. I go to sit beside him on his rented Scottish sofa. I watch him drinking a cup of tea. I wonder what he is thinking.

'Hey, Joe, hasn't anyone ever shown you how to knot a tie?' Kenneth asks him, apropos of nothing. Sweetly, Joe is wearing a tie – *for Kenneth's benefit?* I wonder – but it is clumsily done, the knot as big as an apricot.

'I didn't have much tie-knotting advice when I was growing up,' Joe replies. He leans forward to help himself to a Tunnock's Teacake. 'I know tying a tie is a rite of passage and everything . . .'

'Hmm,' I say. He has always had the unconscious knack of making me feel guilty. I regard him sitting there, preoccupied with the white, rubbery insides of his teacake and considering – what? San Francisco? His girlfiend? His teacake? I think: *He looks like his father*. He has exactly the same expression that I remember, and quiet smile and length of leg. He has that cowlick and those eyelashes. And he is tall: fortunately, he has not inherited my own lack of height. It is always so curious to be reminded of his father when in different circumstances I would have forgotten him. Maybe he would have crept into my head, briefly, once every few years. A bloke. A bloke I slept with in 1979.

Zigzag

Mary's dress is more of a flowing affair than Martha's. It has more grandeur, with medieval-ish, bat-wing sleeves and a nipped-in waist. Sally has used nearly four skeins of silk on it and it is still not finished. She likes to get the colour-changes as subtle as she can. That is why she has so many embroidery silks. In Martha's face, for instance, there are six different shades. You need that many to get the expression of envy right.

Embroidery Times, the sewing magazine that Sally subscribes to, is full of useful advice about such techniques. The gradations and the subtleties. It also features things called 'makes'. The 'makes' it suggests this month are:

an embroidered plastic-bag holder

an embroidered, reusable Christmas cracker to fill with your own little gifts ('How about some home-made fudge or tree decorations?')

an embroidered apron

an embroidered greetings card

The world of embroidery is a kind world, a womanly world, full of gift-giving and the consumption of time. Time measured out in stitches and pricked fingers. Sally and Pearl often laugh at the more curious 'makes' in *Embroidery Times*. The embroidered egg-cosies and the embroidered bag in which to keep one's embroidery threads. The Zen-ness of an embroidered embroidery-bag! She never makes these 'makes'. But sometimes she wishes she was the sort of woman who did.

*

Rowena Cresswell's mother used to subscribe to magazines. It is one of the few things Sally feels she would have in common with Rowena Cresswell's mother. She used to get *Woman and Home*, *Woman*, *Woman's Realm*, *Women's Weekly*. She kept them all in a polished wooden magazine rack between the sofa and the television. She bought them on a fortnightly basis. It seemed like a kind of aberration, the amount of money she would spend on these publications, which all advocated the same things: plumped-up cream cushions, candles, highly-complicated dinner-party recipes involving lasagna sheets and roux sauce; adverts for shoe racks and leather-bound encyclopedias. Mrs Cresswell's lifestyle, Sally supposes, must have mattered to her a lot. The ordered calm of it. The unchanging neatness. It is an ambition which Sally can comprehend now. The Cresswells certainly lived in a nicer house than the Tuttles did, at the expensive end of town. Unlike the Tuttles' house, all the houses on Rowena's estate were detached and they all had names. The Willows didn't actually have a willow tree (it died shortly after they moved in) but it did have a very green, spongy lawn and a lot of bright, blowsy flowers in the flower beds. Custard-yellow tulips. Scarlet gladioli. The house was new, built in the early Seventies, with fake, old-fashioned tile-cladding. Sussex-red. Mr Cresswell was an undemonstrative man but from time to time, in the summer and early autumn, he would sit in his traffic-noisy garden, drinking beer and playing Frank Sinatra songs. 'New York, New York' bellowed aggressively across all the neat lawns of the neighbourhood.

'. . . start spreading the news,/ I'm leaving today,/ I want to be a part of it . . . ,' sang Sinatra, as people's washing twirled around on their East Grinstead Whirly-birds.

Mr Cresswell was overweight. Mrs Cresswell was very thin. Even when Sally knew her, she must have been ill. Her legs gave no form to the blue trousers she wore. She used to work in a gift-shop café, serving buns and scones with a silent sadness. Rowena and Sally used to go and watch her sometimes after school: they would sit at a table in a corner of the café and eat discounted flap-jacks. Mrs Cresswell never spoke to them as they sat there: she seemed unable to combine work with any semblance of banter. Not even 'How was your day?'

Occasionally she used to look across at Sally with an expression that was hard to fathom: a combination of irritation and pity. Her fine, fair hair was scraped tightly into a bun, wisps escaping from it like a badly-built nest. The other women all seemed quite jovial as they plodded around behind the counter, slathering margarine on to white rolls and wrapping buns in clingfilm. But Mrs Cresswell was not. Mrs Cresswell looked pained. Disappointed.

When, some evenings, Sally went round to tea, Mrs Cresswell spoke to her in a slow, exaggerated voice, as if she was slightly delinquent.

'And what are you doing for your O-levels again, Sally?'

'English, Maths, French, Chemistry and Needlework.'

'How nice. Needlework. And what a good idea, to focus on five. Five is all anyone needs, isn't it?'

Rowena told Sally once that her mother had been an aspiring 'career woman': she had been heading for greatness in the legal profession. But then she had met Rowena's father and got married and had Rowena and her ambitions had been shelved amidst the ornaments.

Rowena's was one of the few houses Sally ever visited. After school they would let themselves in at the wobbly glass-fronted door, warble a reedy 'Hi,' then leap straight upstairs. They would sit in Rowena's room, which smelled of new pine furniture and hoovered carpet, and discuss the dilemmas of their hearts.

'So are you going to go for it then?'

'What? Go for what?'

'You know. With Colin. Are you going to, you know . . .?'

Sally remembers this particular conversation. It'd had, she supposes, particular relevance. She remembers thinking of Colin Rafferty and blushing and blushing and turning to reach for something, anything, a distraction. A record. She picked it up. *Ever Fallen in Love (With Someone You Shouldn't've).* Rowena had an eclectic mix of singles which even at the time struck her as odd. How could someone like both the Buzzcocks and Supertramp?

'You've gone puce,' observed Rowena.

'Thanks.'

'You have, though.'

And Sally had stared down at the record sleeve.

'I –' Rowena began, and she stopped. Then she said, 'It's just you clam up about him. Ever since we met him. You always go all thingummy, Sal. I know he's the love of your life and everything . . .'

Sally did not reply. She looked around Rowena's room: at the china-headed Pierrot doll staring tragically into the night; at the make-up box and pink slippers; at the tips of the Cindy dolls' feet peeping over the top of the wardrobe. She thought, 'I have a boyfriend called Colin Rafferty.' And a new image of him floated spectrally, heroically, into her mind.

'I will tell you,' she said. 'It's just, I mean, we haven't . . .'

'It's all right,' Rowena sighed, and Sally gazed, hot-faced, through the picture window at the almost technicolour garden beyond.

Occasionally, Sally spent the night at Rowena's house. She remembers pulling flannelette sheets over the mattress of the Cresswells' clanking Zed-bed; standing in the bathroom in her *Love is . . .* pyjamas. She remembers the tiny details that separated Rowena's way of life from hers. The little silver dish containing Mrs Cresswell's jewellery (Sally's mother never took her wedding ring off); the over-large rubberwood fruit-bowl (at home they had a cut-glass trifle bowl); the woven place mats (they had cork boards with pictures of parrots); in the garden, the sprinkler on the lawn (the Tuttles had a watering can). At suppertime Sally would feel like a prodigal daughter, returned from a life of hardship. The four of them would sit around the table in the 'L' of the dining room, eating casserole from large beige dinner plates. Mr Cresswell would eat in total silence. Mrs Cresswell would talk about the woman who used too much washing-up liquid in the gift-shop café. Outside, Mrs Cresswell's windchimes would clank in the breeze, the wires twisting around each other in a way which Sally felt must irritate her.

From time to time she would give little presents to Rowena. Pencil-sharpeners, 45 rpm singles, pretty hairgrips. She also used to give presents to Colin Rafferty. She didn't have a clue about aloofness then, about sangfroid. She was just besotted and would bring these offerings to him, like a cat bringing dead mice to its owner. She bought him a corkscrew and a pocket knife and a badge; she brought him a beautiful green feather and a shiny pebble. Things like that were imbued with meaning – with eternal significance. *Whatever happens, this means I will always love you. This time in our lives will always be . . .*

In all the time he knew her, Colin Rafferty gave her one thing: a postcard bearing the picture of an old Scottish fishwife, gutting herrings. Maybe giving presents heavy with poignancy was not something that men did.

French Knot on Stalks

I first met my husband in Rouen, on something the head of my department insists on calling a 'jolly'.

Jollies consist, in almost every country I have visited, of middle-aged academics helping themselves to wine and canapés in the dark interior of a chain hotel. The canapés are often alarming: potent, fishy things teetering on small oatcakes, too big to eat in one mouthful and too messy to eat in two.

'I'll go for one of these cherry-tomato things,' people mumble, as if someone is forcing them to eat something *or else*. As if the hors d'oeuvres chef is *having a laugh*.

There is also innocuous jazz played low and a certain amount of flirting, particularly from the married ones.

Before I met Kenneth, I used to hang around at these events with female peers from other universities: we would stand near the bar in our best clothes and perfume and wonder if we were having fun. Was it more fun, more *jolly*, than sitting hunched over our computers and dictionaries and time-sheets? It was certainly a change; a social event for which I sometimes felt ill-prepared. My talent for chat was impeded by weeks of sitting alone in my office, surrounded by dusty plants, unread manuscripts and unmarked papers.

It was also a bit like being at Razzles on East Grinstead High Street. The anxious hovering. The pretending. The smoke and mirrors. It was strange seeing your peers in 'casual' attire, worrying that they might not look cool. *Should we let our hair down? Take our handbags to the toilets?* And we really *had* handbags now, real womanly handbags in which we kept packets of paper hankies, wet-wipes, lipstick, diaries, keys, receipts, business cards, photographs of our children. Some of the young mothers even had a nappy or two secreted bulgingly in one of the inner pockets.

I still have pictures of a baby in my wallet. Baby Joe, summer 1980. I can hardly believe how old this baby is now. The year of the Jolly in Rouen, he was in his last year at university.

On that particular evening it was August but already cold, and the Jolly delegates all seemed tired. The next day some of us would have to sit in a small, airless room discussing the translation of poetry from Hebrew into French, and from French into English. Discussing the nuances. The nuances of the nuances.

'Is anyone interested in seeing the Cathedral?' I asked.

No one was. Rouen Cathedral was too far away – an eight-mile taxi ride from our 'central' hotel. Everyone was too tired. One woman was pregnant and planning an early night.

So I had spent most of the evening looking at pictures of other delegates' children. None of them had children as old as my son. The oldest of the other children was nine. The women were all about the same age as me, but still at the stage of discussing potty training, speaking ability, nurseries, the amusing things children say.

'The other day,' said one of the women (a specialist in French Medieval Literature), 'my daughter wanted to help me mop the kitchen floor. There she was, flinging this mop around and she suddenly looked up and said, "Mummy, when I grow up I want to be a floor-mopper."'

The other women laughed. Some helped themselves thoughtfully to more Bombay mix from a bowl sitting on the bar.

'And I thought,' continued the woman, 'where do girls get these thoughts? That they want to mop floors for a living? What happened to female emancipation?'

Nobody seemed to know. Perhaps, girt about with our motherly clobber – nappies in handbags, maternal antennae twitching long-distance – we were all wondering.

'Well, my son is always careering around with action men and guns,' someone began. And I felt a kind of heaviness in my chest. I have heard the Nature versus Nurture debate about once a fortnight for the past two decades. It has become a kind of phobia of mine.

'It's genetic. Nature,' the women agreed. People always agree that it is Nature.

'How about *your* son?' someone asked, turning to me. 'Does he bounce on the sofas too? Is he always *into* everything?'

'My son is twenty-two,' I said, and everyone stopped, glasses of wine and Bombay mix halfway to their mouths.

'No!' said the woman whose daughter wanted to be a floor mopper.

I felt the little group of academic mothers peering at me in the half-light, their brains whirring, calculating my age. I felt suddenly very envious of them – of the small children they had had at the appropriate age – little children, who were not about to leap off into the world; who still enjoyed bedtime milk, soft toys, bubble-blowing.

'He does still hurl himself on to the sofas, though,' I said. And the women paused for a second and laughed; then suddenly, wordlessly, turned and moved on, like a shoal of fish.

I missed something, by being a young mother. Missed out on mother-peers. When girls my age went out in the evenings, I would stay in my parents' house in East Grinstead with my colicky baby son. We would sit and watch *Life on Earth*. When girls my age went *down town* to look at the make-up counters, I went up the road to buy nappies.

Now, women with sons the age of mine are collecting their

pensions. Some of them have silver hair. Some of them are in their sixties.

I missed something from two different directions.

Kensington Outline

Rowena and Sally used to observe Colin's female colleagues from a distance. These women always made Sally feel rather clown-like in her uniform and over-sized school shoes, while they floated about in their sexy tops, hair flicked and static with hair-spray, little belts pulled in tight around their waists. But Rowena reassured her: Sally was the girl he wanted. Sweet Sally. 'No competition, Sal,' she used to say.

Sally's first few dates with Colin Rafferty were furtive, spent in the pedestrian precinct or in the park during school lunch-hour. Rowena came too, following at a distance to make sure Sally was OK. Colin was a lot older than them, she reminded her. Nearly six years. He had informed Sally of this on their second date. It was quite shocking.

'You be careful, Sally,' Rowena had warned her, mother-hen-like, when she relayed this information on to her. 'You know what they're like.'

Rowena was concerned. Possibly a little startled, too – Sally conjectured – that he hadn't chosen *her*. Because Rowena was prettier than her. Rowena was brighter than her. And once, out of the corner of her eye, Sally had noticed a tiny scowl on Rowena's face as she turned to leave. (Before Colin arrived she would go to lurk behind the silver birch trees at the other end of the park.)

Colin and Sally had had very little to say to each other on these early dates. Their conversations seemed always to be at cross-purposes. He would ask a very simple question, and Sally would gabble an extremely complicated response.

'So. When do you go back?'

'Who? What? Go back where?'

'Your school.'

'Oh. We go back on the sixth. But the fifth is the official first day back, it's kind of the first day for the first and second years. But the sixth is, you know, the actual, you know . . .'

'So. The fifth or the sixth?'

This sort of incoherence would happen perhaps three times during the course of a twenty-minute walk. Then Colin would kiss her, tell her that she was sweet and funny – that she made him laugh – and they would part.

'How was he?' Rowena would ask, catching up with her after Colin had gone.

'Oh, Rowena, he's so nice.'

'Yes, but what did he say?'

And Sally looked up at the blue sky above the bowling green, at the pigeons clattering plumply, noisily up into it. She couldn't quite remember what Colin had said. She also didn't have a clue why he wanted to be with her. *Does he really love me? Am I really pretty?*

'He's . . . so nice,' she said.

'Oh, for God's sake, Sally.'

It was Rowena who suggested London Zoo as a place for the first big date out of town. She had decided, from a distance of a few hundred yards, that Colin was respectable enough to go to London with.

'Zoos are dead romantic,' she said. 'Plus, you won't bump into anyone.'

Sally had pondered this. She hardly knew Colin, really, apart from the fact that he was nearly twenty-two and worked in advertising. But at London Zoo she imagined them openly holding hands, chatting about their lives, wandering along the paths in the cool greenness. Happily pointing out the gazelles and parakeets and laughing at the stick insects. They could really get to know each other there. He would see that she was funny but also serious: he would comprehend the intricacies of her mind. And London Zoo *did* seem like a lover-ish place to go; sweetly poignant. It was like the song her parents played on their record player: an old record on their new stereo.

'Something tells me it's all happening at the zoo – I do believe it, I do believe it's true . . .'

On their way to the station, she noticed a man practising yoga. He was standing on a grass embankment at the side of the road, his long arms outstretched.

'Doesn't he look funny?' she said to Colin.

'Probably a student.'

'So? What's wrong with that? I'm a student.'

'No, you're not. You're a schoolgirl.'

She didn't reply. Flirting, sophistication, maturity, did not come easily. She worried about every sentence that came out of her mouth, in case it meant he fell out of love with her. Their relationship, twenty-one days old that Friday, was suspended on the finest, surrealist thread. How was it ever going to work? Sally looked at her watch. It was nearly eleven o'clock; she should have been in the school library with Rowena, revising. But there was a big romantic sun in the sky. There were pigeons and drifts of orange leaves at their feet.

'Do you think that yoga man's discovering his inner self?' she said, hoping she looked very pretty as she spoke. She pushed her right hand through her long brown hair, inadvertently disturbing several kirby grips.

Colin smiled and walked ahead of her to the pedestrian crossing. Sally watched him go, this man she was in love with. She regarded his hair and his jacket and the way he walked. She thought of his kisses, metallic-tasting and intoxicating. *But why does he love me? Does he think I'm pretty? Does he like my mind?* Heart thumping, she watched as Colin began to cross the road. And she lagged behind for a moment. 'I will give him some space,' she thought. 'I will be mysterious.' It was childish, to go rushing after him all the time. So, loitering on the pavement, she turned to watch the yoga man again; to have her own fascinating thing to observe.

But the yoga man had stopped. He was standing there frowning.

'This is not a public performance,' he said. 'I am not a performing seal.' He glared at her with peevish blue eyes and she felt, somehow, that he knew her secret.

By the time they made it to Victoria station she was as nervous as a rabbit. And Colin was in a funny mood. He had that inscrutable air about him, looking around the crowds with his vacant, angelic expression. They walked out of the station into a high wind which blew paper bags around their heads.

'I hate the wind,' Sally said, her voice raised.

'Why?' Colin shouted back. 'It's exciting! Beautiful. Like you!'

Did he say that? She thought she heard him say that. He had a clear, high voice, some of his vowel sounds occasionally betraying an exciting Northern origin. Speaking to him Sally used to try taming her own twanging, Southern vowels, but it never lasted. Like Miss Button, Colin had made a few remarks about her accent. He had once said it was a 'gutbucket' accent, and she didn't even know what he meant. Unlike Miss Button, though, she hoped that Colin thought of her accent with tenderness.

Rowena's presence, that day in 1979, would have been a comfort, a buffer, like those nets of corks that people sling over the sides of barges to stop them crashing into the riverbank. Unmoored, though, precarious, they spent the morning floating around – Covent Garden, the Strand, along the Embankment.

They crossed trafficky roads. They walked beneath avenues of autumn trees. They sat on a green curlicued bench beside the Thames before walking across to Trafalgar Square to stare up at Nelson's Column and three pigeons sitting on his three-cornered hat.

'Did Nelson fight the French?' Sally shouted.

'Yes. Don't you know anything?' Colin replied, before abruptly hoisting himself up on to the plinth of one of the lions, placing his left foot at the base of its tail and pulling himself on to its back.

'Colin!' Sally screeched, feigning delight.

Colin didn't reply. He leaned back against the lion, put his hands beneath his head and closed his eyes.

'Does your friend know anything?' he asked into the wind.

'Who? Rowena? Know anything about what?'

'About life. About history. About the battle of Trafalgar.'

'No more than me.'

'Does she know what Nelson said before he died?'

'Don't think so.'

'Kiss me, Hardy.'

'Sorry?'

'Or was it Kismet?'

'Sorry?'

'What's your school on about, then? What do you all pay your fees for?'

'I don't know!'

You are wonderful, she thought, gazing up at him. *You are wonderful and funny and you have such long eyelashes.*

Colin lay there for a full five minutes, his eyes closed, while the wind blew down the back of Sally's neck. She waited, looking around – at the pigeons again, across to Big Ben in the distance, up at the National Gallery and the steps and the tourists taking photographs.

'Shall we go and get a coffee, then?' Colin asked suddenly from his vantage above her. And he sat up, slid down from the lion, jumped off the plinth and took her hand in his. Sally's heart sprang like a frog.

'I know a place near here,' Colin said, and without speaking further they walked across the square, over the road and down the steps into St-Martin-in-the-Fields. They sat in the crypt, drinking coffee. Sally peered around at the headstones mortared into the walls. There was a leaflet on the table informing them of the fact that a band ('The Cryptics') would be playing there at 7.30 on Saturday evening.

'Could be cool.'

'Yeah.'

She was not sure if it was quite normal to drink coffee in a crypt but she approved of anything she did with Colin. And nothing was normal now, in any case. She, Sally Tuttle, who occasionally still sported a plait, was going out with a twenty-one-year-old man! And when he spoke to her, when he kissed her, it was thrilling but not normal.

When they had finished their coffee they walked up Charing Cross Road and looked at the bookshops. They went into a little shop and bought a paperback on the Metaphysical poets. Then they queued for ages in Foyles to buy another very small book for Colin, on marketing strategies.

'How stupid,' Sally said, about the queuing system.

'It's a time-honoured tradition in Foyles,' Colin retorted. 'Queuing. You wouldn't last a second in Russia.'

'Wouldn't I? Why not?'

'Haven't you heard of the bread queues? Haven't you heard about the way they queue?'

'No.'

And he looked at her. Then he said, 'Never mind. That's why

I like you, honey. Sweet and innocent.'

In the National Portrait Gallery they looked at the paintings for a while – Beatrix Potter, Henry VIII, the Queen, and then got the lift down to the shop. They peered together at the postcards and the cases of coloured slides, Colin's hand sliding lower and lower down Sally's back. She didn't know how to respond to this hand, so she ignored it; she stood, wooden as a figurehead. *Last time I came here*, she thought, *I was with Mum and Dad.*

The women behind the till were discussing lunch.

'That café on the corner does nice rolls,' one of them was saying, into the echoing vaults. 'And what are them things? Spinaca-something. Spinacafrittas?'

'Mm-hmm.'

'Maybe when you go for your lunch break you could pop up there, and . . .'

'Excuse me,' snapped Colin, 'I hate to interrupt but can I just get this?'

And he moved his arm from its new location around Sally's shoulders and pushed across the counter the card bearing the portrait of the Scottish fishwife.

The women looked at him. They did not blink. Then one of them said, 'Certainly, sir.'

'A woman after your own heart,' Colin said when he gave the card to Sally. 'Don't you think she looks like you, in that scarf?'

Sally looked at it. The shawl did look quite a lot like the blue scarf she possessed, the one she wore to look alluring.

'Thanks,' she replied, knowing she would cherish the card, even though the fishwife looked very earnest and not at all romantic. This was the first – and last – thing he ever gave her.

By the time they had been in London for a couple of hours Sally was exhausted with the effort of being happy. She felt like hiding in a phone box to give Rowena a call. Without her she felt out of her depth, a little fearful. *What shall I say to him, Rowena? What shall I say?*

But Rowena wasn't there and she would have to work out what to say on her own. How to be. How to be someone's girl-friend, sitting on the stop-start Tube train, her hair clinging statically to the sleeve of his coat.

They made their way towards Regent's Park, walking hand-in-hand along the pavements, their breath coming out in little cold clouds. They sat for a while on another curlicued bench and Sally rummaged around in her yellow hessian bag for the poetry book she had bought.

'I wonder, by my troth, what thou and I did till we loved? Were we not wean'd till then?' she read out loud, leaning back uncomfortably, her blue woollen-tighted legs on Colin's lap. She stopped and wondered if she had done the right thing: *maybe reciting poetry to him will make me look odd or earnest or –*

'Your voice is beautiful,' Colin said, his eyes closed against the autumn sun.

In a gutbucket way, Sally nearly replied. And she remembers how she had stroked his hair, where it was soft, at his temples. She read on, and wondered what *snorted we, in the seven sleepers' den* meant.

'Oh look, Colin,' she exclaimed suddenly, stopping again to point out a small passing dachshund wearing a crocheted overcoat. Colin turned his head. Then he shivered, sat up, and banged his hands together.

'Small things please you, don't they?'

'I thought he looked cute in that coat. My mum crochets.'

'Your mum does what?' Colin laughed. He took a cigarette out of his top pocket and lit it with a Swan Vesta.

'Does it feel weird,' he asked, taking a puff, 'bunking off school?'

'No,' Sally lied, thinking not of school but of her mother and father, who were both so proud of her and her place at St Hilary's. She had let them down. 'Anyway,' she said, getting up from the bench, 'life's weird whatever. Whatever you do.'

'Weird,' Colin replied. 'Weird weird weird.'

'Even the word weird,' she said, 'sounds weird. If you say it enough times.'

And, alone, she began to laugh.

They reached the Zoo shortly after three. But it was not like the song on her parents' record player. It was not *all happening.* Their illicit day in London had gone flat. Even the wind had dropped, to be replaced by a cold, sleety rain. *Maybe he's realised he's too old for me, Rowena. Maybe I'm not posh enough. Maybe he's thinking he should be with someone who –*

Her stomach rumbled loudly. 'Whoops,' she said, placing a hand over her belly.

'What was that? Concorde taking off?'

'Ha!' she replied, and could think of nothing more to add.

Now things were going decidedly wrong. It felt as if they were sobering up after too much cider. Sally was clumsy, klutzy, a common girl with noisy insides. Colin had become testy, verging on unkind. And the animal enclosures were smaller and more boring than Sally had imagined. Surely, she thought, a twentieth-century zoo should be nicer than this, with swaying trees and long grass for the animals to hide behind. Where there would be leafy retreats. But no: this zoo was just like they always were. Like the awful concrete zoos in her old Peter and Jane books. *Look, Mummy! Look, Daddy! A bear!* The polar bear shuffled back and forth in his small square; the hippos stood at the gates of their pens like strange cows; the arctic hare sat alone and stared through the bars, its fur a dry, yellow-white, like a badly-washed-out paint brush.

Standing by the flamingo cages Sally thrust her hands, star-like, up to the mesh. 'Look!' she exclaimed. 'The flamingoes match my nails!'

Some chagrined-looking owls in the neighbouring cage turned their heads to look at her.

'You've frightened the owls,' Colin snapped.

'Sorry?'

'You've frightened the owls,' he said again, looking up at the two birds sitting high in the branches. It seemed at that moment that he much preferred the owls to her. They were wise and she was stupid. *Patione et consilis*, she thought suddenly, remembering her school badge. But before she could think of anything appropriate to say, he had turned and begun to walk away.

Think of something, think of something.

'I'm just going to find a bog,' she called. Colin and the owls turned, round-eyed, to watch as she stalked off.

But there wasn't even any sanctuary in the Ladies. She had been in there for half a minute when there was a knock on the door and a man walked in.

'Mind if I just come in to clean, love?'

'No, no, that's fine,' Sally replied, wiping her eyes quickly and watching in disbelief as he crashed in with a mop and a bucket of water and a sign saying 'Male cleaner in attendance'.

'Having a nice day?' the man asked convivially, looking at her in the mirror. 'Seen the elephants?'

And he revolved the extremely dirty-looking mop around the bucket, then slapped it down on to the floor tiles.

'They're great,' he said, 'the elephants.'

Star

I'm used to being on my own; slightly *abnormal*. I'm used to people scurrying off when I tell them about myself. People pretend to be cool, unshockable, but they're not. They comment in an interested way about the fact that I, *Rowena Lockhart, MA, PhD, tutor and translator*, gave birth at fifteen. And then they move on. It happens wherever I go. Rouen was no exception. That evening in Rouen, I found myself standing alone, cradling my third wine glass and contemplating going upstairs to my room for an early night.

I had already glanced across the Function Suite to assess the other women, the ones with small children. They were sitting at a low table now, laughing and drinking coffee. Impenetrably alike. Normal. I thought about sitting on my neat hotel bed upstairs and watching the elevated TV, maybe even going over the presentation I was meant to give the next day. I certainly did not feel like joining the normal mothers.

I was, in fact, slightly drunk: not a good state for a single mother. Not a good state for anyone on their own. *Must curb that tendency. Should have had more of those vol au vent things.* And I had been about to put my empty wine glass down on a passing tray, I had been about to head for the stairs, when there was the sound of a man's voice.

'Mesdames, messieurs, dans cinq minutes le tour de la cathédrale va commencer . . .'

A large, rather handsome man was standing in the middle of the room. His accent was good, but not brilliant. Canadian but not French–Canadian. He looked down at his watch. 'Cinq minutes, mesdames, messieurs . . .'

The sight of this man for some reason made me feel cheerful. Why? I looked at him, my vision very slightly blurred. Maybe it was because he had a true kind of jolliness about him. He was tall and slightly overweight and he looked as if he didn't take events like this too seriously. He was not earnest. He did not like earnestness. He was wearing a creased suit. I smiled at him. The man noticed me and smiled back. Then he turned, walked past the women with the handbags and disappeared.

I didn't know where to look. The man's departure was so surprisingly abrupt that it had brought tears to my eyes. It seemed an unkind thing to do, after smiling at me. Cruel. I stood and watched my empty wine glass being carried with others on the tray into the kitchens and felt a familiar sensation – a desolate feeling that I have been prone to for years.

But then, just as suddenly, the man had returned. My heart lurched again with renewed hope. He walked back into the room, past the women with the handbags and straight up to me.

'So,' he said, as if we had already been introduced, 'have you seen the Cathedral yet?'

I felt myself blush, embarrassed by my watery eyes.

'Not yet. Well, not this time. The last time I saw it I was fifteen,' I replied in a rush. 'I came here on a school exchange,' I added, thinking of my old friend Sally Tuttle, *la famille Duval,* the trip to the Bayeux Tapestry.

The man smiled at me. He seemed to want me to continue talking.

'It doesn't actually seem that long ago now I'm back,' I said. The man had greyish eyes, very clear and kind.

'Well,' he said, 'it probably hasn't changed much. But there's a coach trip, if you're interested. To see it floodlit.'

'It wasn't floodlit when I last saw it.' I noticed that I was slurring my words.

'Things do change, then. Things progress. I'm meant to be organising folk,' the man said. 'I'm the organiser for the evening. Look, it says so here.'

And he pulled forward the badge on his collar.

'So. If you want to come, the coach goes at ten. From the front of the hotel. It's got *Vacances Monet* written on the side.'

'It would, wouldn't it?' I said.

'Yes,' he smiled, 'it would,' and he touched my arm very briefly as he said goodbye, but in a friendly, possibly even kindred-spirited way.

At five to ten I went down to the hotel foyer and got on the coach. It was half-empty: there were a couple of elderly lecturers on board, and a few academic parents with their sleepy children, making me miss my once eight-year-old son. It was all very polite. Very cultured and civilised, everyone in groups of two, three or four apart from me and the driver. The driver and I were units. The driver sat on his seat, a cigarette in his mouth. I peered out through the coach window at the neon bar sign and the plate-glass hotel doors. It was cold – a clear, black sky with stars. I wrapped my *Jolly-appropriate* shawl more tightly around my shoulders.

Fly, Attached

She discards things too easily sometimes. Holds on to them for years, and then just lets them go. Sally thinks about Rowena Cresswell's green dress and regrets her decision to leave it in the dress agency.

The sky outside turns a greyish-orange as she stands in John Lewis's haberdashery department, deliberating over the tapisserie wool and the Pearl Cotton No. 5. Sometimes it worries her a little: this inability to make decisions. *Should I choose the sea-green or the leaf-green? The azure or the cobalt?* She is the kind of person who can waste a lot of time deliberating over things like this. Adjusting her expression to one of serenity and hope, Sally picks up all four shades of green *coton à broder* and moves towards the Pay Here counter.

She misses her train back home and has to wait thirty-five minutes for the next one. She sits on a bench with her bag of threads and her bag of rejected clothes. She does not feel like a leading practitioner in the field of embroidery.

It is getting dark now. She thinks of her daughter and hopes she is wearing enough layers to cope with the cold: these days Pearl never seems to appreciate the requirement for layers. Sally has not, of course, had time to buy anything to wear herself, for the embroidery conference tomorrow. No life-enhancing new coat. No practical handbag. And now, sitting at Victoria station with her old coat and her handbag with too many straps, she suddenly has thirty-five minutes of time; potential clothes-shopping time in which she can do nothing. Visiting Sock Shop will not suffice. So she remains on the bench. She sighs and looks at her lap, her unsatisfactorily pointy knees beneath her woollen skirt. She wants something to occupy her hands. She is not used to sitting with empty hands. She reflects that, that morning, she had stuffed the post into her handbag on her way out of the house, and now she gets it all out to read. She opens the envelopes quickly, one after another, resting them on her lap. There is a letter from the Ecclesiastical Arts Foundation, a letter from the Embroiderers' Guild, a Damart catalogue, a flyer about hearing aids, an electricity bill and a wrongly-addressed postcard: picture of a waterfall, some rocks and a spindly tree. She turns it over.

> Hardraw Force, Yorshire Dales National Park.
> At nearly 90 feet, this is claimed to be England's
> highest unbroken waterfall. Brass band contests
> are held annually in the gorge at its base.

> *Dear Grandad*
> *This is near where we are staying. We went for a walk here yesterday and Mummy fell in. Hope you are well.*
> *Love, Celeste.*

Sally pictures the scene – some poor woman toppling into a shallow stream, a brass band playing in the distance. She looks up and smiles at an elderly woman in a tracksuit who has come to sit on the bench beside her. The woman, mumbling something to herself, peers surreptitiously at Sally's letters. Sally shuffles a little further up the bench.

The letter from the Ecclesiastical Arts Foundation describes how *thrilled* they are to have commissioned an artwork from her. The letter from the Embroiderers' Guild expresses how *thrilled* they are to have booked her for a talk, in Edinburgh, on the art of embroidery. Sally does not know how to respond to so many thrilled people. It is not something she has ever had to do. She pictures herself standing in a Scottish hotel room, her English voice twanging on, competing with a coffee percolator on a side table.

The elderly woman in the tracksuit sighs and gets up again. A pigeon comes and pecks at some old French Fries which are stuck to the floor.

Sally looks at the catalogue from Damart. Even Damart is very pleased with her.

> *Once again we are delighted to invite you, Ms Sally Tuttle, one of our most valued premier customers, to our next Special Events Day. Make any purchase and we'll be delighted to give you absolutely free* A FABULOUS FLORAL TABLECLOTH AND MATCHING NAPKINS!

Damart catalogues, like *Embroidery Times*, punctuate Sally's life at regular intervals. She and Pearl are fond of these too: of their 'winter-busting' socks and knickers; of the models' resilient smiles and strange willingness to be seen in rosebud-decorated lounger suits.

Now two men are having an argument outside Tie Rack, clumsily prodding and pushing each other around, hands hard and angry. It is the sort of incoherent male argument that suddenly escalates, becomes wild and bloody and frightening, injuring innocent bystanders. Sally watches as two men in uniforms come to separate them, and they all plod, shouting at each other, down the platform. After a while another woman comes and sits beside her, listening to some very loud music on tiny black headphones. *Tsh, tsh, tsh.* Her boyfriend comes to join her. 'Shove up,' he observes. He is also wearing headphones. They sit side by side, listening to their headphones.

In East Grinstead the sky is a pure grey, almost beautiful if you looked at it objectively. East Grinstead itself is not a place of great beauty. There is the little cluster of old shops in the High Street but the majority of the town is without pretension. Over a lot of it seems to hang the disappointment of the suburbs. The stigma of being near London, but not London. The failure of being Sussex but not rural Sussex. All the shops seem to sell the same things: plastic buckets, galvanised shovels, dog bowls, cassettes, baby clothes. Walking past Woolworths, Sally glances through the window to see an elderly woman hovering by the pic'n'mix, petrified with indecision.

Let me not become like that.

She looks at her watch. She pictures her hotel room in Edinburgh, her floral sponge bag, her dressing gown, her change of clothes.

Sally's parents live in a new bungalow on the edge of town, not far from the Cresswells' old house. Their bungalow is small and easy to maintain. They have a doorbell that goes 'ding-dong,' an ivy growing up a trellis, tartan slippers in the porch and painted glass butterflies suspended from a small ornamental sorbus tree. In their living room they display framed examples of Sally's work.

She is late now, and there is only just enough time, before she has to leave again, for a cup of tea. Not for the plate of sandwiches that she can see waiting on the kitchen sideboard, or the small glass of sherry, or the iced Madeira cake.

'I'm really sorry, Mum,' she says. She hangs on to her bag of embroidery silks and feels guilty.

Her mother is wearing a roll-neck jumper and a tweed skirt and looks very elegant. Almost chic. She can do that, much better than Sally. Her hair is thick and still with a lot of ginger in it. Her nose is aquiline, her eyes dark.

They drink tea. Her mother has always made the best tea Sally has ever drunk, just the right strength and temperature, in a white, rose-patterned cup. And while they drink she talks about one of their neighbours, Mavis, who is in hospital with her leg in traction.

'The doctors say it might be suspended like that for weeks,' she says, leaning against the worktop. Hanging on the clothes-dryer above her head is her old white bathrobe.

'Surely not weeks?'

'That's what she said the doctors said.'

From the living room Sally's father, whose feet, resting on a pouffe, she can just make out around the edge of the door, says, 'Days. It was days, love.'

Sally goes to her parents' house once a week and worries that her dad is getting distant, that her mother is getting anxious. ('How's your work going, darling?' she asks, playing with the rings on her wedding finger. 'How's the shop? And the embroidery? Are the evangelical people happy?' Her mother can't quite believe that, for a living, her only child spends her time sewing. And then there is her love life. Her unfortunate relationships. 'When are you going to find yourself a nice man?' her mother asks sometimes, as if Sally is twenty-two. 'Maybe,' Sally replies, 'I am never going to find a nice man.')

Her mother looks at her. 'How's Pearl getting on at school?' she asks.

'Fine. Busy. She's still rehearsing for that concert.'

'We're hoping to come along to that.'

'That's nice. She'd be really pleased.'

Pearl plays the flute. Currently, she is rehearsing for a concert at the end of term. They are playing dreadful things: something patriotic by Elgar, and *The Ride of the Valkyries*. In rehearsals she sits between her best friend Caroline and a girl called Avril who is so tall and thin that she folds up like a music stand.

'Has she got a boyfriend?' Sally's mother asks.

'Not to my knowledge,' Sally replies, obscurely irritated.

'Can't you tell?'

'It's not always obvious. *You* couldn't ever tell, could you? Anyway, I don't think she'd –'

'I could tell when you were acting strangely, darling. I could tell that.'

'Oh. And do you think Pearl's acting strangely?'

Her mother sniffs and is quiet for a moment. 'Maybe.'

'What makes you say that?'

'No reason really.'

'So why say it?'

'It was just an observation, darling.'

'You and your observations, Mum,' Sally says, more snappily than she intended.

'Well, you're always so . . .'

'So *what*?'

'So head in the clouds.'

'What?'

Her mother says no more. She has always been slightly irked by Sally's dreaminess. By her apparent lack of motivation. *Is it a generational thing?* Sally imagines her thinking. *Do they all hover about like this, waiting for something to happen?* Maybe it is to do with the war. Her mother was one of the baby-boomers born in the Forties, when people seemed to be so much more constructive. She was a young girl during the 'make-do-and-mend' era. Sally's grandfather used to put cardboard in his shoes to make them last longer. Her grandmother saved small lengths of string.

Now her mother begins to move around the kitchen, rearranging things and humming. 'Don't Sit under the Apple Tree.'

'Don't Sit under the Apple Tree' is a sign. A sign for what is coming next.

'Seen John much lately?' she asks, taking the cling-film off the plate of sandwiches.

'Not much.'

'Just thought your paths might have crossed.'

'No. Not recently.'

'Haven't been in touch much then?'

When she met Pearl's father Sally was twenty-seven: a disappointed, underqualified young woman who had left school too soon; a young woman sitting in a corner of an adult education class with a huge embroidery frame and a basket of tangled wools. John was a welder: an artistic one, tutoring a workshop. They first spoke to each other in the canteen, halfway through their classes. He was interested in the embroidery Sally was doing, a rather complicated zoo scene. It involved owls, polar bears, flamingoes. He told her that embroidery was not unlike metalwork in the patience required, in the intricacy, and invited her to look round the studio where he taught Metalwork for Beginners.

'Interesting,' Sally said, looking at the pile of molten pewter he was working on.

'It's called *Woman Sighing*.'

'I know how she feels.'

And he looked at her with admiration.

John was entirely different from Colin Rafferty. He was not upsetting. That was the main thing. And he did not make her blush or dream. He was slightly overweight, quiet, with a lot of dark, messy hair. He did not have mercurial wit, social poise, grace. *But*, Sally thought, *he has something truer, more lasting than that.* He did. She was with John for less than a year before she became pregnant. This was not her intention at all. Nor John's. 'Oh Christ,' said John.

Becoming pregnant was, at the time, a huge mistake. And it had made her think of Rowena all over again: her former friend Rowena Cresswell, who had begun by then to alter in her memory, to become almost a fable. 'The Friend who Changed'. She had not seen her for nearly thirteen years by that time. Now, feeling exhausted and sick at ten weeks gone, looking in the bathroom mirror at the noticeable swelling of her bare stomach, Rowena Cresswell was clear in her mind again: her face, her clothes, her smell, her way of speaking. Fifteen-year-old Rowena Cresswell, before she betrayed her.

Sally's mother doesn't ask any more about John, although she likes talking about him. She has always rather liked John, despite the fact that he went off with another woman years ago. He and Sally had discussed marriage, they had gone as far as checking out the registry office, and then he went off with a weaving instructor called Miriam. Miriam wove very complicated self-portraits using cardboard, brass tacks and black cotton. She made Sally think of a bower-bird, all energy and indignation. After a while she started to weave portraits of John: unappealing images with huge noses and dark expressions. She gave them titles like *The Irresolute* and *Why?*, and John retreated, puzzled and a little frightened to a one-bedroom flat in Chingford. He has remained there ever since. Pearl sees him most weekends. Sally sees him perhaps once every two months. She has still never quite forgiven him for leaving them. And sometimes she thinks of him in his small, messy flat in Chingford, and feels sad that she let him. But she does not have the right skills, she has come to realise: her relationships never go as planned. They are not the burnished, sparkling things she once dreamed of. They have been tangential, lop-sided, amazed at their own existence.

The wind bends the sorbus tree in her parents' garden and all the glass butterflies make a jangling noise. Sally peers past, into the street.

'I have to go now, Mum, or I'll be late for Pearl.'

'Well,' her mother says, 'sorry it was so short and sweet, darling. I suppose we won't see you till you get back.'

'No.'

'Well, I hope it goes well.'

And something makes her heart tighten.

'I don't know what I'm going to say, Mum.'

'Just say what you'd normally say.'

'But I don't normally say anything about my embroidery.'

Her mother walks around the table to give her a hug. 'Tell them why you do it, love,' she says.

And Sally leans into her perfumed, familiar jumper.

'Sometimes,' she says, 'I don't even know.'

Pearl

She named her daughter Pearl because she thought it was a pretty name. Unusual. It has a shimmering, peaceful quality and it alludes to something precious, which, of course, she is. A pearl is something beautiful that has emerged from a tough time. When she named her, she did not think of its overtones of old women, of old women who were young when beehive hairstyles and kohl eyeliner and Capstan cigarettes were in fashion.

Pearl.

Iridescent. Moon-like.

She thought also of that line in *Othello*, that moved her once in an English lesson at school, Rowena's chair empty beside her:

> *. . . then you must speak*
> *Of one that lov'd not wisely but too well;*
> *Of one not easily jealous but, being wrought,*
> *Perplex'd in the extreme; of one whose hand,*
> *Like the base Indian, threw a pearl away*
> *Richer than all his tribe . . .*

'So you're going to be mother-of-pearl,' John said when Sally had finally made her mind up about the name. (They had agreed that she, having lumbered enormously about and given birth, should be the one with the final say.) 'Nacre.'

'Sorry?'

'Nacre. Mother-of-pearl. You see it in crosswords a lot. That's about the only time you see it.'

'Oh.'

John had wanted to give their daughter a more normal name. Something not open to mockery at school.

'It won't be mocked at school,' Sally said, when Pearl was about three weeks old – pale, beautiful, whole, priceless. The idea of her going to school one day seemed ludicrous.

'It will get mocked,' John said.

'No it won't.'

Since then she has been known as Surly Pearl, Pearly Queen, Furball, Pert, Pearldrops, Burly Pearl (despite being as willowy as a tree).

'Mum,' Pearl said to Sally when she was about twelve and had taken briefly to calling herself by her middle name, Emma (which John chose), 'why did you have to give me such a stupid name?'

'It's not a stupid name,' Sally retorted, upset.

'Yes it is. It's an old-lady name. You get Pearls in bingo halls. Pearls with false teeth.'

'You get Julias with false teeth,' Sally said, thinking of an elderly neighbour she used to visit as a girl, whose teeth made a clattering noise when she spoke. 'Or Catherines. Or Sarahs.'

'Yes, but you don't think of them with false teeth, do you? Or in bingo halls.'

'I can't see this conversation going anywhere useful,' Sally said, peering back at her needlework (her tower-block picture).

Recently, though, she is pleased to say that Pearl likes her name again. She seems to have grown proud of its unusual quality. It is a *jolie-laide* kind of name. An ironic name. It is, she says, *cool.* The kind of name, Sally admits now, that requires a pretty girl to carry it off. But thankfully she is pretty.

Pearl is late. And her phone is switched off. This is nothing new. Her life is more of a mystery than it used to be, but Sally accepts that: that is how a girl's life is. She knows she will just have to stand on the platform and wait for her.

While waiting she approaches East Grinstead station's only-functioning Photo-Me booth. She needs a passport-sized photo for the little laminated conference card she has been told to expect by the Embroiderers Guild. She combs her hair quickly in front of the small rectangular mirror, steps into the booth and selects the background curtain colour – *blue, not that dreadful orange.* She adjusts the height of the little round stool, her legs absurdly visible beneath the tiny privacy curtain, places £4.80 in the slot, smiles her big smile and waits for the flash. Nothing happens. Apart from a small, blinking red light which says PLEASE INSERT MONEY.

'I have inserted money,' Sally mumbles to the booth.

She leans forward and bangs the coin slot. The sign does not stop blinking. She presses the *rejected coins* button. Nothing happens.

After a short while she sees a pair of legs stop on the other side of the curtain. She notes with sinking heart the jeans and expensively ugly trainers of an East Grinstead youth.

"Snot working,' says the voice belonging to the legs.

'No.'

She sits for a moment longer. Then, £4.80 and all dignity gone, she gets up from the little round stool, pulls back the curtain and steps out of the booth. The boy has disappeared.

She walks over to a bench and sits beside a large woman eating chips. She continues to wait for her daughter.

Someone has hung a plastic Santa Claus from the main doorway of the station, and his feet keep banging people's heads as they walk past. There is a smell of cigarettes, damp paving, lavatory cleaner.

People get off trains, find each other, hug, kiss and depart, and Ms Sally Tuttle (43, single mother, award-winning embroiderer) is still waiting. She imagines her daughter dawdling somewhere, having some conversation with her friends. A conversation that seems relaxed but is, she knows from experience, fraught with tension.

She looks at her watch. Four fifty-five. After a lull a uniformed man walks around her very deliberately with a large-headed broom.

'Not on the train, love?'

'She'll turn up,' Sally replies. She watches the broom as it picks up station debris: tickets, leaflets, hot-dog wrappers.

Then after five unfathomable minutes or so there she is, ambling across the empty platform towards her, and Sally's heart lifts. *Pearl. My Pearl.* Pearl has, she fears, inherited her father's slightly drifting walk and Sally's lack of self-belief. She is carrying her flute case and her spongy plastic school bag. She is wearing a pair of incredibly baggy green trousers. They remind Sally of the air-filled pyjama trousers she and Rowena Cresswell had to practise life-saving techniques with, in the school swimming pool.

'Hi Mum.'

'Hello, sweetheart.'

Wearily, Pearl hands her a plastic carrier bag. Another plastic bag to carry.

'Oh.'

'Do you mind? Just for a bit.'

'I suppose not.'

Sometimes Sally doesn't know quite what to say to her daughter, who has become a little distant lately, a little surly even. Her voice, as a child, was as clear as running water, but these days she always seems to mumble. Sally hears her talking to her friends on her mobile phone sometimes, and she doesn't understand what she is talking about. She looks at her, her once smiling, once little girl. Her pony-tailed child with the blue wellingtons. She remembers when she used to paint pictures for her: Mummy smiling resolutely through forests, across beaches, over hills.

Pearl's mascara has gathered in dark smudges beneath her eyes.

'Anything wrong, sweetheart?'

'Nope.'

'Good. Well. Let's get home for a cup of tea.'

Sally says nothing about her day spent adrift in London's haberdashery departments. She does not mention the little girl's comment ('Mummy, is that lady cross?'), or the worrying array of embroidery silks, or the sense, the sense as she skulked around the Gütermann cottons and the Lucky Lady button cards, that she should not be here, she should not be doing this. She just grips the two plastic bags in her right hand and looks around the station at the people walking back and forth. Passengers. People on affirmative, life-changing journeys.

'So how long are you away for again?' Pearl asks. 'For your embroidery thingy?'

'Till Saturday. You sure you don't mind me going?'

She peers at her daughter. She has hardly ever left her overnight. Maybe three or four times since she was a toddler. There has never really been the need.

Pearl says, 'I'm going to stay with Dad, aren't I?'

'Yes, I know, sweetheart. I know, technically you're –'

'Chill, Mum. It's only for one night, isn't it? It's your big break and stuff. And I'll be at school all day anyway.'

Sally wants to kiss her cheek but they are in a station and her daughter would be embarrassed.

They go to wait at the bus stop. Sally feels suddenly tired. The fingers on her right hand have stiffened into a needle-holding position. Her back is bent like a peasant woman who has been digging up turnips all day. She does not feel like a woman on the brink of a professional break. When the bus arrives the two of them climb on and sit, wedged together on a small plaid-patterned seat. Pearl stares through the window at the denizens of East Grinstead. A woman in a pink jacket is pulling a tiny, tiny dog along the pavement. Two schoolgirls in uniform wait at the pelican crossing, cigarettes between their fingers. And Pearl turns her head, not wanting them to notice her sitting there with her mum. Sally doesn't say anything. Perhaps it is to do with her years of service as a clothing alterations expert; her years of restraint and seriousness; of sticking pins into waistbands and lying about people's figures.

Her sewing room is the smallest room in their house. The floor is covered with a pink spongy carpet which the landlord chose. When Sally puts the radiator on in the winter, the room smells of the pine shelving unit and the cheap wardrobe in which she keeps her frames and unused canvases. It is a Nordic smell suggesting forests and fjords. Her finished canvases are propped up in ranks jutting into the room. Her cows, her moonscapes, her fields, her people.

When they get home she glances into the room, at her sewing table under the window, and the vase of red carnations she has put there. The flowers perfectly match the scarlet embroidery silk she is using to create some little red flowers at Martha and Mary's feet. There is something pleasing about that. Beside her basket of threads there is a photograph of the three of them: Pearl, John and Sally, sitting outside a pub in Yorkshire. 1997. Pearl has a tendrilly fringe and gap-teeth. John is puzzled and putting on weight; and there is Sally, with the big smile on her face, and her arms around them both.

There is not much else. Little things. Haberdashery. Beside her shelving unit is a piece of card with six green buttons sewn on to it. There is her box of sequins. And there is her pincushion with its pony-tailed Chinese men. Yellow, turquoise, scarlet and pink satin, pierced over the years by thousands of pins. She has always loved this pincushion. Her mother gave it to her when she was sixteen and needed little cheerful things. The men are holding hands, their fingertips – triangular points – stretching across an almost impossible gap.

'When do you want to eat, Mum?' Pearl calls from outside the door, and Sally turns and walks out of the room. 'Have I got time for a shower before supper?'

'I should think so,' Sally replies vaguely, 'It'll give me time to . . .'

And Pearl, standing on the narrow landing, silently switches on the bathroom light as if it's a magic trick. They both peer into the bathroom: at the framed dolphin-embroidery above the bath; and at the array of shampoo and conditioner bottles.

'Macaroni cheese do?'

'Yeah.'

'Right,' Sally says, hovering in the doorway. Sometimes, she reminds herself of her mother.

In the kitchen she chops three small, overripe tomatoes, her heart tight as a winding engine, anticipating the talk she has to give. *What if I can remember nothing, what if I stand there transfixed?* And she has so many things to say to Pearl before she leaves in the morning: *Don't forget Dad's picking you up tomorrow. Make sure you take your flute in for rehearsal. Are you sure you've got my mobile number? And are you sure, are you really sure you don't mind me going? Because I can cancel, easily, sweetheart. I just have to give them a . . .*

'Have you got any homework?'

'Not much.'

'Well, make sure you do it, though, sweetheart.'

'Yeah.'

Pearl spends thirty minutes in the bathroom and another forty-five in her room again, drying her hair with her interminably droning hairdryer. At last she returns to the kitchen, bringing with her the plastic carrier bag.

'So. I thought you might like this,' she says, handing Sally the bag.

'Oh! This is . . . exciting.'

Sally wipes her hands on the front of her apron, takes the bag and brings out its content. A book. A paperback book entitled *Memories of the Blitz.*

She is not quite sure what to think. 'Thanks very much,' she says.

'I just thought you might like it,' Pearl says again. 'It looked like your kind of thing.'

'Did it?' Sally replies. She feels a little alarmed. 'I don't remember the Blitz, darling,' she says. 'It's more, like, Nana's era.'

Pearl looks at her. 'I know that,' she says.

Sally touches her cheek and sits down at the table to look at the book. She turns to the photographs in the middle. There is a picture of a double-decker bus in a bomb crater. Another one of a small girl wearing a gas-mask. She is sitting on her mother's lap. Her mother is also wearing a gas-mask.

'Thanks very much,' she says again. 'It's . . . great.'

Pearl always mocks her for using that word. *Great.* And for using the words *brilliant*, *appalling*, *gym-shoes* and *hi-fi.*

She wonders if Pearl imagined she might do embroideries of the Blitz. It alarms her a little, that she might think that.

Pearl is sitting in her chair now, contemplating the dish of macaroni cheese. She doesn't speak for a moment. Then she says, 'I'll probably go round to Nana and Grandad's while you're away.'

She picks up the jug of water and pours herself a big tumblerful. And Sally notices that she is blushing. Her face, for no apparent reason, has become a little pink.

Sally picks up a serving spoon and slices into the macaroni cheese.

'Maybe when I come back we could do something nice,' she

says. 'It'll be Saturday. We could go up to town. Maybe we could go shopping? Or go to the pictures?'

'Yeah, maybe.'

And they fall silent again. They eat. Four houses along, the gadget-orientated young man starts up his new electric drill. He is doing something to his bedroom window frame.

'So,' Sally says. Sometimes it is so much effort being a resourceful mother.

And after a moment Pearl puts her fork down.

'I'm actually quite tired, Mum,' she says. 'Do you mind if I just go to bed?'

'Oh –'

'I'm just going to lie down, I think, if you don't mind. I've got a bit of a headache.'

'But –'

Pearl stands up and pushes her chair under the table. 'Night, then. See you in the morning.'

'Oh.'

Sally stares up at her daughter, a few thick strands of macaroni pronged on to her fork. She feels baffled. Uncomprehending. She feels middle-aged and upset.

'Well,' she says, 'OK. Night, sweetheart. Thanks for the book. It'll be great for . . . research.'

'I thought you'd like it.'

And Sally wants to get up and hug her. She wants to say something light and kind, something witty about the macaroni cheese, but her daughter has already left the room.

The fridge clicks and hums. The clock on the cooker ticks. Sally sits at the table and listens to her daughter walking about the house in her slippers.

She does not go straight to her room. She goes into the bathroom. Then, after a few minutes, Sally hears her walking across the landing into the sewing room. She does not normally go in there. Sally sits still, unmoving, and wonders what she is doing. There is the sound of drawers being opened and things being moved around. Sally hears an incomprehensible clanking noise and her sewing machine is pushed to one side. A drawer is opened in her little shelving unit. *What is she doing? What is she doing?* Then there is the sound of something falling, something shattering, and Pearl cursing under her breath. Sally frowns. She sits and waits for Pearl to come out with shards of glass or china in her hands, looking for the dustpan and brush. But she doesn't. After another five minutes or so, Sally hears her slink out quietly, like a cat-burglar, and into her own room.

Sally remains at the kitchen table for over half an hour. She feels fragile, like an eggshell turned upside down in its cup. *What is she doing? What is she not telling me? Should I phone Mum? Should I phone her school? Perhaps I should phone John?*

She gets up and dials John's number, but there is no answer.

She is about to head upstairs for bed when she hears Pearl's door opening again. Sally sits and watches her reflection appear in the window. She is creeping along the dark hallway, carrying a waste-paper basket.

'Hallo,' Sally says.

'Oh,' Pearl exclaims, halting, like a field mouse alert to an owl.

'I broke your vase,' she frowns, walking further into the room with the waste-paper basket. 'That blue one.'

'Oh, Pearl.'

'I was just looking for something in your sewing room. In your little filing cabinet.'

'What were you looking for?'

'Nothing. Just a needle. I've got a splinter.'

'Have you? Let me see.'

'It's OK. I got it out.'

Sally looks at her. 'I thought I heard you crashing about in there,' she says. 'You didn't damage my embroidery, did you? Didn't get glass on it? Or water?'

'No. It's fine,' Pearl says. 'I'll . . . get another vase.'

She puts the waste-paper basket on the floor.

She's tired, Sally thinks, she's very tired. 'You had a long day,' she says. 'It makes you over-tired and then you bump into things.'

'I suppose.'

Sally thinks: We are like Robinson Crusoe and Man Friday. Alone on a desert island. And not even speaking the same language. The skin beneath Pearl's eyes is tinged with grey. She stares through the window at the streetlights.

'Do you think I'm pretty?' she asks.

The phone rings some time after eleven when Sally is in bed, under her duvet, wearing the slippers, the leather-soled Aztec slippers she has owned since she was seventeen. It is John on the phone. He says, 'Hi. I dialed 1471.'

'Right.'

'So. Is Pearl coming to stay tomorrow or what?'

'Yes,' Sally replies, squinting in the sudden yellow light of the anglepoise. She glances across the room, at her spare embroidery frame, her needle case, her basket of threads.

'So you're going to Edinburgh then?'

'Yes,' she replies, looking up at her luminous ceiling-stars.

'It's not particularly convenient.'

'Well, I'm sorry, but I did tell you weeks ago. This is, you know, my big break.'

John sighs. 'I was meant to be going out tomorrow night,' he says.

'Well.' She is aware of a loose piece of wool inside her left slipper, beneath the arch of her foot. 'You'll have to rearrange it, I'm afraid.'

He sighs again.

'A date, was it?' Sally asks, wiggling her foot.

But John does not reply.

She can imagine him roaming around his studio-apartment in Chingford – bearded, a trail of banana skins and old coffee mugs in his wake.

'I'll pick her up from school, then,' he says.

'Thank you. Tomorrow. Friday. Do you remember what time school finishes?'

'Of course I do.'

'OK then.'

Sally holds the phone against her ear with her shoulder, reaches down under the duvet, pulls off her left slipper, turns it inside out and breaks off the strand of wool. She has strong, professional, thread-snapping hands. Her slippers, these days, are an assemblage of snapped threads.

'I'm only away a day and a night,' she says. 'I'm sure you can pick up your romantic life when I get back.'

And John nearly does not say goodbye. Then, at the last moment, he does. They are mature people. They are forty-four and forty-three.

Before going to sleep, Sally calculates how many years she has owned her slippers.

Stem Outline

Sometimes I still wonder about my old teachers. About the despondent Miss Haugh, the *upwards-and-onwards* Miss Gordon, and Miss Button, peculiar Miss Button. I think in particular about Miss Button. Her fierceness. That man I saw her with once, in town, in a sports car. And her habit of confiscating sweets. Where did she put all those sweets? I wonder, too, why she chose those particular blouson patterns for us all to sew. Was it because the end result was so profoundly ugly? I recall mine was a stripy orange material, and Sally's had little blue flowers on it. Nobody, not even the prettiest girl, could have looked good in a garment like that.

'She has a warped mind, that woman,' I remember once mumbling to Sally Tuttle. And we looked across the room at pretty Miss Button, sitting behind her desk in a new cashmere sweater. Miss Button beamed back disconcertingly, took a sweet from a confiscated packet and popped it into her mouth.

'D'you think she's in lurve?' Sally asked. 'She looks all perky today.'

'Dunno.'

After Sally had started seeing Colin Rafferty I remember being embarrassed about the word *love.*

I looked down at my sewing pattern. *Pin front interfacing to wrong side of front yoke.*

'What is a front yoke?' I asked. 'Is it – ?'

'Rowena Cresswell,' Miss Button's voice interjected, 'unless you get on with your work *in silence* you will have to leave the room.'

Miss Button used to like lobbing harsh pronouncements, like hand grenades, into the torpor of a late afternoon. The thing about Miss Button was: she was sarcastic, but she wouldn't let you join in with the sarcasm. She knew the other teachers were ridiculous but she wouldn't tolerate *us* saying so. She was young, but she was *so much more mature* than we were.

She had a curious, stalking walk too, I recall – a gait of immense self-importance which used to impress and slightly frighten me. I remember her stalking in her quiet shoes down the corridors, through the Resource Area, past the portrait of our school's noble, bejewelled benefactor. In class she would pace like a caged and beautiful peacock up the rows of spotty, sweaty schoolgirls. At lunchtimes she would prowl past the desolate octagonal tables. 'Enjoying your rice pudding, girls?' she would ask.

She also had a very soul-destroying habit of taking apart your work. She was even rumoured to take work home with her, to unpick at her leisure.

'Hopeless girl,' she would reprimand someone who had mangled her blouson pattern, lopping off notches and shearing along the wrong lines. 'Shoddy, shoddy work.'

And she would glare at the girl, her eyes a dark, beautiful brown.

Sometimes, I remember, when she was bored at the end of the day, she might lull us all into a false sense of camaraderie by engaging us in girlish conversation. She would sit on her desk, impeccable even at four in the afternoon, and discuss men. She would criticise the East Sussex Comp boys. She would talk about the Robert Redford film she had just seen, or muse on the failings of the day's youth.

'The problem with boys today,' she would say, 'is they have no sense of style. Half of them are unwashed and they walk around in those awful down-at-heel shoes. Don't they? Those grotty, grey shoes.'

Then she would flex her own beautifully-turned ankle, incline her head towards the window and gaze at the street beyond, as if yearning for the impossibly exotic existence which she knew was waiting for her.

Sally Tuttle and I sat side by side, secretly counting the number of times Miss Button used the word 'grotty' and jotting the number down in our rough books. Once, it reached as many as fourteen in a triple lesson. Miss Button was contemptuous of everyone. Although there had been that man in that low-slung sports car. 'I suppose he wasn't too grotty,' I thought, brushing my fringe back, my bangles jangling down my arm.

The other day I described those blousons (*very easy / très facile*) to Kenneth. The waistline, I told him, had actually ended at mid-buttock and was elasticated, creating a bulging, balloon-like effect. The cuffs were also elasticated. The neckline was high and boxy. The finishing touch was a bow attached to the collar.

'Attractive.'

'Certainly was.'

'And do you think Miss Button would have worn one?'

'Not if you'd paid her a million quid.'

Appearance mattered a lot to us then. The details mattered so much that sometimes you could overlook the larger picture. Sally Tuttle and I worried incessantly about our skin tone (greasy / 'combination'), teeth (not straight enough), hair (too fine / too mouse). We discussed how far we could take in the sideseams of our skirts before the teachers noticed. And at breaktimes, meeting in the school toilets, I remember how we fussed endlessly with the important detail of our hair. We used to try to give it more 'volume' by bending forwards until it trailed against the ground and our faces reddened; then we would pull it into a tight bunch and snap in a hairband. When we stood up again, our ponytails would be ridiculously high, and our hair would bounce, *bouffant*, above our scalps. We resembled gonks. The look of 1979.

I remember taking magazines into school, with titles like *Hair*, *Hairstyles* and *Style*. Sally and I scrutinised the photographs: pictures of grim-faced young women beneath perms and huge black fringes.

'Look at that one!'

'Look at her!'

'What would your mum do if you came home with a perm?'

'She'd wig out.'

This was the term before we were supposed to sit our O-levels. By this stage, I recall, girls had begun to realign themselves, to seek out kindred spirits. There had been a sudden pause, a suspension, a sort of quiet luminosity for a week or so, when there was the potential for anything to happen. It was like the end of childhood. It was like the Red Sea parting for a brief moment before everyone scuttled, terrified, for the banks of friendship. And then the seas had crashed in again, covering the poor singletons who had not made it. Help me! Save me! But it was too late. It was almost too awful to watch: the closing-in of the waters.

The washed-up, waterlogged girls still lurked at breaktimes, alone or in clinging, ill-matched groups, while Sally Tuttle and I marched magnificently around. We were the chosen ones: we had made it out of the Red Sea. And we were both grateful. *What would we ever do without each other?* Neither of us could envisage a time when we would not be together. Sometimes, there would be something that niggled. Some little comment that irked. But we knew we would still be meeting up for chats about men and words when we were ninety. Giggling in our rocking-chairs. I suppose, at the age of fifteen, girls know no better.

Rosette Chain

Nearly everybody Sally knew had come to her embroidery award ceremony. She was very touched. It was like a wedding without the cake or the confetti or the groom. Plenty of sparkling wine, though. Sally drank too much of it and was so overwhelmed she hardly spoke all evening.

John made up for it. John, when he has had enough to drink, becomes very convivial. After the speeches and the clapping and the presentation of the cheque, he came to find Sally, and put his arm around her shoulders. He was wearing a shirt with a jolly, abstract print. He smelt quite pleasantly of sweat. His eyes looked watery and a little pink. He kissed her on the lips – a nice, rather alcoholic kiss – and said, 'You and your sequins, Sally.'

'I know.'

'You and your sequins.'

'I know.'

The rest of the event is already a bit of a blur. Sally's embroideries, arranged on the walls, swam in and out of focus. The peacock, the elephant, the tower block. The elephant, the tower block, the peacock. Everyone wore nice clothes – wool, silk, linen – and stood for ages in a queue, waiting for the chicken satay sticks and peanut sauce. Wine glasses clinked. Waitresses yelled. People got quite exercised about the satay sticks.

Sally has never been good in crowds. *What to say, what to say?* She has always been shy, and considers herself very fortunate to have ebullient friends who can usurp the limelight. Even as a girl, her friends were much more outgoing than she was. Rowena, for instance. Sally doesn't really know how that friendship happened. But somehow she had been scooped into her embrace. With Rowena, she felt bright, clever. And Rowena altered too: her accent plummeted, her syntax slipped. Maybe that was why Mrs Cresswell never liked Sally.

'These sodding patterns always say they're very easy,' she remembers Rowena whispering to her in Needlework one afternoon. 'They always say *very bloody easy*, but they're bloody not.'

And Sally looked at the blouson pattern instructions spread out across their desk. At the pencil sketch of a woman, diaphanous, her legs as insubstantial and curved as raspberry canes. She was about to say something about the awful word 'blouson' – it was one of *those words* – when Miss Button's voice cut across them.

'I think you'll find, Rowena,' she said, striding across the room towards them, 'that they *are* very bloody easy. Only a *simpleton* could get this particular pattern wrong. Although looking around this class . . .' she added, and then, perhaps thinking better of it, she stopped talking and returned to her desk, to continue unpicking someone's work.

'Rhiannon Clark,' they heard her spit, 'when will you understand the difference between petersham and bias binding?'

Everyone looked up. Rhiannon Clark was standing by Miss Button's desk, morose, her face pink, her blazer too tight. She was evidently not a girl for whom petersham would ever be important. Why could Miss Button not see that?

'What a cow,' Sally whispered to Rowena. Once, Miss Button had returned her homework to her – an essay on the care of delicate fabrics – covered in coffee stains. Sally had imagined her laughing and wiping coffee away with the back of her hand.

'Do you think she's actually the Wicked Witch of the East?' Rowena whispered.

'All I know is she's a cow.'

And Rowena nodded seriously and began to cut out her collar interfacing with the coveted class pinking shears.

Miss Button was particularly unpleasant that day, Sally remembers. She had eventually reduced Rhiannon to tears – a miserable wreck sitting beside her sewing machine, her Kwik-unpicked garment in her hands.

'She's pure poison,' Rowena said, the blades of her scissors slicing comfortingly against the nylon. And for some reason Sally was very happy when she said this. Rowena was so sure of her likes and dislikes. And Sally was one of her likes.

'She's probably lonely or something,' she conjectured. 'Or frustrated.'

Rowena smiled. 'Frustrated spinsters are the worst. D'you want the pinking shears for your interfacing?'

'Yeah.'

'For your lovely blouson.'

Sally smiled.

'When I've made mine,' Rowena said, 'I have plans to waft about in it across the fields.'

'I'm planning to wear mine next time I see Colin.'

From her elevated desk, Miss Button made a point of ignoring their conversation. Perhaps even *she* knew there was no point breaking into one of their flights of fancy.

They left school together, to walk to the bus stop. It often rained and they never seemed to have umbrellas.

There were a lot of school pupils at that bus stop. The girls stood and talked and the boys stood and punched each other. Most of the girls had highlighted hair and heavy eye make-up. Most of the boys wore parkas.

'I've got loads of spots today,' Sally said, suddenly alarmed at the prospect of meeting Colin that evening.

'Use some cover-up,' suggested Rowena – a girl with the kind of matt skin that seemed impervious to everything, including adolescence.

'Hi,' a boy said to Rowena, and she turned. Mark Malone. A tall, thin boy who had a huge Adam's Apple and played the oboe in his school orchestra. He and Rowena had once, briefly, gone out together, Rowena waiting for him outside the church hall where his orchestra rehearsed. He had been sweet, she told Sally, but she had eventually deemed him to be unsatisfactory. Rowena knew how to deal with men. She could end relationships with a definitive chop, like a martial arts move. Paul Woodman, Shaun Dale, both skillfully tackled and discarded. Now Mark Malone. Poor Mark. He had looked handsome at discos in his long white school shirt, which went impressively blue in strobe lighting. In plain daylight, though, you couldn't help noticing his spots and his Adam's apple. 'People who play music are often quite serious, don't you think?' Rowena had said, and Sally didn't know how to reply. She had felt rather sorry for Mark Malone, standing forlornly at the bus stop in the mornings, trying not to look at her. Rowena had been, she felt, a little harsh.

'Oboe-boy again. Poor thing, look at him,' she observed loudly. And the two girls turned and watched as he moved away, to stand alone, Malone Alone with his oboe, at the other end of the bus stop. It was funny, Sally thought, how you never liked people who liked you. Who liked you too much.

She worried that this might be the case with Colin, a man she loved beyond measure.

She was beginning to rearrange her evenings now, to be with Colin. They had moved from meeting in the park to his flat. And at some point, Sally felt sure, they would have a very profound conversation.

Colin's life, though, was a mystery. Who were his family? Where did he come from? He told her, between kisses, that his mother was Italian – a great beauty and a former opera singer. She had sung, he said, at La Scala, Milan.

'What's that?' Sally asked, and he looked at her and said, 'God, you're ignorant, aren't you?'

His father had been very handsome, apparently – 'More handsome than me,' Colin said – and had acted in Hollywood. But he didn't see him any more. 'I don't really want to talk about my dad,' he added, softly.

'Oh,' Sally frowned. Colin seemed to have led such a full and, in some ways, tragic life that she didn't know how she could possibly be alluring enough for him: a girl who lived in a close at the wrong end of East Grinstead. A girl whose family ate fish fingers and Arctic roll. She looked around Colin's room: at the posters he had put on the wall above his bed. A picture of a naked, rather green-looking woman. Another poster saying 'I have nothing to declare except my genius'.

Why did you come to East Grinstead? Sally wanted to know. He seemed to have had such a glamorous upbringing that she couldn't understand why he would want to come here. The son of a Hollywood actor and an opera singer, living in East Grinstead? Working in an office beside the pedestrian precinct? Walking past the municipal bins and the swing-park?

Colin sighed and blinked his beautiful eyelashes. 'We fell on hard times. My dad had a terrible . . . fall . . . from some theatre scaffolding.'

And he looked as if he might cry.

'Oh,' said Sally, leaning her head against his arm.

His first Saturday job, he told her eventually, over the course of one evening, had been in a bakers, of all places – *Crumbs*, the bakers in the High Street. It had since closed down. He was fourteen. And he described, comically, how he had stood all day behind trays of macaroons and éclairs and apple turnovers. 'There were these fat blokes,' he said, 'who used to shuffle in every day for pork pies and stuff.' And Sally giggled. There were not many people who could make a Saturday job in a bakery look amusing – almost *necessary*, somehow – but Colin Rafferty was one of them. He imitated the way the fat pork-pie men spoke, and she giggled again and hoped her hairgrip was not pressing too much against his upper arm. Colin *had* gone on to greater things, of course: to his job in the advertising agency where he was presently engaged on an advert for a new brand of yogurt. *Yogopot.* He was still working on a slogan, he told her, and had whittled it down to three:

Yogopot for Pots of Taste
I'm potty for Yogopot
There's a Yogopot at the end of the rainbow.

But still, why? Why did he . . .?

Colin gazed down at her. She gazed back and was on the point of leaning up to kiss him when he smiled and said, 'Your hair looks very flat today, m'dear.'

Her heart clunked.

'Sorry?'

'Your hair,' he repeated. 'Very flat.'

He was good at doing that, she recalls: altering her happiness with one carefree comment. It would send her into an instant panic, make her wretchedly scrutinise her appearance when she got home. It would make her visit clothes shops after school, struggle into T-shirts in the changing rooms, look glumly at herself in the dark mirror. *Am I pretty enough? Do I look old enough? Why does he want to be with me?*

And her face would peer back at her, shifty and unsure. Somehow, all the other girls in the changing room seemed slimmer, older, more tanned. They all had Strip-waxed legs. They all had long, wavy hair.

Twelve ninety-nine, she would think, looking at the price tag on the shirt she had taken in, and wondering if she could ask her mother for a loan.

Rowena used to go shopping with her at the weekends but sometimes her presence would make her feel even worse. She would hang loyally on to the handles of all her plastic bags and say 'He'll like you in that,' as Sally pulled some cheap, ribbed top over her head, the seams already coming apart. 'Very sexy,' she'd add.

They liked irony but it sometimes escaped them.

'So how was Colin? Did you have a snog?' Rowena asked her once in the middle of Miss Selfridge's underwear department.

'Rowena!'

Irritated, she had turned and glanced at a middle-aged woman standing by the sale bin. She was pulling out pairs of primrose-yellow knickers.

'So did you?' Rowena asked.

And something had made her not want to tell her.

'Are you really in love with him?' Rowena asked.

Sally did not reply.

Fern

I leave my son and husband putting houseplants into boxes. An umbrella plant, a weeping fig and a dried-out maidenhair.

'Where are you off to?' Kenneth asks as I am standing in the doorway of the flat.

'I've got a bit of a headache,' I say. 'I just thought I'd go for a walk round the block.'

'Do you need some Paracetamol?'

'No. Thanks.'

I look at the plants. I feel too tired to place words into sentences.

'So. See you in a bit. Won't be long.'

'Do you have your mobile with you?' Kenneth calls as I am closing the door.

I met Kenneth too late to really contemplate having more children with him. I already had a son and Kenneth had two daughters. I was thirty-nine by then and he was nearly fifty, and it would just have been exhausting. Our relationship is predominantly to do with the mind, not the body. Not with nappies and baby-wipes, babysitters and school catchment areas.

When I used to feel particularly bitter about my lot (aged eighteen with a two-year-old son and no qualifications, no job), I viewed men with suspicion. All men. I remember, once, taking Joe to a swing-park on the southern edge of town, one of those depressing swing-parks with its inevitable squeaks and adolescents. All the other parents in the swing-park were mothers – all engaged with their children, all holding their hands on the dangerous bits and encouraging them down the slide. All except for one young man, who was lying flat on his back on a bench. His daughter had tagged on to the children of one of the women. He seemed to have assumed that an unknown woman in a bobble hat, already dealing with her own small children, would also look after his daughter. There was something so infuriating about this that I thought '*Right!*' and strode over to the man.

'Excuse me.'

The man opened his eyes.

'Is that little girl in the pink anorak your daughter?'

The man peered across the tarmac.

'U-huh.'

'Well.' And now I couldn't think what to say. My anger had overtaken my plan of attack.

'I just thought you ought to know,' I said, 'that she was right at the top of that tree over there.'

I turned and pointed to a huge elm tree, a diseased one probably, its branches sticking out like the rungs of a ladder.

'And,' I continued, 'she would have fallen if that woman over there' – I pointed to the woman in the bobble hat – 'hadn't very carefully coaxed her down.'

The man considered me for a moment.

'Well, that was very kind of her to coax her down,' he said. 'My daughter's always getting into scrapes.' And he smiled. 'Shouldn't you be in school?'

My heart thumped.

'*That* is *none* of your business,' I hissed, turning on my heel and, dragging Joe by the hand, striding across to the little awkward squeaky gate and leaving the swing-park.

I hated men. I hated them all. I didn't want my son to grow up like that and taught him, as well as I could, how to be considerate. How not to hit. Or head-butt. How to say please and thank you.

And he was often gentle and polite. But then he would also do these things which I could not stop. Nature, not nurture.

Girls are more intelligent. That is my opinion. But somewhere along the line, around the age of, say, fifteen, some of them will do something stupid. Some of them will find they have shackled themselves to an impossible situation.

My mother helped as well as she could with Joe, but she was ill by then, thin and unsure. She bought him things that were too old: jigsaw puzzles with fifty pieces when he was two. Junior science kits at three. My father retreated slightly after Joe's birth, embarrassed by this new, unexpected relative which was not even in control of its own limbs.

It was hard for my parents: they waited fifteen years for their daughter to grow up, only to find themselves with a grandson.

I like Edinburgh; I have been here before, on lecturing trips. I spoke at a conference here a couple of years ago, on the French correspondence of Mary, Queen of Scots. 'Are you calling it Mary's French letters?' some wag in my department inquired. I fixed him with a scornful look.

I know the city's geography these days, and can orientate myself by the views. I suppose I have never quite got over the excitement of city life. It is such a contrast with the town I grew up in. I love the all-night buses in cities, the department stores, the restaurants, the delicatessens. I love the posters, the leaflets, the curious events. In our hotel this morning, I picked up leaflets advertising the Chinese State Circus, a weekend archery competition on the Meadows and a display of rain-dancing in the museum. And tomorrow, in the hotel itself, there is going to be an 'embroidery fest'. An *embroidery fest!* The phrase made me laugh. It is like the concept of a 'power breakfast'. The passion! The drama!

Reading the blurb, I also noticed a name in bold font which I recognised. Jeremy Bowes. Dr Jeremy Bowes would be attending the embroidery fest, giving a keynote speech on medieval French tapestries. And I found myself smiling, all on my own, in the hotel's lobby. Jeremy Bowes, that old charmer! Jeremy Bowes, possessor of a bargello waistcoat, whom I have encountered over the years in stuffy academic offices across Europe. And at Jollies, of course, over the stuffed olives and pretzels. Somehow, he has always managed to work his way, cat-like, into almost every cultural exchange on offer. Jeremy Bowes! I picture him, dressed in his expensively modest suit and that waistcoat. 'Enchanté,' he says, stooping slightly to bestow a kiss. He gave a lecture once in a museum in Paris, on the underacknowledged skills of medieval women. That was the first time I met him. I remember looking around the audience and witnessing the collective melting of female hearts. It was like spring snow plunging off an Arctic shelf. I pity all the middle-aged women who have not yet encountered him. Jeremy Bowes is one of those men that women often fall in love with. He is an original, in his expensively casual clothes; he is carelessly handsome. He is sympathetic. And he always focuses all his attention on the (female) person he is addressing.

It's funny, the way people orbit each other without ever knowing how close they are. I've never fallen for Jeremy Bowes, but I do hope I bump into him in one of the hotel's corridors. I hope he'll be wearing that waistcoat and those boots.

The slope of Calton Hill looms, yellowish-green to my right. I cross the road at the pedestrian crossing and walk past five squat bronze statues in the shape of pigeons. There is a cast of some pigeon feet where the sixth statue used to stand. A long-faced busker is standing beside the pigeon statues, strumming a banjo and singing a cheery tune. 'The First Cut is the Deepest'.

'I would have given you all of my heart,' he sings merrily, 'but there's someone who's torn it apart . . .'

His banjo plinks. His dog lies beside him on a tartan rug.

My own heart feels too full, like an overstuffed filing cabinet. I think of Joe packing plants into boxes in his flat. *I need to not mind that my son is going to live in San Francisco.* Because I know what it is like to have anxieties pinned on you. Too many anxieties pinned upon a person can be damaging.

So I mustn't mind my son's departure. He is going to be a satellite son now, a phone-call son. A son living in an unimaginable suburb on the West Coast of America. Maybe he will own a hot-tub, a fast car, go jogging, get married, have an affair, drink root beer.

Now I can't think which direction I should be facing. I have always had terrible bearings. And how long have I been out? What time, exactly, did I leave Joe's flat? There are spots of rain in the air and the dampness is filtering through my coat. I stop walking to try and work out where Joe's flat is. The busker is smiling at me as he sings. I throw a fifty-pence piece into his cap.

'You've a kind heart, hen,' the man says, and I feel ashamed.

I turn and walk on, down Leith Walk. I hope it is the right way. But after five minutes, after I have walked past a pub called the Boundary Bar, a tattoo parlour and a number of boarded-up shops, I doubt it.

I am turning back, panicking a little, when my mobile phone rings in my bag. A silly tune: 'Bobby Shafto's Gone to Sea'. Joe programmed it for me. Relieved, I take the phone out and answer it, at the end of 'silver buttons on his knee'.

'Rowena?'

'Hi.'

'Walking purposefully or wandering aimlessly?'

'Walking purposefully, of course.'

'Amazing. Because you forgot your *A-to-Z*. And Joe's address. And the hotel key. You left them on the edge of the bathtub.'

Kenneth is not like a lot of men. He is practical. He carries with him useful pieces of information: addresses, phone numbers. This is not to say that he is boring. I have discovered, over the years, that the men you think are exciting sometimes turn out to be the boring ones. And vice versa.

'So. Here's Joe's address,' Kenneth says, reading it out.

'Thanks.'

I write it down in my diary with a biro miraculously stowed in my bag. 'Thanks. I'll ask someone for directions.'

'See you then,' says Kenneth. 'Oh – and could you get a pint of milk? Joe seems to have run out.'

'OK. Kenneth?'

'Hello?'

'Shall we go out for dinner tonight? The three of us?'

'That'd be nice.'

'Maybe we could book something. Because we haven't really had a posh dinner yet, have we, and he's . . .'

'Yes, I know.'

I pause.

'Well, anyway,' Kenneth says. 'We've got to take those plants to Oxfam before it shuts.'

'Sorry? Oh. OK.'

I had almost managed to forget about the plants –

'Dinner's a good idea.'

'Yes.'

– and now I feel sad again at the thought of Joe saying goodbye to them.

Twisted Chain

On the morning of her flight, she opens her wardrobe and looks at the empty space where the green dress used to hang.

'I've had a bit of a clothes clear-out,' she says to Pearl in the kitchen. 'Some of my old dresses and things. They were just hanging there, unworn. And I know you wouldn't have wanted them.'

'Mm-hmm,' says Pearl. She is sitting at the table reading a magazine.

'Cup of tea?'

'Mm-hmm.'

Pearl sits so still sometimes while Sally rushes around. She looks at her monkish daughter (hood up again) and smiles and is aware of a kind of pulling-away. They are like people on small ice floes which have begun to move apart.

When she was younger she used to float around her parents' house like Pearl, interminably philosophising. Life was a puzzle. *What? What was life about?*

Actually she still wonders.

'Bra,' she says as she packs her rucksack at the end of the table, 'knickers, socks, notebook, needle cases . . .'

She really has no idea what to take. She has promised to take her embroidery as part of her 'illustrated talk,' but there is so much of it now, with so many threads and needles stuck into the canvas. 'Mary and Martha' will take up half her luggage allowance. And what is she really supposed to talk about? Embroidery silks? Types of canvas? Stitches? Sequins? The letter she received from the Embroiderers' Guild mentioned 'an informal discussion, lasting no more than twenty minutes, about your current work and what the award has meant to you.' But now she is not sure *what* it means to her. How can she articulate that? It was nice, yes, it was nice to get the money and the accolade. What more can she say? She can't stand on a stage for twenty minutes saying it was nice, like that woman – who was it? Lady Mary someone? – whose famous last words were 'It was all very interesting.'

Pearl shifts her position at the table, away from the thud of luggage.

'Don't forget your gym shoes tomorrow,' Sally says, a pair of folded socks in her hand.

'Why do you always think I'm going to forget things?'

'I don't. I was just reminding you, sweetheart.'

She pauses, trying to collect her thoughts.

'If Dad's not about much you can always go to Nana and Grandad's after school. If you feel like it. They'd love to see you.'

And she comes round to Pearl's side of the table and places her cheek against her hooded head.

'What's wrong?'

'Nothing.'

'Sure?'

'Yes.'

'Because –'

'Nothing's wrong.'

Before setting off for the airport she leaves Pearl a list on a Post-it note.

My mobile number
My hotel number
Nana and Grandad
Dad's new number

'I won't be away long,' she says brightly, her heart tight. She feels tearful. 'You can always go round to Nana and Grandad's.'

'Yes. You did say, Mum.'

'Because I know Dad's quite caught up with work at the moment . . .'

She thinks of John, metal shavings clinging to his beard. Waiting for their daughter in his small, messy Fiat. Flux on the dashboard. Cupcake cases in the side-pockets.

'What's wrong?'

'Nothing.'

Sally clutches the yellow Post-it note. She is comforted by lists: dates, numbers, plans.

The bus takes the long route through town. They drive very slowly past the shops. Today some of the staff in Woolworths are arranging a Christmas display. Fibre-glass reindeer and polystyrene snow. A shop assistant is struggling with a large, plastic sledge.

Sally has never actually gone to Woolworths for any of her haberdashery requirements. She is unwilling to walk through the doors. It is, she supposes, because Woolworths was where Rowena and Colin had first spoken to each other. *All in the past now, of course, all in the past.*

But she still remembers how perturbed she was, how high and abnormally cheerful her voice had sounded that day.

'Hi, Ro!' she had chirped as she and Colin had walked in. Because there was no way to ignore her: Rowena had been standing right there in the pic'n'mix aisle. Confident, indisputable, scooping Black Jacks and Fruit Salads into a stripy paper bag.

Rowena had looked up. 'Hi, Sal,' she said.

'This is Rowena,' Sally informed Colin, frowning at the Flying Saucers dispenser, selecting her own paper bag and hurling a huge pile of them into it.

Colin looked at Rowena. 'I've seen you before,' he said, 'hiding behind a tree.'

'Oh,' said Rowena.

Don't look at me, don't look at me.

Colin looked at Sally.

'Hot in here isn't it?' he said.

'I've just remembered,' Sally replied, throwing the scoop back into the Flying Saucers. 'I need some blank tapes.' And she scuttled off, crab-like, to the music aisle. Hiding behind a display of Commodores albums, she skulked while her heartbeat slowed and her face cooled down. She watched Rowena and Colin talking to each other. What were they saying? Were they talking about her? And now, oh God, they were laughing! And Rowena was putting a Black Jack into her mouth in that sweet, nonchalant way she had!

Woolworths was where it began to go wrong, that's what it is. It was where her best friend began to change.

Sally had picked up a pack of three blank tapes and stomped back to the pic'n'mix aisle. It was all too bright, too bright and glaring under the fluorescent lights, but she had to go back.

Colin did not seem to notice her return. He and Rowena were still talking: they were joking about the identical bored expressions of the women behind the tills. *They are sharing something I am not a part of. I have never joked like that with him.*

'Hi, Sal,' Rowena said.

'Hi,' she croaked. 'I found some.'

'Sorry?'

'Blank tapes. I'm going to tape Colin's Clash album.'

'Oh.'

'Are you?' Colin asked her. He seemed rather annoyed.

Rowena looked at him, smiled and said, 'Not my cup of tea, the Clash.'

'Really?' Colin smiled back. 'You're missing out.'

'I don't think so.'

'Somebody should enlighten you.'

'Should they?'

This happened on a Friday, Sally recalls: the last Friday of September 1979.

Colin had been waiting for her that evening in the Rialto foyer, leaning against the window ledge, looking at the leaflets advertising East Grinstead's cultural life. The scar on his hand made him look old, experienced. Sally felt alarmed suddenly, jangled, out of her depth. She hesitated, wondering whether to let the heavy glass door swing back again.

Then Colin smiled and waved.

'Hi,' she warbled, her voice cracking slightly. She cleared her throat and walked towards him, a big, lip-glossed smile on her face.

'Hi,' he chirped, offhand. He was wearing his worn grey coat and he had not washed his hair; it was lank and dull, but that did not matter. Things like that were what she loved about him. Of course, *she* couldn't get away with greasy hair. That was not the point at all.

'Why do you wear such a long scarf?' he asked, apropos of nothing.

She tried to think of a quickfire response.

'They keep your neck warm,' she blurted.

'I can do that.'

There was a short moment of staring and silence.

'*Apocalypse Now*'s sold out,' he said.

'Oh. That's a shame.'

'So. We can either watch *The Black Stallion* with a load of kids,' Colin said, looking up at the billboard, 'or we could go for a pizza.'

'Well, seeing as you've painted such a tempting picture,' Sally replied, rising to the challenge, 'shall we go for the pizza?'

And she took his proffered hand and felt temporarily sophisticated. The thought of watching some horse-related story in the dark was vaguely comforting, whereas eating pizza with Colin Rafferty would, she knew, be a challenge. She would have to be scintillating and beautiful and mysterious all the time she was tucking cheese strands into her mouth, and the idea exhausted her. She would be constantly scared that her sophistication would slip; or that someone, some friend or relative or acquaintance of her parents – some *spy* – would notice them. 'Hello, Sally,' they would say, propelling themselves towards their table.

'Shall we go to Caruso's, then?' Colin asked.

'OK,' she piped, hurrying in his wake, aware that she had an eyelash in her right eye and wondering if it looked bloodshot. It felt bloodshot. She shouldn't have borrowed Rowena's eyelash curlers.

Caruso's was hot and red and white. The lights glared unromantically on the tables, around which sat groups of young men out for a night of beer and cheap food. There were very few romantic couples. None, in fact.

'Table for two?' asked a waiter, striding quickly towards them and looking as if he would not take no for an answer. He led them to a table near the till and drew back a chair for Sally.

'Thanks,' she gushed, unused to this kind of service. Male attention, with an undertow of suggestiveness.

The waiter handed them some menus as big as Bibles and retreated.

Sally inspected the cheap options: the salads and the starters. A *tortellini in brodo* was 95p. A mixed green salad was 60p. She looked up again to ponder her choices and to gaze around the restaurant. After a moment she realised that Colin was staring at her.

'What?'

'Your eyes.'

'What about them?' she said in alarm.

'They're beautiful.'

'Thanks,' she said gruffly, wrapping her ankles one-and-a-half times around the legs of her chair.

'You look as if you're going to cry,' Colin said.

'Do I?'

'Yes. You often look as if you're going to cry.'

'Do I?'

Colin took a last, silent look into her beautiful eyes and then looked down at his menu again.

'I'm going to have the Pizza Quattro Formaggio,' he said, putting on an Italian accent, at which point Sally burst out laughing.

'What?' Colin asked, slightly tetchily, and her laugh stuck and subsided.

'I don't know.'

She cleared her throat, the laughter abruptly spent. *You're going to chuck me now, aren't you?*

But all through the antipasti and the bowl of olives, he didn't. All through the pizza, he didn't.

She never told Rowena about the meal in Caruso's restaurant. She never mentioned the huge menus, the waiter, her bloodshot eye. *'Oh God, Rowena . . . and we were sitting there on either side of this little table and I had this bright red eye and he said . . .'*

But she didn't. Something was changing.

By that time, Colin had begun to occupy about eighty per cent of her waking thoughts in any case. She thought of him every hour of every day. She thought about:

his sense of humour (surreal, sometimes slightly cruel)
his smooth skin
the scar on his left hand
his grey eyes

his off-hand manner

his reasons for loving her (she tried not to wonder about this too much).

But most of the appeal of Colin was almost indescribable. He was carefree, light, Peter Pannish, insouciant as a boy. But he was also twenty-one, which meant that he possessed mature things. He had a briefcase, cork-bottomed place mats, large, expensive wine glasses, a washing machine. And he did not live with his parents. He lived in a flat above a kebab shop on the edge of town, and Sally felt a thrill at being there. Colin would clear a space on the kitchen table and she would put two plates on it and some stainless steel cutlery. It was like being married.

'A bean boiled is a bean spoiled,' Colin observed one afternoon, as he stood by the cooker, supervising a pan. He buttered a couple of slices of white toast and poured the beans over them.

'So how was needlework today, dear?' he asked. 'Fascinating?'

'OK. Except I sewed up the pocket and had to Kwik-unpick it.'

'Kwik-unpick?' Colin said, incredulously. Then he laughed. 'What's the point of needlework, exactly? It's hardly useful is it?'

'What makes you say that?' Sally replied, sitting down at the table and pulling at her over-the-knee socks. Colin could sometimes be rather aggressive about the direction of her life, even though he had only been part of it for the previous two months.

'There's plenty you can do with needlwork,' she said.

'What? Make cushion covers?'

'If you want to.'

Colin had done his A-levels in 1974, in General Studies and Economics.

'Needlework is not a career option, Sally,' he said, with the wisdom of a man six years her senior.

'Why not? My mum –'

'It just isn't,' he interrupted. 'Unless you want to make bloody cushions all your life. It's just totally useless. You failed your mocks anyway.'

'Thanks for reminding me,' she said, shocked by his sudden cruelty.

'Colin,' she said, 'are you – ?'

'What?'

'Do you . . .? I'm just . . . Sometimes I'm a bit worried that . . .'

'Worrying's bad for you, dear,' Colin said flatly. 'Stop worrying.'

And so she stopped worrying. She was very obedient. Colin's voice was high, boyish, but his words were unequivocal.

'So,' he said, after a moment's pause. 'I've decided on a Yogopot slogan.'

'Great.'

Colin smiled and breathed in. '*There's a Yogopot at the end of every rainbow.*'

She did not think this was the best slogan. She did not think it was a very good slogan at all.

'It's the one that sticks in your mind, isn't it?' Colin said. 'And that's what advertising's all about.'

'Yes.'

'Anyway, that's bloody Yogopot out of the way. Guess what I'm working on now?'

'I don't know.'

'Maybe I shouldn't tell a nice girl like you.'

'What? What do you mean? Go on, Colin, tell –'

'Condoms.'

'Oh.'

'It's great,' he said. 'You get all these free packs.'

'Oh,' she said again, aware of someone in the flat next door, hoovering their carpet. Bashing the hoover against the skirting board. She wondered if Colin had all those free packs there, at that moment, in his bedroom.

Colin began to laugh. 'Don't look so scared,' he said more kindly. 'Come here.' And he walked towards her and put his arms around her, folding her up roughly, like an octopus.

'You're nice,' she said into his armpit.

'You're nice too. So. Why don't we go to bed? It'll be lovely.'

'Not yet.'

'What are you worried about?'

'Nothing.'

'So why don't we?'

'Not yet.'

'You've got to do it some time. Someone's got to show you. I bet loads of girls at your school have . . .'

'I know, but . . .'

It was late. Nearly ten o'clock. Her parents would be home by now, worrying. She had said she would be home by nine. In the flat next door, the hoover was being pushed around a more distant room.

'You've got to do it some time,' Colin said again. 'You've got to do it with someone. So it might as well be me.' He paused. 'You love me.'

'I do. I do. But . . .'

When the bus arrived, nearly ten minutes late, Colin gave her an unexpectedly brief, dry kiss, like a Russian politician.

'See you tomorrow,' he said. 'Hope your parents forgive you.'

Then he patted her backside and watched her get on the bus, stumbling a little as she made her way to the back seats. She tried to make her profile look enigmatic and beautiful. But he had already turned and walked away. He had not stayed to smile or wave. She watched him turn down a side street as the bus drew away. A middle-aged woman sitting on the back seat was staring at her in her school uniform, evidently amazed that she was capable of kissing a grown man.

Couching

In our hotel room we sit on a small, red sofa and listen to the quiet tick of some nameless instrument. *A thermostat?* we wonder. *The mini-bar?*

We look up at the rose picture on the wall and speculate whether it is a Redouté. We discover two CDs that a former guest lost down the back of the sofa. *The Cutter and the Clan. Tubular Bells.*

'Someone will be missing those,' says Kenneth. 'Better hand them in to reception.'

'Hmm.'

The CDs make me feel a little depressed. I put them on the arm of the sofa, get up, walk into the en-suite bathroom and shut the door. It is warm in here and smells of pine. I take off my clothes and drop them on the floor-tiles. I look at the small bottles arranged on the little wooden ledge. *Out of Eden* Shower Gelée. *Out of Eden* Shampoo. *Out of Eden* Moisturising Cream.

In the shower, I unzip my sponge bag and use my own shampoo.

'So. What shall we do this afternoon?' Kenneth asks when I return, my hair wrapped in a Royal Burgh towel. He is listening to the *Tubular Bells* CD. There is a drone of notes and the occasional chanted word.

'I don't know,' I say. 'Go to bed?'

I am weary, after too much translating of late – too many complicated sentences about nineteenth-century hand-looms. Weary, too, with the effort of getting here. Hotel rooms always make me feel like this in any case; the sight of the bed makes me want to get straight into a pair of practical pyjamas and hide between the laundered sheets.

'Let's have a look at this folder of Interesting Ideas,' Kenneth suggests, hauling out a large pink file from beneath the coffee table.

'Nothing that involves a big trek,' I say, sitting down beside him. I lean my head against the sofa back.

'So,' says Kenneth.

'Glockenspiel!' intones the CD.

'Do you really want this on?'

'I think it's kind of soothing. So . . . there's the Tron Kirk. There's the castle. There's the museum. Or the botanic gardens.'

'Yes, but they'll all be closed and it's freezing anyway.'

'We could go out for lunch. Or we could eat here, where we will be offered "a superb dining experience in sumptuous surroundings".'

'Hmm.'

'Just some sandwiches then? Room service?'

'That sounds not too exerting.'

Kenneth looks at me. 'What's wrong?'

'Nothing.'

'You look sad.'

He thinks I'm thinking about Joe. But I'm not.

I'm actually remembering a ten-minute bus journey undertaken one Sunday in East Grinstead in 1979. A journey I made in order to meet my friend Sally Tuttle. It had been a number 18 bus, and I had been sitting on it with a Tubular Bells album in a plastic bag by my feet.

Colin Rafferty had got on the bus. That is why I still remember the occasion: he had suddenly been there, at the top of the bus steps, buying a ticket. And I had looked up and felt alarmed.

Colin had not acknowledged me straight away; he had just

come and sat down in the seat in front of me, and the bus had roared on, down London Road. I continued to stare, pink-faced, through the window. *Look nonchalant, look nonchalant.* I clutched the handles of my plastic bag and tried to think of the homework I was supposed to do: an 800-word Chemistry essay. Then, apropos of nothing, Colin Rafferty had suddenly turned, leaned one arm casually over the back of his seat and said, 'Hello, Sally's friend.'

I flicked a quick glance in his direction.

'Hello,' I replied, bunching both hands into fists around the plastic-bag handles.

Colin smiled and I noticed his teeth.

'So. Where are you going?'

'To see a friend.'

'Anyone I know?'

'Just a friend.'

'Wouldn't be someone I know, then?'

'Maybe.'

And then he said it: the thing that stays in my memory. 'Do you know, Sally's friend,' he said, 'you have the most beautiful eyes.'

And he smiled again, and turned back in his seat.

I sat rigidly and regarded the back of his head. The bus droned and clanked on. My head throbbed. I felt oddly paralysed. I wished, more than anything, that Colin Rafferty would get off the bus.

Then, after a couple of stops, he did. Without looking back at me or even acknowledging my continuing existence, he stood up, walked down the aisle and descended the steps. He turned the corner of a street and disappeared.

I spent the rest of the afternoon sitting in Sally's bedroom, not telling her what had happened.

'I'm really not sure about this,' I remember Sally saying, picking up the sleeve of my Tubular Bells album to look at the notes. 'I really don't like the way he says *Glockenspiel* and stuff. It's a bit bloody peculiar.'

'Hmm?'

'I mean: *Glock-un-shpeel*! What's that all about? It's a bit bloody airy-fairy isn't it? You ought to listen to the Clash.'

'Hmm?'

'Anything wrong? You've gone all mopy.'

'Just tired, Sal.'

After our wine (white, slightly sour) and sandwiches (ham, tuna mayonnaise), Kenneth and I leave our room to go in search of the hotel's embroidery exhibition. We walk along carpeted corridors, down hushed staircases, past vases of flowers, pewter bowls of pine cones and brass plaques indicating room numbers. We walk into a room marked Function Suite and then into another marked Conference Hall. A lone man in a T-shirt that says *I'm with her* ⇨ is staple-gunning pieces of paper to the walls.

'Is this where the embroidery exhibition is meant to be?' Kenneth asks.

'We're behind schedule, pal,' says the man with the staple-gun. 'I can't see me getting this on the walls before the back of midnight.'

'You're not staple-gunning the embroideries are you?' I ask, alarmed.

The man looks at me. 'No,' he says, 'I'll not be staple-gunning the actual artwork.'

At his feet is a box of photocopied pictures. Beside him is a wooden frame supporting a large embroidered canvas. It is turned the wrong way round, the stitches neatly finished off in reds, greens and blues. I can make out the shape of a face, clothing, the soft glitter of sequins.

'Could we take a look at the embroideries?' Kenneth asks.

'Best not, if you don't mind,' the man says. 'I don't really want to touch them, pal, with my butterfingers. Best if you come and see them tomorrow.'

And we walk away, back up to our room.

'Never trust a butterfingers with a staple-gun,' Kenneth observes in the lift.

I don't reply. I am thinking of the art of embroidery: the innocent pull of thread through cloth.

Chain Twisted, Detached

21 OCTOBER 1979

Chemistry
Physical and Chemical Changes

A *physical change* is a change in a substance which does not result in the formation of a substance with a different chemical composition.

A *chemical change* is a change in one or more substances which results in the production of one or more substances of different chemical composition from the original substances.

You could have put this more succinctly, Sally!
Where are your experiment results? Conclusion?

Everyone worked in pairs and they were always a pair, Sally and Rowena, hunched over the gentle heat of the Bunsen burner. At their experiments bench they peered at the copper sulphate crystal they were supposed to grow. It was not nearly as symmetrical as everyone else's. It was wonky, and made them laugh. Chemistry was always funny. There was some mixture, some chemical composition that Miss Haugh kept talking about. *Fehlings.* Pronounced failings. That made them laugh too.

'So. He's quite witty, isn't he?' Rowena said, mid-morning, and Sally froze.

'So. When are you going to tell your mum and dad about him?'

'I'm not.'

Rowena twiddled the gold stud in her earlobe. She peered at Sally through her plastic goggles. Her eyeliner had run. She looked pale: off-colour, weighed-down.

'They'd wig out, Ro,' Sally said. 'They'd think he was too old. They'd probably ban me from seeing him or something.'

Rowena shrugged, stuck a piece of Sellotape on to their badly-formed crystal, and placed it into their 'Experiments' folder. A couple of weeks earlier, as she had threatened, she'd had her hair permed. She'd had it done at Hairizons, the trendiest hair-dresser's in town. The curls had smelt slightly of ammonia and looked solid, almost as if they had been carved out of wood. Sally was a little unsure about whether it *worked.*

'Do you think he thinks I'm too young?' she asked.

Rowena sighed. 'It's what you think that matters,' she said. 'It's just, I . . .'

'What?'

'Nothing. Doesn't matter.'

And for a while they didn't say any more. They peered at their copper sulphate crystal and tried to think of ways to describe it.

Then Sally broke the silence. She wanted to say something nice, because it was frightening her, this misunderstanding, this veering off the track.

'You're lucky,' she said. 'Your hair's so thick it just stays put. If I had mine permed it would just go all limp, like Rhian-anon's.'

'You should get *something* done to it, though,' Rowena snapped. 'You've had it long all your life.'

'No I haven't. You haven't *known* me all my life,' Sally retorted, flicking the end of her plait. Something was altering, definitely; something was fading away.

'A perm would give it more volume,' Rowena said.

'It doesn't need more volume. I'd end up looking like Kevin Keegan.'

'Well, if you don't watch it, Sally, you'll end up looking like Colin's daughter.'

And Rowena turned back to her chemistry book.

Sally sat, her plait heavy and childish against her back. She felt a strange kind of pain appear and expand beneath her ribcage. She thought of the two sea lions she and Colin had seen at the zoo; the way one of them had just seemed to get bored with the other and suddenly flopped its great hulking body off the concrete ledge and into the water.

She looked down at the copper sulphate crystal, at its chipped, bright blue edges. Then she reached into her school bag, got out a Black Jack, unwrapped it and crammed it into her mouth.

'Anyway. You should be careful, Sal,' Rowena said, her head bowed over her book. 'Y'know, if you . . . You'd have to make sure he wore a thingummy.'

Sally chewed and chewed, aware of a blush advancing up her neck, over her cheeks, across her forehead.

Rowena stopped talking and looked up. 'Blimey, Sal,' she said, 'you've gone really red.'

'Well, wouldn't you? If someone started talking about *your* love life in the middle of Chemistry?'

Rowena glanced at Miss Haugh, pensive, woolly-haired Miss Haugh, struggling with a malfunctioning Bunsen burner.

'What love life?' she said. 'I don't have a love life.'

They worked in silence for a while, eyeing the clock while Miss Haugh intoned sadly about chemical reactions. In ten minutes they would be in different classrooms, considering, respectively, the use of symbolism in *Madame Bovary* and irrigation in the Nile Valley.

The bell rang, and there was an instant, alarming surge of chairs being pushed back, of noisy conversations drowning out Miss Haugh, of flat-footed trudging to the classroom door.

'See you, then,' Rowena said, swinging her bag over her shoulder.

And Sally watched her disappear through the doors and up the stairs. The burden of maintaining her oldest friendship made her feel tired, world-weary, like the parent of a difficult child.

*

24 OCTOBER 1979

French
<u>O-level Prep Essay Title</u>
'*Madame Bovary is fundamentally selfish. Discuss.*'

She saw her again at lunchtime on Monday, through the glass pane of the Needlework room door.

'Hi, Ro,' she said, guardedly, and Rowena looked up. She was definitely, Sally thought, looking a little run-down. Sickening for something. Pale, with dark circles beneath her eyes. She was sitting beside a plate of sandwiches that Miss Button had arranged mysteriously and rather ineptly beside one of the Bernini sewing machines.

'How was Geography?' Sally asked.

'Stuff about gum trees.'

'Oh well. It's over for another week.'

Sally looked down at the sandwiches. A row of white triangles and a row of brown triangles.

'What are these doing here? Are we supposed to eat them?' she asked, and Rowena frowned and didn't reply. She looked, for some reason, as if she might cry.

'I think they're left over from some sixth-form session,' she said eventually.

'What?'

'The sandwiches. Miss Button said we could help ourselves. They make me feel a bit sick, actually.'

'Do they?'

'Yes, I –' she began, and then stopped talking.

'Well, they look pretty grim,' Sally said impatiently, looking at the way the sandwich fillings oozed out a little over the edges. Sandwich spread: some awful, unrecognisable yellow paste. She thought of the jokes Colin might have made about it. But she could never think up jokes like that. She could only ever remember the one about the koala bear falling out of a tree.

Rowena suddenly put her hand up to her mouth. 'I think I'm going to throw up,' she said.

'Really? Are you OK?'

'No.'

'Eat up, girls,' said Miss Button, perky, contemptuous Miss Button, suddenly appearing at their side. Because, as far as she could tell, they were just loitering in the Needlework Room for no real reason. They were, really, Sally supposed.

'Not for me thanks,' said Rowena, her face ashen. Sally glanced at her with alarm.

'We were just trying to work out what was in them. The sandwiches,' she said.

Miss Button looked at her and then at Rowena. She frowned, and Sally thought of the word *moue*, which they had just learned in French.

'The school cooks spent a long time preparing those sandwiches, Rowena Cresswell,' Miss Button said. 'For your delight and delectation. You should make the most of it. There's not usually such a thing as a free lunch.' And she sashayed back across the room in her little soft, practical shoes.

Sally looked at Rowena. Rowena looked at Sally.

'I'm OK, I think,' Rowena said, 'Just came over a bit funny. So . . .'

But she suddenly put one hand up over her mouth, her other over her stomach, and sat there, her eyes closed.

'You all right? Would a Black Jack help?'

'Shut up,' Rowena replied, through her fingers. She sat silently for a moment. Then she looked up. 'Sorry, Sal,' she said. 'I'll be OK.'

They moved away from the sandwiches to stand by an open window, through which the desolate cries of breaktime could be heard. Tentatively, Sally put her hand on Rowena's arm and glanced around at their other schoolmates. They all seemed to be having a cheerful time. They had all, Sally realised, suddenly found their own place – over the past few weeks, while she was not watching. They had all sorted themselves out and now presented a kind of united front. They had found their own best friends. Nuala Odette, a very pretty black girl with dozens of braids, had joined up with Alison Smith, who was small and pastry-white; troubled Natalie Craven had a confidante in motherly Emily Banks. Even Rhiannon Clark had, in recent months, transformed herself from being slightly weird to unaccountably popular. People no longer called her Rhian-anon. Her chosen friend was Wendy, a shy girl who had now grown bolder, like a hyacinth blooming on a sunny window sill.

Sally turned back to Rowena.

'Sure you're OK?' she chirped. 'Not pregnant, are you?'

Rowena breathed in.

'So. You're not going to throw up in Maths or anything, are you?'

'No. Sally –'

'Yeah?'

But before she could continue, the lunch bell rang.

'What? Are you OK? What's wrong?'

'It's OK. It doesn't matter.'

'Sure? You can talk to me, honey pie.'

'It's OK. I'll tell you later.'

Through the window Sally could see a collision of schoolboys on the pavement outside, all pushing each other and swearing.

Flinging little fire-crackers on to the ground, to make the girls scream as they walked past. All of them, without exception, lacking beauty, irony, sophistication.

She turned back to Rowena, leaned forward and touched her friend's shoulder briefly, the way she might have patted the side of a horse.

Her love for Colin had started to expand by this time, to increase without warning. Of course he loved her! He wasn't interested in Rowena: she felt ashamed for suspecting it.

Something in particular had triggered her confidence: the comment he had made about her eyes.

'Your eyes are so beautiful,' he had said, brushing her cheek with his finger. 'So blue and so sad. And with the slightest, cutest little squint.'

'Squint?' Sally replied, horrified.

'Are my eyes squint?' she had asked Rowena a few days later during lunch break, as they stood in the queue for Vegetarian Goulash.

And she wondered why Rowena had had such an angry expression on her face.

'What on earth are you talking about?' Rowena said.

'Do you think my eyes are squint? Colin thinks they are.'

'Haven't you got more important things to think about?' Rowena snapped, declining a plate of orange stew and stalking back to their table with a side plate, a knife and a Golden Delicious apple.

Hurt, Sally chose to sit somewhere else. She sat with Christine Pringle and Susan Temple and discussed their shared love of Supertramp.

At the time she thought it was because Rowena was jealous. She really thought that was why they were falling apart.

*

She was supposed to have gone back to Rowena's house that evening: the day of the goulash and the Golden Delicious apple. But, still angry, she told her she didn't feel well and went home. She felt a little hollow. Bleak. She let herself in to the house and roamed around for a while, eating toast and watching children's programmes: *Jackanory. Paddington.* The feeling of hollowness did not go away. And neither of her parents was in to cheer her up. Her mother was cleaning some big house in the posh part of town, her father was on late shift at the sorting office.

After she'd finished her toast she switched the television off. The house was terribly quiet. Nothing moved. And suddenly she felt a kind of compulsion, a magnetic pull towards somewhere else. Someone who understood. Colin. *My soulmate. My kindred spirit.*

Now she didn't hesitate. This was the only thing to do. She hardly even stopped to check her reflection in her bedroom mirror – just briefly, to brush her hair (washed for the second time that day) and to reapply shimmery eyeliner at the corners of her eyelids. To wonder about her slightly squint eyes.

Then she flew down the garden path to the pavement, up to London Road, past the station, down a long flight of steps and on, the soles of her feet crashing against the tarmac. She ran past the library, the pet shop, the supermarket, her old primary school. She pounded through the streets towards Colin's flat. *I love you, I love you.* It was cold and raining now, but she had put on her mother's big trench coat because it looked dramatic – like a coat in a film she'd seen once. And she was wearing her hair long and loose and wavy from the plait. But her big feet in her big shoes – she could do nothing about them. Her big shoes went slap, slap through the shiny puddles. And beneath the rain her scalp tingled with apprehension. *In ten minutes I will be there.* She was wearing her best knickers and new white bra. She had already Strip-waxed her legs and applied Nivea moisturising cream to her arms and shoulders. Now she imagined herself running up the worn stone steps, past the sign that said 'No Hawkers, No Salesmen'; she saw herself arriving at his door, knocking on the peeling green wood. Waiting. And then, when he opened the door, she pictured herself falling into his open arms.

'Sally, what's wrong?' he would say. 'What's the matter?'

'Oh Colin, I love you. I love you . . .'

Slap, slap, went her shoes through the broken-coloured puddles.

'Where's the fire, love?' asked an old man she nearly flattened as she ran past.

'Sorry,' she shouted back over her shoulder, and continued to run, past the neon restaurant lights, past closed shops, past the new roundabout, past people clutching dreary plastic bags at East Grinstead's bus stops. They stared as she ran on, towards the dim orange lights of distant London. It was five-thirty, dark and cold, and she felt that she was at the beginning of something. Colin's flat was almost within her sights now: the small, white building above the kebab shop, the dark, depressing stairway, the smell of tomcats. Here was the municipal bin and the lamppost and the lone, brave little silver-birch tree. She had run so fast that she was here even earlier than her racing brain had calculated. The clock on the hotel said five-forty, and she knew it was five minutes fast.

And now she was doing what she'd imagined. She was looking at the peeling paint and the sign that said 'Beware, you are entering the house of a genius.' She was looking at the metal door handle, knocking on the door; hearing him walk towards it.

And here he was, opening it.

'Wh–' he said.

This was the point at which the imagined and the real collided, and she was not prepared for it. She was actually a little unsure what to do next. She had not envisaged Colin with that expression on his face. She had not captured the smell of Heinz Winter Vegetable soup emanating from the kitchen; or pictured the damp grey underwear flopped over the radiators. In her imaginings, the door to the bathroom had not been open, with its view of an economy-sized pack of salmon-pink toilet rolls and the broken-seated toilet. Undeterred, she strode straight down the hallway, past the broken-legged table and into his room. Her eyes were wide, all-seeing. She felt wild, almost insane, rainwater dripping off her mother's trench coat. Tonight she was going to proclaim her love; she was ready emotionally, spiritually, physically –

'What are you wearing that for? What the hell's the matter?' Colin was asking in a not very affectionate voice. She noticed how white his face was.

'Oh Colin,' she began, and as she spoke she glanced down at the carpet, because some curious object at her feet had suddenly caught her attention. For a second she couldn't quite understand its significance – why the sight of it should appall her so much. Colin's flat was such an incongruous setting for it, and it looked so ridiculous and out of place that she almost laughed. It was lying on the floor at the foot of his bed: Rowena's stripy orange blouson (*very easy / très facile*).

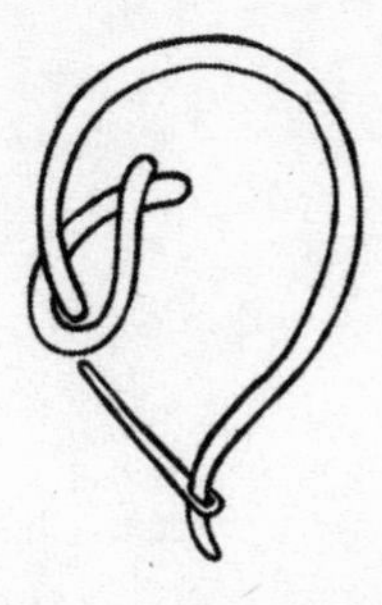

Know what is meant by the International Textile Care Labelling Code, and how you would care for the items you have made. Understand the importance of labels.

The Guide Badge Book, 1998

Petit Point

I'm an airport regular. I fly to Paris at least four times a year, and have become the sort of woman who pulls her wheeled luggage through town, irritating the local residents. I own 'crushable' dresses and scarves that double as sarongs or 'evening cover-ups'. I own noise-reducing headphones, a travel iron, magnetic chess, a palm-pilot on which I sometimes play Solitaire.

Together, Kenneth and I have been to over half the countries in Europe, as well as parts of Africa, South America and Iceland (a trip I made, a very cold trip with Joe, aged eight, and someone called Craig Pinski. We saw whales, the Northern Lights, a sulphurous, mud-flinging geyser around which delicate butterflies congregated. That was the holiday when Craig Pinski told me he couldn't see me any more because he would never be able to commit; it was a problem he had; he had forgotten to tell me about his commitment problem.)

After breakfast (muesli served from a silver bowl; dates; thick yogurt; nice coffee), I phone Joe. He sounds slightly hungover. His voice is low and flat. Maybe he was up all night after we left, drinking whisky.

'Are you OK?'

'Yes,' he replies, defensively.

He suggests a visit to the Botanic Gardens, which is a good place to go, I suppose, if you have a headache. Airy. Optimistic. I would have done this with my parents, I think, as I put the phone down; I would have shown them the ponds and banana plants and the Chinese lanterns. I would have taken them to admire the ferns and the winter jasmine.

I consult our *Guide to Edinburgh*. Then Kenneth and I put on our coats, pick up our bags and leave the hotel. We get on a 23 bus, career fast down The Mound, across Princes Street, up a short hill and down a long one, past art galleries, corner shops, antique shops, round a bend and – quick – get off the bus. Joe is already waiting for us at the gates: there he is, tall and quiet, *my son, my son,* and not wearing a warm enough coat. It is just gone eleven on Thursday 27 November. He is not even going to be with us for Christmas. I hurry towards him, to give him a hug and kiss his cheek.

The sky above is flat white. We peer into the fine drizzle.

'This is known as a haar,' Joe says.

'A-hah,' says Kenneth.

'So,' says Joe, and we all turn and troop silently through the silver gates and into the gardens. Signs point us to the Rockery, Café, West Gate, Demonstration Garden, Glasshouses. Everything today seems glassy, silvery, intangible. Even the flowers. The flower beds seem to be filled mainly with young mothers extricating their children from beneath low-spreading trees. On the lawns toddlers pick up damp leaves and pine cones and chase the pigeons. Squirrels canter fatly past.

'It's a nice place, the Botanics,' Joe says. 'A nice place to come and think.'

I expect he used to come here with his girlfriend, on summer's evenings, hand in hand.

'Where shall we go then? The Rockery?'

'How about the glasshouses? It's nice and warm in there.'

And we wander on, past red-leaved trees, purple autumn crocuses, a pond with swans, until we come to a door marked 'Glasshouse Experience'. Kenneth pulls open the door and we step inside, into the jungly warmth of the tropics. It is a kind embrace.

'It's fantastic on a day like this,' Joe says.

It reminds me of the Jardin des Plantes in Paris. The scent of leaves and ferns.

I pull off my scarf and gloves.

England was oddly hard to leave. It was a wrench, twenty-two years ago, to give up its parks and pavements, its daily walks. No more school! No more college with its vending machines, its linoleum floors, its student bands! No more Tetley's tea-bags! No more home!

We were impoverished in Paris for a while, me and Joe, but it was not like *La Bohème*. It was not moving. To begin with, my grant cheque did not come through. My French bank account had yet to disentangle itself from red tape. I broke out in stress-related eczema during our first week there, and had to spend most of our minuscule funds on a French version of Betnovate cream. Then Joe contracted hand, foot and mouth disease – something I had previously thought only occurred in livestock. He was ill for a week with a fever and a different type of rash. He blamed me for this unsatisfactory turn of events. He didn't want to be covered in rashes in France. He didn't want to visit the Orangerie or the Jardin des Plantes: he wanted to take his bike to the park in Maida Vale, the one that always smelled of wallflowers in the spring.

'I'm sorry, darling,' I used to say, stroking his hair and trying to resist the urge to scratch my own rashes, 'I'm sorry. But we can't go back just yet. Not just yet. Let's give it a bit more time.'

'Why?'

'Because we've only just got here.'

'But why can't we go back?'

'Because . . . we've got to give it more time. You have to, sometimes.'

I had nothing comforting or reasonable to say. No justification for my words or actions. What on earth were we doing here? At the age of twenty-two I felt the weight of being a selfish mother.

We spent the first two weeks before the start of my course wandering the streets. Moving from A to B because there was nothing else to do. One day we got caught up in a carnival in the eleventh arrondissement, squashed against people's backs and legs. All around us was the sound of drums and whistles, the smell of sweat and marijuana. People looked down at Joe and put out their hands to him. I hung on to him so tightly that he complained I was squashing his fingers.

By the end of our first week I concluded I had made a dreadful mistake, removing my son from England for *this* – a poor, unstructured life in a foreign country. We stopped being able to afford Métro tickets and spent our time wandering around a local market, confronting stalls full of pigs' trotters and skinned rabbits ('Look, Mummy – meat with eyes!'). We walked to the Pompidou Centre and Les Halles, our footsteps echoing around the underpopulated shopping-malls. We sat and ate an approximation of English sandwiches in formal, unaccommodating parks. Joe sat seriously by my side and watched the huge numbers of dogs and their owners that Parisian parks seemed to contain. 'What is the French for dog?' he asked, wrapping his chewy crusts into small, clingfilmed bundles. He seemed very small and pale. *What if he hates school in France? What if he detests it here?* I used to buy very cheap oranges and apricots and biscuits and bags of bread for him in the grubby and *non-touristique* market. Ramshackle pigeons barged against our feet. Stall-holders tried to sell me glass bangles and plastic necklaces, telling me how pretty they were, and how cheap.

At the beginning of our second week my grant cheque came through. We went to the *laverie* a couple of blocks away and dry-cleaned our fusty, rented duvets. With the change, I bought Joe a small toy lion which he christened Gary.

'That's a nice name for a lion,' I chirped brightly, wondering if his choice of an exceptionally British name said something about our being in France.

'Bonjour, Gary,' Joe said to the lion.

Joe seemed fine in fact, after a very short time. He did not resent me. And the people we met on the streets and on the dark oak staircase of our apartment block began to seem kinder. 'Ça va, mon petit? Ça va, le p'tit m'sieur?'

He had never liked English primary school anyway.

I missed my parents. I was homesick for their house. The polished piano, the clean carpets, the magazine rack, the big sliding door into the garden.

In the evenings, after Joe had fallen asleep on his fold-out bed, I would sit in our tiny kitchen and look through the window at the empty sky (our apartment faced the wrong way for a view of the Eiffel Tower). In the courtyard below, people hung out their washing or shouted or kicked footballs around. It sounded almost like home. But I didn't know anyone. I would sometimes write a letter to my cousin in Wolverhampton or Jane King (a girl I'd met at a mother-and-toddler group) or Susan Temple (a girl I had known at school) or listen to the World Service on the radio. I thought about Sally Tuttle, my old best friend. I mourned my parents. Sometimes loneliness seemed almost like a physical presence, sitting in front of me.

I pulled myself together after a while.

My course began.

I found a place for Joe at a local school.

I bought:

a stove-top percolator
some cushions
some picture books
some pot plants

I met a guitarist called Julien at a bookstall on the Left Bank. I bought:

a radio-cassette-player
some wine glasses
a reproduction of a painting by Manet
a potato peeler

The store cupboard became populated with new tastes: pots of tarragon and packets of madeleines and dried mushrooms and couscous. Some evenings I would look across at Joe, asleep on his fold-out bed and think: *This is a way to exist; this is one of the ways.*

'Look at that red flower,' Kenneth says as we are walking through the Temperate Room. He stops to gaze at it. 'Just like a pom-pom,' he says.

I am turning to smile back at him, to say 'Isn't it calm in here? Isn't it lovely and peaceful?', when suddenly it is not: there is suddenly an extremely loud noise – so loud that I am aware of a tiny, primitive twitching of the bones in my ears.

For some reason I feel instantly, oddly, upset. The noise – a young, human wail – is so out of keeping with the tranquillity.

'That's quite a pair of lungs,' Kenneth says, 'for a baby.'

'Babies have the biggest lungs,' I reply.

The sound is coming from the room next door.

The three of us do our best to ignore it. Quietly we walk past the pom-pom flowers, the tree-trunks covered in bright green moss, the creepers, the purple orchids – and over a bridge beneath which huge Coi carp flail and splash. But the screaming continues. We stop on the bridge and look down at the carp. The largest – a white, cantankerous-looking one with orange, cow-like splotches – must be nearly two foot long. We lean over the railings, watching the fish swim beneath us, before heading for the Aquatic Room walkway.

But the scream is even louder here. It is more a series of screams. And then I realise it is not coming from a baby at all. It is coming from a young child, about three years old, who has her head stuck in the walkway railings. Her parents are crouching on the walkway beside her, white-faced and resigned. They are not attempting to ease her head out; they have presumably already tried and failed. They have curious expressions on their faces: a mixture of fear and fatigue. The girl's older sister stands next to them, twisting a huge, illegally-plucked banana leaf between her fingers. The three-year-old continues to howl. In the jungly surroundings, it is like the sound of a monkey.

I am not sure what to do.

'Is there anything we can do?' I ask the child's mother as we approach. The mother looks up. There are tears in her eyes. She looks only a few years younger than me.

'They've phoned for the fire brigade,' she says.

The little girl's father has his hand through the railings and he is stroking his daughter's hair. All I can really see of the girl is her mousey hair and her pink anorak. The father looks withdrawn, as if he has mentally removed himself from the proceedings and is sitting in some café somewhere, reading the football scores.

'We could –'

'No, we're fine, thank you,' says the mother.

And I want to say something comforting, something to help. *I know what it's like*, I want to say. *You have to watch your children doing these things. It starts so young. And you just have to watch them.*

'In twenty minutes it'll all be over,' is all I can come up with. I reflect that this is exactly what the midwife told me when I was giving birth to Joe. I remember that I didn't believe her.

The woman looks at me. 'Oh God,' she says.

'Well, if we can be any help,' Kenneth says, 'we'll be in the next room.'

And the three of us hurry, as fast as we can, away from the scene where we are not needed. Three mature people who don't get themselves into scrapes. We go into the Aquatic Room, where we stand, silently, and look at dozens of tiny fish vacuuming themselves to the side of the tanks, their mouths perfect grey Os.

'Poor little girl,' I say. 'Poor woman.'

'They'll be dining out on that for years,' Kenneth says. 'The day little Susie got her head stuck in the railings.'

'Did I ever do that?' Joe asks. Sometimes he still asks the kind of questions he would have asked at the age of eight.

'I got my head stuck in our banisters once,' Kenneth says. 'My dad had to saw one of them off. I don't remember it.'

'Fortunately.'

'Blanked it out.'

'They shouldn't be more than four inches apart,' Joe says.

We remain in the room with the little glass-kissing fish for quite a while. Maybe ten minutes. Tranquil fish. Zen aquatic snails. After a while there is the wail of a siren in the gardens, and a fire engine appears and stops outside. Men run in with equipment. There is the buzz of cutters, the clang of a felled railing, the wails, the sobs, the murmurings and finally the gradual, gradual cessation of noise.

When we emerge discreetly from the Aquatic Room, the little girl is sitting in her buggy, still as a statue, transfixed, but still managing to suck a lollipop.

Burden

END OF TERM REPORT, DECEMBER 1979

Geography. Effort: D. Attainment: D
Sally will have to pay much more attention and complete her homework assignments if she is to qualify for her course next year.

English. Effort: D. Attainment: C
Sally's absence from class is beginning to form a pattern. If she were here more often, she might understand the difference between irony and sarcasm.

Mathematics. Effort: E. Attainment: E
Sally's grasp of algebra and trigonometry remains tenuous in the extreme. Correct answers seem to be arrived at haphazardly.

Needlework. Effort: A. Attainment: B
What a difference! Sally has worked really hard in the past few weeks, completing her blouson and skirt before the end of term. Her work is invariably neat and methodical. Well done, Sally!

The teachers were not supposed to refer to 'the situation' at all. They were not supposed to mention it. But Miss Button, trendy Miss Button did.

'That stupid girl,' Miss Button said one day when Rowena was away at an antenatal appointment. 'What a waste of a good brain.'

Rowena would sometimes look at Sally from across the playground. And sometimes, despite her monstrous betrayal, Sally wanted to run across and hug her, say 'It's OK, it's OK, I forgive you.' *I knew, really,* she wanted to say, *I knew deep down, when we bumped into you in Woolworths.*

Because she missed her. She missed her so much that her eyes welled up with tears when she thought about her. But now there was this thing, this bulge, this *result of reproduction* which only a few months ago they had sniggered about in Biology lessons. There it was, turning Rowena Cresswell into someone else. Puffing up her face. Thickening her waist. *What have you done, Rowena?* And inside her was Colin's child. Sally's boyfriend's child. Even her betrayal faded in the light of that.

Within just a couple of weeks, their estrangement had become too frightening, too established to do anything about. Sally was at a loss to know *what* to do. She was so shocked she couldn't even properly hate her. She pretended to be ill and stayed away from school for a whole week, embroidering a frog on a lily-pad, until her mother marched her to the bus stop one rainy morning. (Rowena had not been at the bus stop: her mother had started driving her to school in their Volvo.) And when Sally got to school she discovered that, in her absence, Rowena had been scooped up by two motherly sixth-form girls – girls who had always had that irritating, serene look on their faces when they went up to the altar during Communion. Now Sally would see them at break, plodding about the playground in their sensible shoes, Rowena between them, duplicitous as a cuckoo.

Nobody really knew what to say. There was no precedent. This was a nice school. It was not 'that awful comprehensive' down the road. What was the best course of action? Expulsion? Or understanding? It was 1979. The teachers took so long wondering what to do that it became 1980, and Rowena's pregnancy was becoming undeniable. She wandered around the playground with her sixth-form minders, untouchable, her stomach beginning to swell beneath the blue nylon of her school blouse. She was somebody else now. *Not Rowena.* And now Sally *did* start to hate her, particularly after she had her hair cut – a short, brutal cut, like a signal of contempt. No more prissy perms and wedges for *her*. It seemed she had abandoned her taste in wishy-washy hairstyles. She seemed, Sally thought, almost triumphant, flaunting her pregnancy, her short hair like a flag. Her school skirt, the fastening undone to accommodate her stomach, grew tight around her legs. By late winter, when the rest of their class – chaste, good girls – were wondering if she would become one of those extraordinarily huge pregnant people – *God, maybe she would* die *giving birth!* – she left, never to return. It was the most exciting departure anyone had ever made. Even more exciting than dying.

Nobody seemed to know who the father was. Nobody except Sally. She sat quietly, without Rowena, in Needlework, meticulously hemming the cuffs of her blouson. Needlework had become a kind of solace. A consolation. She could bury her head in the material; she could watch the push and pull of the needle, and make the pinking shears purr. She could comfort herself with the feel of silk, with the words *voile*, *georgette*, *organza*, *petersham*, *linen*, *wool.*

At home her parents sat, non-plussed, on their Dralon sofa.

'What's going on, Sally?' asked her father.

'What do you mean, what's going on?'

'You used to get good reports.'

'Well, I don't know what they're all on about. I haven't done anything different.'

'At least she's good at Needlework, Bill. Maybe . . .' her mother began, and then stopped, confounded. She sighed, bent, and picked up a piece of fluff from the carpet.

'I haven't done anything different,' Sally said again, and she stood up and left the room. She went upstairs to her bedroom where she sat, listening to the tapes Rowena had recorded for her and staring at all her belongings: her Pierrot doll, her cheap guitar, her *Jackie* magazines, her make-up box, her basket of threads. For years, she and Rowena had sat there together; Rowena had sat on that bean-bag, talking about everything, from God to leg-warmers. And latterly, Sally thought – it slowly dawned on her – they had talked a lot about Colin. Rowena had even blushed; had looked shifty at the mention of his name.

She was sleeping with him! She was having sex with him!

And obviously they were not even using his free condoms.

She couldn't stop thinking about the consequences of sex. It had changed Rowena totally. Pregnancy had turned her into a navel-gazer; someone who no longer cared about the outside world. Someone who no longer spoke to Sally. She wished she could ask her what it was like. Was she happy? Or scared? Did her mother condemn her or cosset her? Had she taken her to see someone at the Marie Stopes clinic or knitted her tiny pastel-coloured cardigans? And how did it feel, what was it like, to have a stomach with a *baby* inside it? A baby that *moved*? She'd heard that they *moved around* in there! And sometimes you could see little outlines of hands and feet through the skin! Was that true or was that some myth? Sally patted her own flat, uncaressed belly and tried to imagine. At school she went to Biology classes where they were having sex education lessons, and from which Rowena, already educated, was excused. She learned about the reproductive life of a frog, its sad little body splayed out on a wooden board.

Colin, she didn't actually care about so much. His importance had shifted, like the ace in a pack of cards. From highest to lowest value in one switch of games. He had vanished, in any case; had disappeared overnight, sidling away through the night-black suburbs to who knew where – Reading? Scunthorpe? Italy? – and there was nothing Sally could do. She missed him of course, she missed him physically, in her chest, as if a part of her had been wrenched away with him. A sudden, awful hurt. And visions of Colin floated around her head: there he was, at Razzles. There he was, in his beautiful, awful coat. There he was, lying on the lion statue at Trafalgar Square. But then, after just a few weeks she couldn't picture him clearly any more. His face began to grow hazy and indistinct, and this struck her as the saddest thing that could happen to someone: the forgetting of a loved one's face. She couldn't picture the exact contours and angles any more, the curve of his lips or the colour of his eyes. His face was a vague shape, a memory of something loved. It was a deprivation. It was not fair. But Rowena had known him better than she ever would.

The town was empty, a void. She walked past the Cresswells' house and couldn't bring herself to look up at the lit windows. She told the teachers that, no, she couldn't give Rowena the lesson notes she had missed. She dialled her number and then put the phone down when her mother answered. She dialled Colin's number and sat with her ear against the receiver, listening to the single, continuous, humming tone on the other end of the line. She imagined his empty flat above the kebab shop. She lay on her bed on top of her old, lanolin-smelling sheepskin rug, staring up at the ceiling. Apart from that, she did nothing. She just lay there.

After a while she wondered if her relationship with Colin had been some sort of elaborate joke. She looked at herself in her parents' wardrobe mirror and saw herself reduced; not a mysterious young woman but a schoolgirl with gangly legs. Of course, of *course* this would happen. How could he have found her attractive and Rowena not? *But that could have been me!* she kept thinking. *That could have been me, with that stomach and that baby!*

A 'To Let' sign appeared outside Colin's flat, and she couldn't help observing, childishly, how it would have said *toilet* if there had been an *i* in it.

Sometimes she used to imagine she would bump into Colin. Surely it was inevitable? And maybe when she did she would forgive him. Or perhaps he would fall in love, unrequited, with the wise, witty beauty she had become. He would be some unspectacular thirty-two-year-old man, balding, possibly fat, and she would be twenty-five, gorgeous, talented, cruel. Maybe she would bump into him at a swing-park one day. He would be wearing a hideous two-tone padded anorak and pushing his awful snotty child back and forth, back and forth on a swing, and she would not even recognise him until he uttered the words *How could I have let you go . . .?*

Rowena gave birth four months after she left school. It was early April, a day full of pink and white blossom. Sally discovered on the grapevine that the baby was nearly a month early, a five-pound, five-ounce boy whom she named Joe. Rowena had given him her own surname. Joe Cresswell.

Occasionally Sally would see Rowena pushing Joe Cresswell around in a pram, up East Grinstead High Street. Or sitting in the Me-n-U café with her mother, the baby in her arms, A-levels abandoned, the punk hairstyle grown out too. Sally's heart always blanched when she spotted them. The baby looked tiny and pink, like a prawn, its head flopping as if there was something wrong with it. Rowena and Mrs Cresswell always seemed to be arguing.

Sally left school herself a few months later, her life haphazard, insubstantial, papery as a sewing pattern. She stayed at home, cloistered behind the safe, fern-leaf-splattered walls of her parent's house. She sat in front of the television on Thursday nights, watching *Top of the Pops* and *The Generation Game* and eating too many Ritz biscuits. She had unfinished O-levels in five subjects. She did not have a single friend.

Her father sat on the sofa beside her sometimes, marvelling at the discordant noises emerging from the bands on *Top of the Pops*. ('Is this singing? Do they think this is singing?')

Her mother used to come quietly into the living room, walking across their squeaking autumn-leaf carpet, bearing trays of Bourbon biscuits and cups of tea. 'Here y'ar, darling,' she used to say, frowning. There was something wrong with her daughter but she didn't know what it was.

'You're not pregnant, are you?' she asked one evening.

'No, Mum,' Sally replied tetchily – by now her grief had turned into a kind of permanent tetchiness. She reached forward for another biscuit. 'I am not pregnant.'

It was not Colin she missed, after all. It was Rowena. It was Rowena she thought about. Alone in the kitchen, she would go to the phone and dial Rowena's number again. She knew Rowena's number better than her own. But she would put the phone down before the first ring, imagining their silence, or their anger, or the wail of Joe Cresswell in the background. Three times their own phone had rung and it had been Rowena; but Sally's mother had answered and Sally had pretended to be out.

Eventually Rowena and her son moved away – to London, Sally heard – to live in some flat in Maida Vale. And then on to somewhere else. While Sally continued to drift around the house, collapsed on the furniture.

'Come on,' her mother used to say. 'You've got to buck your ideas up.'

Her mother wanted her to snap out of it, whatever it was. She plumped down beside her one afternoon, a month or so before Christmas, and said, 'What are you planning to do with your life, then? Eh?'

'Dunno.'

'Because you can't hang around doing nothing, can you?'

'S'pose not.'

'What happened to Rowena? You never talk about her these days.'

'Dunno.'

'Can't you think of anything to do?'

'Nope.'

So she found work. She began to work at the Country Kitchen, donning her mob cap and her puffed sleeves every morning. And in the evenings she came home and picked up her canvas, her needle and her thread.

Cross

There are many ways in which a girl's life can go wrong.

Or, there are a few ways, but the ways are like waves, building up momentum as they progress. Gathering up seaweed, rubbish, shipwrecks, oil slicks, dubious sailors in their wake. Sailors with tattoos on their arms proclaiming undying love.

My son has always made friends easily. He used to bring some of them home for tea back in England: big, space-invading schoolboys in smelly shoes. I remember all their names: Luke, Max, Chris, Simon. I remember the things they used to like eating, their obsession with trainers and small electronic games. When they were very young they called me Mrs Cresswell. When they grew older they didn't call me anything. They looked at my smooth skin and unmotherish figure and some of them blushed.

Usually I don't worry any more about the potential pitfalls in my son's life because he is past the age of stupidity. The time to worry about male stupidity – physical stupidity – is over. He is twenty-seven. He has always been more academic than sporty in any case; not one of those boys that goes abseiling or potholing or freefalling. He has never been interested in situations involving sheer drops or tight spaces. But he could always run fast, do trigonometry, clear the high jump.

Another reason not to worry about him: his appearance. He is a nice-looking man, his features even and open. He does not have the hang-ups that I used to have; that all the girls at my school seemed to have. When he was younger he never even seemed to care very much when he got spots. I remember caring a lot. I remember the hours Sally Tuttle and I used to spend in front of mirrors, fretting and wondering. About our spots and also about our hair. Was it better like this, or like that? Better with a side parting? Or a middle parting? Or no parting at all?

Joe is lucky because (a) he does not mope around for hours in front of mirrors, and (b) he has not inherited my straight, straight hair.

Instead he has his father's waves and kinks. Curls I used to long for. When he was still a baby people sometimes described his curls as 'angelic', which made me simultaneously proud and envious. He had these dark golden, bouncing curls. He had, the hairdresser used to inform me on my visits to Fringe Benefits, 'hair to die for'.

'You see the way Joey's hair stays in place?' she said, attempting, with a cylindrical brush, to flick some life into my hair. 'People pay a fortune on perms to get their hair to sit like that.'

'Really?' I replied, thinking how strange it was to describe hair as *sitting,* like a patient dog.

'That do you?' the hairdresser asked then, bending down towards my face and pulling two strands of hair across my cheeks, to check they were the same length. They weren't, quite.

'That's great,' I replied. 'That's lovely.' And I smiled in the mirror. I didn't have a clue what I should do with my hair or my life.

I visited Fringe Benefits for over a year but my conversations with Lorraine never really got past the subject of how lovely my haircuts were. I was no good at conversations with other girls any more: a part of me, at that time, had closed down. Sometimes I thought I might begin a conversation about something – my plans to go back to school or to sixth-form college – but my nerve would buckle as soon as I saw the other clients ranged around the walls like wilting foxgloves beneath the lilac hairdryers.

I should go somewhere else. I've been coming here too long.

'So, what would you like today, Rowena?'

My own flat, nice toys for Joe, a career, some fun, a boyfriend, a girl friend.

'Just a trim today please.'

Lorraine considered and tapped the side of her face with her fingers. She had a silver bracelet on her left wrist, with the letter L attached to it.

'Ever thought of a more flicky sort of fringe?' she said one afternoon. (It was 1982 by now: Joe was two and my old school peers had all started at university.)

'Hmm,' I replied, looking around the salon at the women beneath the hairdryers. At the dried-out Easter cactus plants, the curled magazines and the cups of tea. It felt as if nothing had moved in there for years.

'Go on,' Lorraine coaxed, 'have a bit of a change.'

I had an hour to spend at the hairdresser's before I had to relieve my mother of babysitting duties (babysitting was a huge strain for all concerned).

'OK,' I said, 'it's about time I had a different look.'

'Your little boy's lucky, isn't he?' Lorraine observed, pleased that she had persuaded me. She pinned my hair up at the back and gently pushed my head forwards. 'Them curls.'

'He gets them from his dad,' I replied wickedly into my plastic grey cape.

'Really?' Lorraine asked, her voice fading away. She cleared her throat, embarrassed. Everyone in that part of East Grinstead knew about the posh schoolgirl who had the baby, but pretended not to.

'So,' Lorraine said. 'I'm going to do a sort of flicky look at the front, and short at the back.'

'OK.'

Far away, in the distance, a radio was playing Bob Marley. *No woman, no cry*. Someone turned on a hairdryer. Someone laughed.

I remember leaving the hairdresser's that day, running because I was late and Joe would be crying and my poor, ill mother would have on her long-suffering face. I remember turning the corner by the butcher's shop, putting my hand up to the shortness at the back, the new flicks at the sides, and thinking, 'I could be different. I could be different.'

The hairdresser helped me make that decision. She must have transmitted something through her silver scissors, along my hair and directly into my brain.

I began to think more clearly in those weeks. In a notebook covered in yogurt, I wrote down my achievements and plans:

I've got:
1. Maths and English
2. An A in French O-level
I could:
1. Go to sixth-form college
2. Study French

(*University?* I wrote in brackets. *Nurseries? Grants? Check library, newspapers.*)

I remember writing this as I lay on my flat stomach, on a tartan blanket in my parents' garden, my son nearby, crashing into the flowerbeds. He was wearing the little jacket I had found in Oxfam – the one that had the typographical error printed all over it: *cutey pi*. He turned his head and smiled at me and said something in infant language about the leaves on my mother's variegated holly. I leaned across and kissed his cheek.

*

My first step towards a career was a course for early school-leavers and people on benefit. It was located in a grey council building in the hinterland of East Grinstead. I left Joe with my parents for the day and clanged up the metal steps, a new card-board folder under my arm.

The course was called 'Steps to a New Career: The Challenge Ahead'.

The tutor (a woman whose name, I recall, was Felicity) was very upbeat. She wore enormous, swaying earrings and spent the whole of the first hour telling us how she had sorted her life out. Her name used to be Dawn, but she didn't like that, she almost shouted, so she had changed it by deed poll. This was an example of how she had Overcome a Difficulty. And this attitude could be applied to finding a career.

We early school-leavers and people on benefit looked at her. There were eight of us. This was part of a government-sponsored 'Into Work' package. Either you attended or you paid back £100. ('You get a free lunch,' the 'Into Work' adviser had told me at my local DHSS office. 'There *is* such a thing. I believe they do quite nice sandwiches.')

Felicity's life story involved four jobs, two years in America and a divorce. 'So,' she said in conclusion, 'that's enough talking from me. Now I'd like you all to introduce yourselves. Let's start with you. Tell us all who you are and what your last job was.'

She turned to the very scared-looking man sitting beside me.

'My name's Bill,' he squeaked. 'I was a joiner.'

But he was better at joining wood than groups like this. He shoved his hands beneath his thighs, turned and looked at me.

'Oh,' I said. I wasn't expecting to be in the spotlight so suddenly. 'I'm Rowena. I'm just a . . .'

But I didn't want to say anything about Joe. I didn't want to say I had left school at fifteen because I had got pregnant.

'A what?' Felicity asked, smiling at me.

'I don't know. I just . . .'

'No no, you never *just* do something, Rowena,' Felicity said.

'OK. I was . . . I am . . . I kind of . . .'

I thought of Joe and felt treacherous.

'I'm a mother,' I said.

'That's better,' Felicity said, looking a little alarmed, her earrings sparkling beneath the fluorescent lights. 'None of us is *just* something. The word "just" is not allowed in this room.'

And she stood up, walked over to the whiteboard, wrote JUST on it, then drew a line through it.

'"Just" has been exterminated,' she said. I almost expected her to throw her head back and laugh, like a villain in a cartoon. Instead, she smiled mildly, sat down again and looked at me.

'Being a mother is one of the toughest jobs there is' she said.

'Yes,' I mumbled, feeling that I might be about to cry. I was aware of the woman next to me bracing herself for an ordeal.

Some events, some days stay in your mind and you don't even know why. I remember that day with great clarity. I remember having to do something called 'Accelerated Learning: Dilemmas and Solutions'. This had involved shuffling around the room until we found someone to discuss a dilemma with. We had to discuss two problems each within six minutes. I grabbed the first person I could find – a curly-haired woman who had once worked in a café. *Her* problem, she told me, was that she used to eat half the cakes before they had even made it on to the counter. 'I did it for weeks before anyone found out it was me,' she said, and I nodded sympathetically, like a priest in a confession box.

'I mean, apart from putting on the weight,' the woman said, 'it meant we used to run out of things to sell by four o'clock.'

I tried to apply my mind to a solution. 'Maybe,' I suggested, 'when you get a new job, you could eat a bowl of cereal or something before you . . .'

The woman looked at me and gave a small, unamused laugh. 'It wouldn't be the same if I just ate something at home,' she said. 'It was the thrill of the chase.'

She looked at her watch. 'That's one and a half minutes anyway. You have to talk about a problem now, duck.'

'Oh God,' I said. I couldn't think of a small enough problem. Also, I really didn't know how I could follow the woman's cake story.

'Go on,' said the woman, 'We all have problems. I'm all ears.' But actually she was all eyes. Her eyes were enormous behind her glasses.

So I talked about getting pregnant. How I had not meant to but it had happened, quick as anything – there was this bloke I had had a crush on, and now I had a twenty-six-month-old son and I had screwed up. And my best friend didn't talk to me any more. I hadn't seen her for well over a year, but time . . . time seemed to have done strange things. It had moved and it hadn't moved.

'I love my baby and everything . . .' I said, instantly regretting what a private subject I had chosen. The tears were beginning to well up behind my eyes, as they often did in those days. 'You know, I wouldn't ever have wanted to . . .'

The woman looked at me. She blinked. 'You're young,' she said, somewhat irritably. 'How old are you?'

'Seventeen.'

The woman gave another short, slightly bitter laugh.

'The world's your oyster, darling.'

'Yes, but it's not, is it? It's not exactly . . .'

The woman picked three shortbread biscuits off the catering trolley. 'Have you tried to patch things up with your friend? Maybe she could babysit for you.'

I found it hard to comprehend how obtuse this woman was.

'It's a bit complicated,' I said. 'I really don't think that's likely to happen.'

'Why not?'

'Because we fell out. She thought . . . We never really talked about it, but I think she might have thought . . .'

I stopped talking. The woman was staring at me, her eyes enormous and uncomprehending. She took a bite of shortbread. I imagined how I might once have talked to Sally about her. The way we would have spoken about it. And a little picture came into my head then, of how it might have been; how different it might have been, if Sally had remained my friend. She could have been like an aunt to Joe. She could at least have continued to be my friend. But now I didn't even know what she did any more. I didn't know where she spent her days. She had left school, apparently, got some job in a plumber's merchants: that was all I knew.

'Quick, we have to swap again now,' the woman said, looking around her at the other couples in the room. Then she launched into a story about going to the vet's with her dog. 'He had a distended stomach,' she explained. 'He looked like one of those airships. He looked as if he was about to explode . . .'

And I listened and looked at the rain bouncing off the window sills and knew something about my life would have to change.

Up-and-Down Buttonhole

Her *award-winning* embroidery was sent ahead a few days ago. Fed-exed, as somebody informed her on the phone. But she could not bear to do that to Mary and Martha: couldn't place them in the hands of some man in a uniform and watch them disappearing into the ether. What if she never saw them again? What if they ended up on the other side of the world, received with confusion by someone in Alaska or New Guinea? So she packed Mary and Martha carefully into her portfolio, covering them in white tissue paper, smoothing the threads on the rough side.

She is on the point of leaving for the airport when there is a phone call.

'Sperlin?'

'Sorry?'

'Sperlin?'

'Oh. No, you've just missed her, I'm afraid. She's on her way to school.'

'Cool. Cheers.'

And he hangs up. Sally doesn't have a clue who he is.

Two more calls follow while she is running around wondering where her keys are. The first is from Sue at In Stitches. 'Nervous?' she asks.

'Extremely. And I've just gone and lost my keys.'

'You'll find them.'

'Ha!'

'We're all rooting for you, Sal. You'll be fine.'

'Thanks,' Sally says, looking up and seeing her keys on top of the bread bin. 'I've just spotted my keys,' she says.

'Told you you would.'

Sometimes she feels her friends have more faith in her than they should.

The third call is from the Reverend Avery.

'How is the, ah, embroidery coming along?' he booms.

'Oh, fine. Yes, it's . . . I think I'm on the final leg of the foreground now.'

'The final leg of the foreground,' Reverend Avery muses. 'Hmm.'

And neither of them seems to know how to continue. Sally looks at her watch. She pictures a plane taking off.

'Are you using sequins?'

'I'm actually getting low on sequins.'

'Low on sequins. Ah.'

The Reverend Avery sounds a little concerned.

'I'd normally order them in bulk,' she explains, 'but I don't want to . . . hang around waiting, and I'm off to Edinburgh today. Right now, in fact,' she adds, the sense of lateness increasing and making her feel slightly sick. She reaches up to the bread bin and grabs her keys. 'So I'll see if I can find a haberdashery department while I'm there,' she says, 'and stock up.'

She is not sure why she is telling the Reverend Avery the minutiae of her embroidering schedule. Or of her need to hang around haberdashery departments every so often, just taking in the colours, the textures, the minutely beautiful cards and packets.

'Well,' she says. 'I have to go now, or I'll miss my plane.'

'Yes. Off you scoot,' the Reverend Avery says tetchily – making her wonder how on earth he got involved with the commissioning of something as fiddly and irksome as an embroidery.

The flight up to Edinburgh is full of people carrying identical conference bags. They are made of black canvas with webbing straps, and emblazoned with the logo *We Get There First.* Sally thinks of the machine operators who embroidered the logos.

She is standing in the plane's narrow central aisle behind an overweight young man in a vented suit. His trouser legs (she noticed, as she walked behind him on to the plane) need lengthening at least half an inch. She resists an impulse to laugh as he tries to push past another overweight young man in a vented suit, and their *We Get There First* bags become wedged fast.

'You *could* wait a minute,' one of them snaps.

'I'd be waiting all day.'

'Excuse me,' Sally says, swerving around them into her seat. She puts her bag in the overhead locker and her portfolio by her feet.

She has always been a nervous flier. She grips the flimsy plastic arms of her seat as the plane rumbles along the tarmac, its passengers rattling and swaying like wooden dollies. It lifts abruptly as if a giant child has picked it up to play with. Within seconds they are thousands of feet up, the land beneath them smugly safe. The engine roars, changes pitch (*Why's that? Why's that?*) and Sally's palms sweat. Beside her a woman sighs and opens a minuscule packet of Planter's peanuts. Sally closes her eyes and tries not to think how far up and how fast they are traveling. Air journeys always seem incredibly foolish, a kind of unthinking leap into the air.

There is a huge crowd of backpackers on the shuttle bus to the terminal, a lot of red Gortex and dangling rip-cords. Sally finds a seat but is nearly flung off it as the driver swerves to avoid something lying on the tarmac. A suitcase. A blue-and-orange checked suitcase, with yellow airport tape wrapped vigorously around it.

Where did that come from? Did it fall out of the sky? Then she sees that it has dropped off a baggage trolley. She imagines the same thing happening to her portfolio and is thankful that she has it with her. She hangs on to its handles, the way she once used to hang on to Pearl's hand.

A man in overalls is standing on the tarmac, waiting to run out and retrieve the lost bag. He makes a gesture to the bus driver, denoting thanks that he didn't cover it with tyre marks. The driver gives him a little nod and a semi-wave and drives on. How polite people in vehicles can be. How civilised, even on the tarmac of an airport, with that little edge of condescension. *Thank you, my man.* Making those little waves, like the queen.

Sally gets off the shuttle bus at the main building. It is three-thirty in the afternoon. Cold. The sky is orange. There is a smell of chips wafting east.

In the nothing-to-declare queue she stands behind a young, pregnant woman. She is about six months *gone* – her stomach has reached that beautiful stage of roundness, that still plausible grandeur. Even after nearly sixteen years Sally still misses that solid state: the validity, the company of another presence with her; the outrageous acrobatics of a baby in her belly.

'Not much fun, all this standing, for you,' she says to the woman.

'Oh, I don't mind,' the woman replies. She smiles at her, as if perhaps Sally doesn't know what pregnancy is like. And Sally smiles back, reminded of that feeling of being unique. Invulnerable. The opposite of what people expect.

A short, swarthy man is standing outside the automatic doors, waiting for her. He is holding up a card which says SALLY TUCKWELL.

'Hello,' Sally says, walking towards him and giving him one of her smiles – the big, confident smile which, she knows, is one of her assets. (Her counsellor Mrs Bonniface said a big smile can do wonders. Over the years she has learned how to enhance her mouth and how to conceal her big ears, her fine hair, her (mother's) nose. She has also acquired something she never thought she would have: a tough shell. Impenetrable as thimbles. She hides behind it at work: her Needlewoman face. *Yes, of course we can fix that, no problem!*)

She is about to say to the taxi-driver, 'It's Tuttle, actually, not Tuckwell' (*I had a friend once,* she thinks, *whose surname was Cresswell*), but then she doesn't bother.

'OK, hen?' the man says, taking her rucksack and portfolio and opening the door of his waiting cab – it smells of vanilla and has a cluster of small plastic grapes hanging from the rear-view mirror.

Sally gets in and sits quietly on the slippery leather seat.

'Ken Embra?' the driver asks over his shoulder as they begin to move. Incomprehension flits like a moth around Sally's brain.

'Do you know Edinburgh, like?' the driver says, articulating slowly.

'Oh. No. I've never been here before,' Sally replies in her south-east English accent.

She looks out of the window at the drab environs of Edinburgh airport. Bungalows – bungalows in Edinburgh? Roundabouts. Shopping malls. A large, purple shack calling itself PC World. It all looks like East Grinstead. Maybe everywhere these days looks like East Grinstead. An aeroplane takes off and crosses the frozen vapour-trail of an earlier one. A big kiss in the sky.

'You staying at the Royal Burgh, then?'

'Yes.'

'That's a fine hotel, the Royal. A fine hotel. Better than all that Ibis nonsense.'

'Oh good.'

*

This is the vocabulary of her new life: *Conference. Delegate. Allocate.* She has been allocated two conference delegates to talk to when she arrives. Their names are typed on her information sheet: Jeremy Bowes and Nora Wheeler. She is due to meet them at the hotel at six, for drinks followed by a dinner. She is intrigued about Jeremy Bowes. The world of embroidery and dressmaking is usually entirely bereft of men. She imagines sitting opposite him and Nora at an octagonal table. (*'And which embroidery stitch do you prefer, Ms. Tuttle?' 'Oh, satin stitch, Jeremy, every time.'*)

As they round a corner, Edinburgh Castle appears, dreamily, on the skyline. Now the bungalows begin to peter out and give way to tall grey tenements. The taxi passes a kebab shop, a stationer's, a costume hire company and a bagpipe shop. There are seagulls in the sky. Maroon double-decker buses. Schoolgirls in blue blazers and kilts. A smell seeps slyly into the cab – a smell she can't place, like overheated Weetabix.

'That's the brewery, like,' the taxi driver says suddenly.

'Oh.'

'It's the malt. But they're pulling it all down.'

'Pulling what down?'

'The brewery, like.'

'Oh. That's a shame.'

'End of an era.'

'Yes.'

The schoolgirls make her think of Pearl. She gets her mobile phone out of her handbag – a phone she has bought especially for the occasion, and on which she has only just got used to pressing the correct buttons. She wants to phone John to see if he has remembered to pick Pearl up from school; but the little screen just lights up, displays a picture of a rainbow and says Emergency Calls Only. Her phone does not appear to be able to connect to East Grinstead. The only person she can call is an emergency switchboard operator. She thinks of Pearl and a tiny electrical charge of anxiety fizzes inside her chest. She puts the phone back in her bag.

'So,' the taxi driver says, 'are you here on business or pleasure?'

'Business. I'm going to a conference. On embroidery. Which is what I . . .'

'Come again?'

The man's left ear seems to move very slightly towards the open window.

'Embroidery,' she repeats loudly, and the word hangs in the cab, unaugmented, gaining too much significance. She looks at her portfolio and her rucksack and her handbag sitting beside her, like three long-suffering travelling companions. She imagines Mary and Martha staring crossly up from their canvas.

'What aspect of embroidery is that, then?' the taxi driver asks, making her jump.

'The history of it,' she replies, raising her voice above the noise of the engine. 'And the connection of Scotland and France.'

'Oh aye, the Auld Alliance,' the taxi driver booms. 'That old chestnut.'

Outside the window a little girl is refusing to hold her mother's hand. Crouching on the pavement while her mother walks away, pretending to abandon her.

The foyer of the Royal Burgh Hotel is pale and cool, with a smooth floor and a lot of glass surfaces. Sally emerges into it through the expensive doors – *taa-daah!* – carrying her portfolio, her handbag and her rucksack. She thinks she probably looks like a too-old student. A man with slicked-back hair is sitting behind the reception desk, his chair so low that his chin only just reaches above the counter.

'Good afternoon, madam,' he says.

'Good afternoon.'

'Would you like someone to take your luggage up?'

'Oh, no, it's OK, thanks. It's very light.'

It *is* light, her luggage, but she feels this was the wrong response. The man looks at her rucksack, her portfolio and her handbag. 'OK,' he says, handing her her room key and directing her towards the lift.

The corridors smell of bacon and lilies and Mr Sheen.

She walks along the second floor, noticing the way all the doors swish against the carpets. It feels opulent, professional. And here she is, in it. She wants to phone Pearl just to tell her what colour the carpets are. To inform her that there is a large pewter bowl bearing pine cones, positioned on a wooden table at the end of the corridor, and three enormous white candles placed, like altar decor, on a window sill. She steps into a lift and notes that it is made by a company called Schindler. And that the piped music is 'Annie's Song'. She wants to tell her daughter all this. All the details of being away *on business*.

Her room is just as she had hoped. Large and beige, with a double bed, a sofa, an en-suite bathroom and a number of innocuous flower-prints on the walls. It is excitingly bland. It makes her feel polished, elegant, important. She looks at the double bed with regret.

She has been picturing this place for months, ever since she got the letter from the conference organisers. She goes into the bathroom. There are five white towels, a transparent shower curtain, a shower cap and a wrapped sachet of Lux soap. There are small sachets of shampoo and moisturising cream. There is a pink carnation in a vase and a matching toilet roll. She wonders about the chamber maid whose job it is to perform daily feats of origami with its top sheet.

The wardrobe in the bedroom smells of citronella and contains eight wooden coat-hangers. There are packets in a lavender-lined drawer in the bedside cabinet, containing a shoeshine kit, complimentary mints and an emergency repair set (two buttons; one needle; four threads). Sally takes off her coat and looks out of the window at the view: the laundry chute and ventilation shafts emerging from the hotel kitchens.

5:00 Arrive
6.00 Meet Jeremy Bowes and Nora Wheeler
7.00 Dinner with Jeremy Bowes and Nora Wheeler

Outside a blackbird is singing – a beautiful silvery evening song – from the top of the laundry chute. She stays at the window to listen for a while, and to look up at the remnant of the moon – very pale and round up there, like a pod of honesty. Sometimes, at home, she can forget to look up for days – weeks even – and she doesn't even know if the moon's full or a crescent. Then, when she does glance up and see it, it's so beautiful she feels ashamed for neglecting it.

Thorn

Late in the afternoon, feeling in need of jollity, brightness, warmth, we walk to a pizzeria. It is not the kind of restaurant or time of day I envisaged. But it has a nice name – Amici's – and Joe has, he tells us, been there several times before. It is up a long hill, on the south side of town. My legs ache.

'It'll work up an appetite,' Kenneth says.

Joe does not talk much on the way. He has been subdued all day. His walk is the same as it has always been: hands in his pockets, eyes on the pavement.

'Anything wrong?' I ask.

'No, I'm OK,' he says. 'Just a bit tired.'

He's apprehensive, I think – about America and his new job – but he doesn't want to show it. Typical man. I glance at him as I walk beside him. He is nearly a foot taller than me. Lanky. I try not to think of him walking lankily along a rubber gangway tomorrow, into a jumbo jet, and flying away.

Kenneth is doing his best to buoy us up. He strides, breathing out clouds of warm air, relaxed in his shoes. He is talking about California in the Seventies, an era which he sometimes seems to regard as recent.

'. . . essentially the time of flower power . . .' he is saying.

'Yes,' Joe replies.

'. . . flea markets everywhere . . . bookstores . . .'

Kenneth's words drift into the cold air. It is freezing.

'. . . but maybe it hasn't really changed so much. What do you think, Ro? Do you think Berkeley's changed a lot since then?'

'Hmm?'

'Lost in thought?'

'Hmm?'

My eyes are fixed on the gum-marked pavement.

The Amici's waiter has a new-looking beard. He is twenty-two at most. Younger than Joe. His eyes are green and shiny like a kitten's.

'Would you like to order some drinks?' he says, and I ask for three beers. It is five in the afternoon but I need a beer.

We are given a table by the window, a rather small one with too much cutlery on it, a vase of red carnations and a large, glass candle-holder cluttering our view of each other.

'Well,' I say, 'how nice.'

'It's not bad, this restaurant,' Joe replies. 'We used to come here quite a lot. We . . . It's . . .'

And he stops talking.

Directly in line with us, on the other side of the window, is a bus stop. Three people are waiting at the bus stop and looking in: an elderly woman in a heavy coat, and two young girls in tracksuits. A man and a dog walk past. The dog also glances in, a wondering expression on its face.

'So. I've got a bit of news,' Joe says.

'Oh yes?' I say brightly, my heart clonking.

Kenneth, who has been sawing away at a rather hard bread roll from the basket, stops and puts his knife down.

'So,' I say, beaming, 'what is it?'

And Joe blushes: something he hardly ever does. I watch the pink rising up his cheeks to his forehead. He looks through the window at the girls in tracksuits.

It will be something about his girlfriend, I think. When someone says 'I've got a bit of news' doesn't it usually mean that they, or someone else, is pregnant? *Is she pregnant? Surely not. Not when people are so open about everything. Not with the pill. Not when . . .*

Joe is looking down at his elaborately-folded napkin. 'It's . . .' he says.

'Hmm?'

'Maybe now is not the right moment, actually. Maybe I should . . .'

'Hey, go on, spit it out!'

'No, it's OK. I'll tell you later.'

'Joe, come on. It'll –'

'Can I take your order now?' the young, bearded waiter says, suddenly appearing like a new set of ten-pins at our table.

I don't know what to say. The overcrowded table looms garishly up at me. Outside the window a bus arrives. The elderly woman and the young girls get on to it and are transported away.

'Could we have a while longer, please?' Kenneth says to the waiter.

I look at my knees. I feel suddenly as cold as tap water.

The waiter looks at me as if I might be ill, says 'Sure' and is just moving away when I hear myself bark, 'No, it's OK.' And I grab the menu.

'I'll have the Pizza Capricciosa,' I yell.

'Oh,' Kenneth says, startled, 'OK, well . . .' And, jolted into action, he snatches the menu from me. 'I'll have the . . . the Spaghetti Napoletana.'

'And I'll have the Linguine della Casa,' Joe says quickly.

The waiter writes down our order, sighs slightly, collects up our menus and walks away.

'Well, that was super-efficient,' Kenneth says.

'Yes.'

We sit around the flower vase. Kenneth looks moody. Joe looks staticky, as if he's just touched an electric fence. I don't know what to say. I think: *My son is going to America tomorrow. And there's something that he can't even tell me.*

It is ridiculous.

It is ridiculous and upsetting.

Any minute now, I think, there are going to be tears.

'So,' I say with forced jocularity. 'When *are* you going to tell us, darling? Over the main course or –'

'I've been in touch with my dad,' Joe says.

'Oh.' I grip on to the wallet in my lap.

'He lives in the States now,' Joe says. 'In New York State.'

'Really? Does he?'

'So I'm going to meet him. For a coffee.'

'Right, well, that's . . . I've always thought it's important you meet him,' I lie. Because I never wanted them to meet. Ever. I just wanted it to be me and my baby. My beautiful boy in his babygro. His father has always been almost irrelevant.

'So,' I say regarding the table with too much cutlery on it, too much *stuff* – candle-holder, wine list, dinner menu, lunch menu, flowers – I want to put my arm out and sweep all of it on to the floor. 'So what's he doing out there?'

'Married with kids. My half-sisters, of course. Ella and Gretel. They're sixteen and twelve. My dad's playing the oboe. In one of the orchestras.'

'Really?'

My voice is over-loud and shaking. Waiters walk noiselessly to and fro.

'So. You have half-sisters?'

'Yep.'

'Ella and Gretel.'

'Yep.'

I nearly say something about their names, something to do with pantomimes. The existence of Ella and Gretel makes me feel obscurely jealous.

I look at Kenneth, who looks back at me. His face is sad with sympathy. The smell of pizza skulks around our table. At the table beside ours some women, about my age, are having a Friday lunch out. They are wearing pretty things: pretty, happy things with straps.

'I'd like the chance to get to know him,' Joe says, looking down at the few inches of uncovered tablecloth. He looks angry. And I never wanted this to be something he'd be angry about, the circumstances of his birth: two teenagers who made a mistake one autumn evening. I told him years ago all I knew about his father, which was not very much. Not enough, evidently.

'I found him on the internet,' Joe says as Kenneth stands up quietly, places his napkin on his chair and makes his way with weary inevitability towards the toilets. 'I looked up Malone and East Grinstead.'

'How . . .' I begin, searching for the appropriate word, 'easy.'

'Yes. It was.'

I look up to see Kenneth open the door of the Signores, knock it against an umbrella stand and a potted fig tree, and disappear.

It is not quite five-thirty.

'*That's Amore*' finishes. '*O Sole Mio*' begins.

Joe says, 'I'm not blaming you or anything, Mum.'

'No. I know you're not.'

'I mean, I know you were young and everything when you had me. I know I was' – he pauses – 'a mistake.'

I look into his eyes. 'You weren't.'

'Yes, I was.'

'OK. At the time. But my best ever mistake.'

'I just . . .'

'I was very young,' I continue. 'I was fifteen. I was very much left to my own . . . devices.'

'I know.'

'I was fifteen.'

'I know.'

'I didn't have you adopted.'

I turn my head. In front of the bus stop, the picture stencilled on the window is of an enormous Italian mamma wearing a chef's hat and holding a wooden spoon. And I wish I had been like that: I wish I had been a comforting mamma with an enormous bosom and an appropriate set of motherly rules. But I was too young. I didn't know what I was doing. 'There was no one to help me,' I said. I suppose I did my best.

Battlemented Couching

Every so often, a vision of the green dress enters her head and she feels a little sense of panic. *What have I done?* Why did she leave something so precious in that horrible shop, then get on a plane and fly to Scotland? Her dress, with that woman's patronising note attached to it? *Green silk, good condition.* Why hadn't she just whisked it back into her bag and left? Too hasty: she has always been too hasty in leaving things behind.

She has made these decisions in her life: really quite small decisions about whether to take up Needlework, say, or whether to ignore someone's phone calls, and they have opened out into enormity. And now here she is, with the life she has constructed for herself. She is Sally Tuttle, forty-three, *embroidery expert,* sitting on a small leather sofa in a Scottish hotel foyer, beside an arrangement of potted plants and a tankful of goldfish.

It is nearly six o'clock. She is waiting for her fellow conference delegates. She keeps looking up at people passing, but they are not the people she is supposed to meet: they walk on and out, into the evening.

After a while she is joined on the sofa by an elderly English couple. The woman sits down beside her, and the man stands and hovers.

'Goldfish,' says the woman.

'Yes,' says the man.

Sally shifts as unobtrusively as possible to give the woman more space: she is a big person, with a spreading lap. She and her husband are wearing almost identical brown corduroy trousers.

And they are both unhurried, careful, conscientious, with neat suitcases. They remind Sally of tortoises. They have built a whole life together, secure in their shells, and have they ever been out of love? Possibly not. Sally tries to imagine herself with a man, thirty years hence, looking dignified and old in a hotel lobby. Looking as if she has spent the larger part of her life with him.

Now a man of about Sally's age walks across the foyer. He looks a little like a man she dated for one night, a few years ago. A bank clerk called Peter. Peter was sound. Normal. Alarmed by Sally's all-encompassing embroidery: the peacocks and the elephants. This man has the same mousily youthful hair, the same bouncy walk, the feet turned slightly inward –

A woman's voice says quietly, 'Sally?'

And she jumps, readjust her limbs, turns in her seat and smiles.

'Nora?'

'Yes,' the woman says, doubtfully.

'Nice to meet you.'

Sally is oddly annoyed that she missed the direction Nora Wheeler appeared from. She stands up and Nora Wheeler puts out her hand. 'Oh!' Sally says, before she can stop herself. It feels odd, shaking another woman's hand. There is not the air of dominance that men indulge in. The smothering male palm. Nora and she just stand, holding hands for a moment, like small girls. Nora's hand is slightly warmer than Sally's.

'I thought I'd be the last to arrive,' Nora says shyly, peering around. She is shorter than Sally. She has pale, round eyes and the sort of hairstyle that appears in 1940s films: neat, shiny, with a side parting. Her suit is double-breasted, blue-flecked, belted.

'Mr Bowes is quite late, isn't he?' she says, looking at her watch.

'Male prerogative,' Sally replies.

Nora has that effect that some petite women have, of making Sally feel too loud. Too prominent, like some building jutting out from a flat landscape.

'Maybe he's got held up,' Nora suggests. 'The traffic's not good.'

'Well. It'll give us a chance to . . .' Sally begins, trailing off. *It'll give us a chance to what?* The journey has wearied her, and the anticipation, and the oddness of being here. She just wants to go back up to her room: she wants to get out her embroidery and work on another section of Mary's sleeve. She doesn't want to be sitting here with Nora Wheeler, shy woodland creature.

'Let's sit here,' she says. 'Hopefully he won't be much longer.'

So they sit on the sofa again, knees almost touching. Nora hangs on to her yellow folder and smiles.

'They're pretty fish,' she says, looking at the aquarium. Then she looks at her watch again. 'Come on, Mr Bowes,' she urges, as if he is the slowest person at school sports day.

They are just debating whether to go on without him, to go to the dining room and hope to see him later, when suddenly there he is – Sally knows instantly it is him – behind the glass of the revolving doors. A man in his late forties with a determined expression and dark hair that flops, cunningly haphazard, across his temples. A decisive man with a leather portfolio and cuban-heeled boots. He looks as if he has never had anything to do with embroidery in his life. How can he have arrived here, in their feminine midst?

They introduce themselves, then stand back for a moment. Sally's smile is too big.

'OK. So shall we find a table?' Jeremy Bowes says.

'Yes,' Nora and Sally reply. Jeremy sets off and they follow.

'This is a good table,' Jeremy states, selecting one by the window and holding chairs out chivalrously, first for Nora and then for Sally.

'Thank you,' Sally says, sitting down and wondering why she is allowing this man to fluster her. She thought she had given up being flustered by handsome men. She looks down at her knobbly knees and then out, through the window. She can't think of anything to say. She can feel her heart beating. 'So,' she says, looking with increasing interest at the very ordinary street beyond the glass. If she cranes her neck, she can just make out the edge of Edinburgh Castle on top of its misty, craggy hill. She clears her throat and holds on to the stem of her empty wine glass. Nora says, 'A-haah!'. Apart from that, nobody speaks. The people of Edinburgh progress, in their anoraks and raincoats, up Lothian Road. You'd never find a beautiful castle in East Grinstead, but you would find people like this. People with expressions like this, in the same kind of anoraks, with those kinds of plastic bags . . .

And then all three of them begin to speak at once.

'I –'

'When –'

'It's –'

Jeremy's observation eventually prevails.

'It's much colder here than in Paris,' he says.

'Paris?' replies Nora, twisting the silver chain around her neck.

'Apparently this is a "haar",' Sally says, suddenly inspired, accepting an enormous menu from an arriving waiter. 'This mist. So the girl at reception told me. A sea haar. It rolls in from the sea.'

'Yes,' Nora says, 'That's what I was saying. *A haar*.'

'Oh.'

Nora and Sally look at each other and for a second nearly laugh. Nora's eyes are bright blue and turn up at the corners.

Nora looks back at Jeremy. 'Anyway. How wonderful,' she says. 'To live in Paris.'

'It is,' Jeremy Bowes confirms crossly.

'Edinburgh's beautiful too, though, isn't it?' says Nora. 'Almost Parisian, really.'

Jeremy purses his lips and says nothing. 'Let's order a bottle of wine,' he says after a moment.

'French, of course.'

'Oui, oui, bien entendu.'

Now Sally feels irrationally annoyed, as if some very small object, possibly not even hers, has been taken away from her. As Nora and Jeremy speak, she continues to gaze out through the glass at the beautiful misty city.

A red-faced man reels past the window, very close, clutching a packet of fish and chips. This, indeed, does not seem very Parisian. In Paris he would at least be holding a baguette.

It happened, now she comes to think of it, as soon as Jeremy made his way out of the revolving door. There was something in the way he looked at them, some kind of recognition. As if he had been stumbling around in a big, perilous forest and suddenly, in the nick of time, found two damsels in a clearing. *'You're here at last! Thank God!'* And he was saved from being submerged in the brackeny undergrowth.

Nora had peered shyly back at him from the bracken. Sally was like the Girl Guide leader, up ahead, with her torch and practical rucksack. A girl who had somehow become cynical with the passing years; lost all her naivety about love.

'The traffic was quite bad this evening,' Nora whispers to Jeremy.

'Was it?' he replies, looking into her round blue eyes.

Nora smiles and plays again with the pendant around her neck. She has no wedding ring, no engagement ring. Sally wonders how old she is. At least her age. 'I noticed –' she begins, but she doesn't continue with what she noticed, because Nora interrupts. 'I speak some French,' she says to Jeremy. 'Some schoolgirl French. Malheureusement, pas très bien.'

'Mais c'est merveilleux!' exclaims Jeremy. Then he adds, in English, 'Believe me, it takes a lifetime to sound like a native.'

'Well, your accent sounds pretty good to me!' Sally quips – Sally, the third member of the party, behind the flowers.

'Ha ha ha,' Nora laughs. Jeremy does not reply. He does not seem particularly pleased with her last comment. He smiles rather alarmingly, then says, 'So. Are you looking forward to the conference, Sally?'

'Oh yes. Yes, very much.'

'And I understand you won a prize?'

'Yes. Last year,' she says, her confidence suddenly plummeting. How infantile, to have won a prize. Like being back at school. She thinks of all those embarrassing headlines. 'That's what I'm going to be talking about,' she says.

'I'm particularly interested in French crewelwork techniques,' Nora says, politely.

Sally beams brightly at them, so brightly that her jaw aches. She wants to say, *I don't know a thing about French crewelwork techniques. I was a school drop-out. I went to evening classes.*

Out of the corner of her eye she can see their three hors d'oeuvres in the serving hatch, illuminated in the pretty yellow light. A man is sprinkling parsley over them and wiping the edges of the plates with a large tea towel.

'There are our starters,' she says, childishly.

'J'ai faim,' Nora replies.

'Me too. All I've had all day is plane food. A strange chicken thing and a slab of cake. Both tasting remarkably similar to each other.'

Jeremy looks at her. 'Plain food?'

'Yes.'

'– ?'

'Food that you –' she begins.

'– eat on a plane,' concludes Nora.

'Of course,' says Jeremy. Then he looks at Nora. He sweeps his left hand through his thick brown hair.

The starters are on their way now: a waiter has picked up all three of them and is progressing, butler-like, across the room towards them.

Sally has chosen mussels. Now she regrets ordering them. The waiter places them in front of her and says 'Enjoy.' She looks down at them.

'Everything OK?' Nora asks.

'Yes,' Sally says. 'Fine.'

'Ah, les moules,' observes Jeremy Bowes.

'They look nice,' says Nora, unsurely.

'Yes.'

This is not what I embroider for, she thinks. *I do not embroider so I can sit at a table with two strangers and talk about how nice mussels look.* She is missing Pearl: she should be with Pearl. *In ten minutes,* she thinks, *I will excuse myself and phone her.*

She clears her throat and places her napkin on her knees.

'So. Do you' – she begins, turning to Nora and realising too late what an undiplomatic question she is about to ask – 'Are you married?'

'No,' Nora replies quickly. 'That never . . . It wasn't . . .' She trails off. She looks down at her plate.

'Ah, but it's not too late, surely?' Jeremy says chivalrously.

Dutifully, Nora laughs. But she looks crestfallen. Sally picks up her spoon and feel tactless. Too caught up with her own life to know how to conduct herself. She looks down at her mussels again. Mussels are not a quiet little dish, to be eaten unobtrusively. Mussels are an event. They make her feel exhausted just looking at them.

'Right!' she says out loud. And she wonders what a really practical woman would do. Her mother, for instance. Or Sue. Her mother or Sue would just get on with it. So she picks up her knife and begins to lever the shells open. They make a cracking noise. Fish-scented steam rises melodramatically.

'You're brave,' Nora exclaims.

'Why? Haven't you ever eaten mussels?'

'No.'

'They're wonderful. You should try them, Nora.'

'Yes, you really should,' Jeremy adds.

But this evening she finds she doesn't have the panache required to eat shellfish. She feels inadequate and working-class. Exposed. The words fall out of her mouth. The mussels sit on the dish in front of her, aghast, affronted.

Now Nora and Jeremy are toying with their starters and discussing their childhoods – and moving gradually closer and closer towards each other. *How can she not see through him?* Sally thinks. He is probably married. He is evidently one of those serial flirts. A married flirt: the worst kind. Although he has not flirted with Sally.

Nora and Jeremy have discovered, through a combination of stumbling sentences and something else – telepathy? intuition? – that they both went to boarding schools. And that they both endured horse-riding lessons on mean-minded horses called Stardust. What an extraordinary twist of fate! Quelle coincidence! Two horses called Stardust! The subject of embroidery has been pushed aside.

'I absolutely detested school,' Jeremy spits. 'I had an absolute horror of school.' He is eating, very fast, a goat's cheese tart with a side serving of 'wild leaves'.

'Yes, yes, me too,' Nora agrees over her big bowl of vichyssoisse. Something has really happened to her now, some unmistakable, undeniable excitement. Sally recognises the early signs of infatuation. Nora's face is bright pink, and she laughs and peers, enraptured, at Jeremy. Now she removes her tweed jacket and is down to a surprisingly low-cut and clinging top, its neckline prettily picked out with lace. Damart, possibly. The pendant on Nora's necklace is in the shape of a sea horse. The skin on her chest is blotchy with emotion. She is one of those mousey women who is daring underneath.

Jeremy has removed his beige corduroy jacket too, and his cream turtle-neck sweater. He is sitting there in a pale blue shirt, the top button undone to reveal a little chest-hair, far up, like a high Plimsoll line. ('And did they force you outside in the rain to play hockey?' he is saying charmingly to Nora. 'Yes, yes,' Nora is saying.)

This abandoning of clothes is beginning to be a bit like strip poker. *There is something subconscious going on here.* Sally is the only person who continues to wear all the clothes she arrived in.

At the far end of the restaurant, a woman in a white halter-neck dress appears in the doorway and goes to stand by the piano. A pianist, already poised on the seat, looks up at her. She pauses for a second, smiles back at him, then launches into a song. 'Every Time We Say Goodbye'. Sally sits on the edge of her chair and listens. The pianist is good. The singer does not quite hit all the notes.

'She's confident,' Sally observes, but Jeremy and Nora do not hear. She lets the comment float in the air, to die gracefully. Then she picks up her soup spoon and takes a sip of bouillabaisse from her dish of mussels. It goes down the wrong way. She splutters and coughs, tears springing into her eyes. Nora and Jeremy are still discussing the two horses called Stardust. Sally blinks and can't see or breathe properly. Nora and Jeremy smile at each other. Sally gasps for air. She begins to be frightened. Then Jeremy, breaking off from his bittersweet equine reminiscences, glances across at her and finally looks concerned.

'OK there, Sally?'

He leans across the table.

'I'm fine,' Sally rasps, her eyes bulging, the tears warm and painful. 'Why do gods above me,' the woman at the piano is singing, 'who must be in the know . . .'

'I'm fine,' she croaks, attempting to smile. But she feels explosive, like an over-blown balloon. She cannot swallow, cannot breathe. Other diners have begun to turn surreptitiously in their seats, to observe the spectacle. *How awful, how awful to die eating mussels in a faraway hotel. Everything unresolved, everything unsaid. My daughter, my work, my loves . . .*

'Oh dear,' Jeremy is saying, ineffectually.

And now Nora Wheeler is taking charge. She has come round to Sally's side of the table and has begun to slap her on the back. 'It's OK,' she says. She slaps Sally's back again. Something gives. Sally gasps and breathes. Jeremy hands her a glass of cool water and she takes a sip. She swallows, clears her throat, holds her hand up to her neck and sits, not speaking. The earrings swing warmly from her earlobes. Nora sits down again, even closer to Jeremy. United in the drama of the moment.

'I'm OK now,' Sally says, wiping her eyes.

'It's awful when that happens, isn't it?' Nora says, referring, Sally knows, not to the fear of dying but to the social embarrassment of it.

She looks at the two of them. 'I'm feeling quite tired, actually,' she says, 'and I've got a bit of a headache. I'm wondering if . . . I don't suppose . . .'

'Why don't you go and have a rest in your room?' Nora suggests, with enthusiasm.

'Yes,' Jeremy adds. 'You'll probably feel . . .'

'Yes, a rest would probably do me the world of good,' Sally says, trying to regain some semblance of dignity. But she feels too tired, and too upset. And tomorrow she will have to get up early, sit in an enormous room full of strangers and talk about embroidery. *I should never have agreed to do this. I should be in East Grinstead, hemming up a trouser leg.*

'I'll go up for a little while,' she says. 'Go and compose myself. But I'll probably come down again for a coffee later. So we can discuss the agenda for tomorrow?'

'Allez vous coucher, Mrs Tuttle,' Jeremy Bowes commands. 'Si, si. Allez. Bonne nuit.'

'Do you think if we tell the waiters, they'll . . .'

'Don't worry about the waiters,' Nora almost shouts, newly boisterous in her eagerness for Sally to leave her and Jeremy alone. 'We'll explain you're not feeling too well. I'm sure they'll –'

'Well, if you really don't mind . . .'

And she gets up from the table and walks away, up the carpeted length of the restaurant, up the stairs, past the framed pictures of Edinburgh (the Castle; St Andrew's Square; Greyfriar's Bobby; the Grassmarket), and along the corridor to her room. She opens the door with the credit-card contraption she was given by the man with slicked-back hair, and pushes her way in. There are all her things. Thank God. Her material possessions. Her coat, her sponge bag, her handbag, her sensible shoes. Her portfolio, her rucksack, her canvas. Her Martha and Mary – who seem, at that moment, to be her only friends.

Four-legged Knot

No matter how difficult a time you are having, there are always thousands of people going about having a perfectly nice day. It is almost unbelievable. Some days are so difficult, so full of angst and awkwardness that you can't imagine that other people are not affected. But they are not. They do not even know who you *are*.

I am looking down at the street through our hotel window. It is ten thirty at night and freezing, the moon hiding behind a pale gauze of cloud. On the street below walks a girl in a black dress, progressing beneath the streetlamps to the bus stop, to begin work probably – some job in a bar or restaurant. Or maybe she is off to a party where she is hoping to meet *him:* the love of her life. She has nearly all her life ahead of her. She waits as a bus driver navigates a maroon bus down the dim green bus lane at exactly the same time as he did the night before. Watching the girl climb aboard is a man sitting on the pavement with his dog and his blanket and his empty polystyrene cup.

You look at them. They do not know your story. And you do not know theirs.

I am thinking about my life with my son in Paris. Living on a street where the cafés had not been trendy and the pavements were often strewn with rubbish – onion peelings and cabbage stalks and halves of orange marinading in the sunshine.

We had lived closest to the Filles du Calvaire Métro station. I remember buying our tickets there at a baffling machine. We used to take the Métro to a lot of places. Montmartre, the banks of the Seine, the Louvre, the Pompidou Centre. One afternoon, we had taken the Métro to St Michel and gone to see the tapestries in the Musée de Cluny. It was the first time I had ever been there, though I have been back many times since. I remember walking through the courtyard with Joe for the first time, past the stone well and the late hollyhocks and thinking how serene it was. A kind of haven: a sanctuary from the noise and all the blindingly-bright, white-shingled parks.

That was where we had first met Jeremy Bowes: at the Musée de Cluny. Handsome Jeremy Bowes had been standing in Room VIII (Salle de Notre Dame de Paris), his backdrop a series of white, headless statues. His embroidered waistcoat would not have looked out of place beside the tapestries in the next room. Seated in plastic chairs were a number of middle-aged women, listening to the lecture he was giving on the museum's tapestries. And even the statues around him seemed to incline in his direction. Into his small, lapel-fastened microphone he was informing them all in quite good French on the meaning of peacocks, periwinkles, necklaces and unicorns.

Joe and I had stood in the doorway.

'. . . et ce paon ici, que vous regardez, celui-ci, c'est . . .'

'Mum,' Joe said, 'I want to see if there are dinosaurs.'

I looked down at my son, my mind momentarily blank. I remember whispering, 'Darling, there aren't any dinosaurs here. This is not a museum for dinosaurs.'

And a few of the women in the audience had turned at this point, and fixed us both with primitive, lantern-jawed expressions of dislike.

'. . .et regardez bien,' Jeremy Bowes was saying, 'la myriade de couleurs magnifiques autour du plumage. Remarquez les petites taches . . .'

'Mum!' insisted Joe.

And after a moment I gave in, released my grip on my son's anorak sleeve and followed him out of the room.

There were no dinosaurs. Not in the museum or in the shop. There were embroidered magnets, embroidered cushion covers and embroidered handkerchiefs.

'Can I have a lollipop then?' Joe asked, casting around for something that wasn't hand-stitched. 'Lollipops are cheap. They're one franc.'

I didn't reply.

'Or one of these pencils?' he said. 'Look, there are kings and dragons.'

'Oh, Joe, I can't keep buying you things,' I said, glancing at the shop's display of *petites surprises* before noticing out of the corner of my eye that the handsome, waistcoated tapestry lecturer who had been in the Salle de Nôtre Dame had finished his talk and was now heading straight towards the shop.

'But Mum –'

My heart skipped.

'Mum, please –'

'Sorry about that,' I blurted to the lecturer, who was now walking through the doorway. 'Sorry,' I said, 'about the commotion just then.'

Jeremy Bowes jumped slightly and looked at me. We were standing beside a bin full of small wooden unicorns and, apparently unsure what else to do, he leaned forward to pick one up.

'I . . .' I began again: 'My son . . .'

He looked at me with his lovely brown eyes, and smiled. And when he spoke, I felt sure it would be something delightful. I was twenty-three and pretty, I suppose, and there, in Paris, without a man.

Jeremy Bowes opened his mouth. 'It *was* somewhat distracting,' he said.

'Oh.'

'The Musée de Cluny really isn't the place to bring a small boy.'

'Oh,' I said again, my disappointment almost as physical as a punch.

'Weren't you ever a small boy in a museum, then?' I asked Jeremy Bowes, holding on to Joe's hand.

Jeremy Bowes looked a little taken aback. 'A museum . . .' he began but then he seemed lost for words. He trailed off. He said, 'Excuse me.' And he gave a curious little nod, turned, walked back to the doorway and disappeared.

We went to see the tapestries after that. I wanted somewhere comforting to go, something reassuring to look at. Somewhere dark.

The textile rooms were dimly lit to preserve the cloth and the thread, and we had had to strain our eyes to see the pictures properly. My heartbeat slowed as our eyes made their adjustments. And then we began to make them out, the colours and the figures. These were the tapestries of *La Dame à la Licorne*: deep red cloths covered with embroidered flowers, foxes, birds, fruits, monkeys, mythical beasts. Fantastically beautiful.

'Look at the birds, Joe,' I said, 'and those tiny flowers.'

And slowly we moved along the tapestries, admiring them in turn, reading the descriptions, pointing out the animals and the flowers, all the way along, until we reached the last one. A picture of two young women. Two friends.

'For a long time,' said the text, *'this particular tapestry defied interpretation.'*

I looked at the picture. I stood and looked. And something, some draught, suddenly caused me to shiver. I don't know why, but standing in front of that tapestry I felt suddenly quite bereft.

'What's your favourite bit in this one, Mum?' Joe asked.

I looked. I considered. 'The ladies,' I said, and I continued to gaze at them – at the two young women in beautiful dresses, one a lady, the other her maidservant. One of them was handing the other a necklace from a casket.

'Contrary to what was once thought, this lady is in fact not selecting, but depositing the necklace into the casket held by her maidservant, and holding it in a cloth, having taken it off. She is thus not in the act of choosing a piece of jewellery, but of renouncing her jewels.'

'I like the dog,' Joe whispered.

'Yes, it's a lovely dog.'

I looked at the dresses and thought of those flimsy, floating styles Sally Tuttle and I had once worn. Sally Tuttle, my lost friend.

Le coeur de ma mie est petit,tout petit,
J'en ai l'âme ravie, mon amour le remplit.
Si le coeur de ma mie n'était pas si petit . . .

A stout woman in pink corduroy trousers trod heavily on my foot, and I glared at her: it seemed a mean thing to do.

'Come on then,' I said to Joe, 'let's go and find a café.'

He looked up. 'Why are you crying?' he asked.

'I'm not,' I said, 'I'm not.'

After that first encounter with Jeremy Bowes, I began to bump into him regularly around the world. At a conference in London (topic of discussion: the storage and handling of valuable works of art across Europe). At a university dinner in Seattle. A few years later, at a book launch in Antwerp. Sometimes I had to translate his papers and pamphlets. But he did not recall our first encounter, he told me, when I reminded him of it. No, he could not recall it at all. I knew he was lying; I saw a little flicker of knowledge cross his face.

From then on he has been one of those people I keep encountering, over the years. In museums, in hotels, on station platforms. Once, in the dairy aisle of a supermarket in Brittany. I had been clutching a lettuce and a cheap box of Camembert.

Well, hello, Rowena!

Why is it people like Jeremy Bowes that you bump awkwardly into over the years? And of others, there is not a sign. Never a single sighting.

Needleweaving

It is eight minutes past eleven. Sally sits in her *delightful room*, her canvas on her lap, a red-threaded needle in her hand. Like a medieval lady waiting for her knight.

She turns on the huge radio fixed to the wall above her bed. '. . . you'll find,' a man's voice is saying, 'that if you wait too long your potatoes will have turned into a kind of mush . . .'

She changes stations. There is something tragic on Radio 4, a lot of sighing and moaning and sound effects: wooden spoons, tin buckets.

She knows what she is doing. From the three counselling sessions she had with Mrs Bonniface, she knows that she is *stalling*. Like one of those horses called Stardust. *Whenever something good happens to me, I wreck it.* Actually, she has never needed counselling sessions to be told that. Her mother has told her for years. At last, she is at the beginning of a new career! She is an authority on embroidery! But what is she doing? She is sitting in her bedroom, sewing. *As per usual.*

She wonders how Nora and Jeremy's conversation is progressing downstairs. Even Nora, shy Nora Wheeler, is making a better go of things than Sally is. She is probably more accomplished at embroidery. She has coiffured hair. She is even flirting, in a curious kind of way, with the keynote speaker.

I should be here with a man, Sally thinks. *I should be getting up in the morning with a man.* And she thinks of John, on an early date in the winter of '83, driving her across London in his beige Cinquecento, changing gear and then, sweetly, putting his left hand beneath his thigh to keep it warm.

Her yellow conference bag is lying at the foot of her bed. Sally leans across and pulls out the conference programme, which has been archly strung together with big yellow wool stitches. On the front page is a typed list of quotations:

Our lives are like quilts – bits and pieces, joy and sorrow, stitched with love

I love sewing and have plenty of material witnesses

I'd rather be stitchin' than in the kitchen

Thinking that she should perhaps, after all, not take the conference so seriously – this is just another homely affair, all about love and stitches – she turns to page two. Page two has the next day's agenda:

9 a.m. Breakfast and Reception

10 a.m. The Embroidery of Courtly Love, by keynote speaker Jeremy Bowes

10.45 a.m. An Embroiderer's Yarn: Sally Tuttle, winner of this year's £9,000 national embroidery award, gives a talk on her experiences as an embroiderer

11 a.m. Advanced Embroidery workshops

12 p.m. Lunch

2 p.m. Feedback session

4 p.m. Conference ends

The phrase 'her experiences as an embroiderer' makes her feel suddenly pale, bloodless. Experiences? She just sits and sews. She takes up trouser legs, a draught blasting under the gap of the shop door. How can she follow a talk on the Embroidery of Courtly Love? She thinks of those beautiful medieval tapestries and all those women who created them. She feels the weight of centuries of silent, female talent. Talent dismissed as hobby. Somebody has changed the title of her talk, too: 'An Embroiderer's Yarn'! It makes her sound like some old sea-dog, full of lies and exaggerations. Or some chatterbox, so easily dismissed, prattling on about her needlework. She remembers what Colin Rafferty once said: *Needlework is not a career option, unless you want to make cushion covers all your life.* And she is dreading that word *feedback*: the questions at the end, which she was told to expect some weeks ago by a woman called Francesca Coutts-Marvel on the other end of the phone. *There'll be a little question and answer session, yup?*

She dreads someone, probably an eccentric woman in a hat, putting up her hand to say: 'And what interested you in embroidery in the first place?'

'Because it was all I had left,' she would say across the hushed room in her clanging accent. Should she say that?

She looks at Martha and Mary and their big, sequinned eyes. *I am actually here,* she thinks, *because I wrecked my chances twenty-five years ago.* She pictures herself running from her hotel room, taking her embroidery with her. She sees herself a few hours hence, like Mrs Tiggy-Winkle, running running running up the hill, all her hairpins coming loose. (*Why! Mrs Tiggy-Winkle was nothing but a HEDGEHOG!*)

She glares at Martha and Mary. But Martha and Mary are just a bundle of threads.

She keeps forgetting that she owns a mobile phone. She forgets that it is switched on and that it is *her* phone making that series of watery, descending notes, like a reed warbler. Her phone, in her handbag, on the chair.

She rushes to undo the zip of her bag and to retrieve the trendy little silver thing from a midden of old paper handkerchiefs, lengths of embroidery silk, Polo mints, make-up bag, purse.

She presses the green button with its sweet picture of an old-fashioned phone; one that would once have been conveniently attached to a wall.

'Hello,' says a man's voice, 'is that Mrs Tuttle?'

'Yes.'

'This is the Reverend Avery. I hope this is a good time to call.'

'Yes. Not bad,' she lies. The Reverend Avery, she reflects, with a stab of shame, is the only person who phones her with any regularity.

'I was just phoning to see how it's all going. How the . . . ha, ha, how Mary and Martha are progressing.'

He sounds edgy. Furtive. There's something wrong.

'It's all going pretty well,' Sally replies. She grips the phone tightly and looks at the hotel escritoire in front of her, at the laminated breakfast menu (*poached eggs, kippers, porridge, croissant, yogurt with a selection of seasonal berries*), the tastefully dull curtains, the framed rose print, the coat-hangers on the back of the door. She could be standing at the bottom of a well for all the Reverend Avery knows.

The Reverend Avery himself sounds rather stentorious, as if he is the one in the well. He is probably in some sepulchral church hall. Or perhaps he is looking at the chilly blank wall in Southwark Cathedral, where Sally's embroidery is supposed to go.

'It was certainly very . . . interesting to hear how you're doing. We were wondering,' he says, 'whether we could perhaps arrange to see how it's progressing. We were thinking we could perhaps schedule another meeting for the, ah . . .' He pauses while, Sally imagines, he flicks through his ecclesiastical diary.

'Actually,' she says.

'Sorry?'

'I don't really like . . . showing people my work until it's finished.'

'Oh?'

'No. It's just a bit of a superstition I suppose.'

'Oh, well, ha, ha, the church is not a place for superstition. Perhaps just this once . . .?'

She doesn't know how to deal with the Reverend Avery. She doesn't know how subservient to be. She supposes he would once have been her patron, and she would have been his impoverished artist. Like the Medicis. Maybe she should do whatever he asks.

'It would be so nice to –' the Reverend Avery is saying.

'OK,' she interrupts. Maybe they want to commission someone else instead. Some knitter or patchworker.

'Oh good,' says the Reverend Avery. 'How about Wednesday the fifth, about 11 a.m.? Back at headquarters?'

'Yes,' she replies cheerily, her heart sinking. She pictures the trip to Southwark Cathedral. The echoing walls. 'That should be fine,' she says. 'Can I phone you back later to confirm?'

'Of course, of course,' says the Reverend Avery. And Sally imagines him putting his hand up, beatifically, in a sign of peace. *He doesn't trust me. Something has happened.*

'Goodbye then,' says the Reverend Avery. 'Work well.' And he hangs up.

Sally presses the little green telephone button and watches the tiny rainbow on the screen bulge slightly, then contract and disappear into blankness. *Richard of York Gained Battle in Vain.* She takes off her shoes and her skirt and gets into bed.

Double Back

Poor Mary, Queen of Scots, imprisoned at Holyrood Palace, half a mile and five centuries away. A Frenchwoman surrounded by Scots, a woman who embroidered her own flame-red petticoats just before going to the scaffold. I wonder what Mary, Queen of Scots would think of Edinburgh now; of the pavements and the clowns and the trendy wine bars.

'There's quite a lot of French names in Edinburgh aren't there?' I observe to Kenneth, flicking through the index of my *A-to-Z*. 'Look – there's a Beauchamp Grove, a Bellevue Crescent, a Cluny Place, a –'

'There's also a whole lot of Buckstones, Burdiehouses and Burnheads,' says Kenneth, peering over my shoulder.

'I was just *pointing out* the connections. The auld alliance and everything. I mean, what's the link with Cluny?'

I think that taxi accident had a strange effect on my memory. My short-term memory has been shunted sideways by my long-term memory. More and more, I seem to remember things from twenty, thirty years ago. It is peculiar. This morning, for instance, while waiting for Kenneth in the hotel lobby, I looked down at the Visitor book on the reception desk and was instantly reminded of the autograph books we used to have at school. We used to write those little rhymes in them:

Two in a hammock attempted to kiss,
All of a sudden they ended like – ꓕHIƧ

By hook or by crook I'll be last in this book.
By egg or by bacon I'm sure you're mistaken.

Schoolgirls don't keep autograph books any more, I suppose. We were a lot more naive then. Nowadays girls have i-Pods and phones with built-in cameras.

Over breakfast I mention the autograph books to Kenneth. 'Did you ever keep one?' I ask.

'Not something boys did.'

'No. I suppose it wouldn't be.'

My autograph book was cream-coloured, I remember, hard-back, with a sticker of a smiling snail on it.

We are sitting – rather late because we were both tired this morning and somewhat down – on either side of a small, white-clothed table in the hotel's dining room. A young couple at a table near ours are trying to get their small son to eat porridge from a teaspoon.

'In it goes,' the young mother says as the boy turns his head. 'Yum yum!'

It makes me want to get up and grab the small son: grab that part of my life again.

'If all the boys lived under the sea,' I say, 'what a good swimmer Rowena would be.'

'Sorry?'

'One of those things people used to write in autograph books.'

Kenneth picks up his glass and takes a sip of orange juice. 'What's up?' he asks.

'You know what's up.'

His eyes are sympathetic. But he is also getting on with his morning. He is, for instance, eating French toast with chocolate spread while he has the chance. A pragmatist. I think of my son. I think of his father, a rather dreamy boy I slept with twenty-eight years ago. I wonder whether to eat an egg. But I am not hungry. I can't stop thinking of my son and the time before my son. Of those autograph books.

All the best, Rowena. We'll come and visit you and the baby. Susan xx

Tunsalov, Rowena. Take Care! Rhiannon xx

We'll miss you in Needlework. All the best for the future, Christine xx

Search, and find the purpose of life and having found it never let it go. Good Hunting! Miss Button xx

The cloth on the breakfast table reminds me of the embroidered one I was given by my French exchange-family when I was fifteen – which reminds me again of Sally Tuttle. A part of me feels almost dizzy when I think of how much there is, how many people there are, to remember.

'D'you know, I think that accident I had did something to my memory,' I say, picking up my teaspoon to crack my boiled egg. 'I seem to remember so much these days, from when I was in my teens.'

'Maybe you're getting old,' says Kenneth.

'Well, thanks.'

'You're welcome,' he says, smiling. 'Anyway, you had a kind of eventful adolescence, didn't you?'

'In some ways. In other ways it was totally static.'

I begin to peel the shell from my egg.

'You'll be OK,' Kenneth says. 'This is a difficult time. With Joe leaving. We're all moving into the next phase.'

'Does life always have to be in phases? In chunks? As if it's a big cake or something? And what are we supposed to do in the next phase?'

'Life as a cake,' Kenneth muses.

Then he eats another piece of chocolate-covered toast. The thing about Kenneth, the thing I love almost more than anything else about him, is his grip on reality.

I can remember what the Number One song was the day Sally Tuttle and I began to make our blousons in Needlework. It was 'Message in a Bottle'. The Police were big that year. Why should that come back to me now, after nearly thirty years? Or the ridiculous word 'blouson' – and the way it made us laugh! Laughing as we pinned the pattern (size 10/12) to the material; removing the thin paper template from the envelope, sewing white tailor's tacks through the large black dots at shoulders, neckline and zip-fastener opening.

Two schoolgirls at their sewing desks.

Sally Tuttle and Rowena Cresswell.

Rowena Cresswell and Sally Tuttle.

We were very close. Like sisters.

And now I begin to remember the daily events in our lives. The way we used to congregate with the other girls around St Hilary's big beige vending machine (it offered tomato soup, hot chocolate, coffee, tea and milk). The places where we sat: on the wall outside the Chemistry block, on the under-stuffed green armchairs in the Resource Area. The walks, in rain and sunshine, up the school drive.

Then there were the conversations about that boy Sally was in love with – Colin. Colin Rafferty. A young man, really, rather than a boy. And quite unsavoury, actually. Up to no good. But handsome. I recall that he had worked in advertising. He and Sally used to slope off together, up to London. I was so jealous. And I missed her, sitting beside her empty chair in class. I worried about her. Her absence always seemed so shocking – *Sally was a good girl!* – and I never knew what to say to her when she reappeared the next day.

'You're not eating much,' Kenneth observes.

'Not very hungry.'

'You should eat. It'll make you feel better.'

'Hmm.'

I watch the young couple beside us hoist themselves up from their table, pick up their belongings – their baby-changing bag, their portable, clip-on high-chair, their plastic bags, their wipes, their baby – and leave the room.

'Cute kid,' Kenneth says.

My mother would always be late back from her shift at the canteen. I remember standing without Sally at the school gates, feeling nauseous and terrified and gazing at the incomprehensible graffiti. I gazed at that graffiti every day, as if it might one day change into something else, a coherent sentence.

Clare is a sexy fish.

Much sexier than Laura.

Nothing would change now. Or rather, everything would. My pregnant state would remain, but my life would become unrecognisable.

My mother's car always appeared slowly. Slowly it rounded the corner. A small blue Honda. I watched as my mother carefully changed gear and reversed the car compactly into the school drop-off bay. I would attempt a smile, lean forward, feel sick and open the door.

'Hello,' my mother said. She didn't listen to music, the way a lot of mothers did in their cars. It was always completely silent in our car.

'Hi,' I replied, getting in and closing the door.

'No Sally today?'

'No.'

The smell of chamois leather made me want to throw up. *I am going to have to tell her*, I thought, looking down at the terrifying, incipient bulge beneath my waistband. (I had already, somehow, told Mark Malone: I had told him on the phone, and the only thing he had said, after about five minutes, was 'Oh Jesus.' We hardly even knew each other. At the school bus stop in the mornings I used to see him glance stealthily across at my stomach as he stood with his gawky, scientific friends. He had exactly the same horrified expression as me, and I had almost felt sorry for him.)

'How are you? How was school?' my mother used to ask, staring through the windscreen. She had had her own secrets by then; something she did not want to reveal herself.

'OK,' I replied.

Every day, I wished I could tell her how things really were.

Joe was given a ticket on the day he was born. Like a kind of bus pass. It was blue, blue for a boy, and tied around his ankle: Baby Cresswell. I remember the sense of unreality – that I had had a baby, and that I had not died. I had thought the last thing I was going to see on earth was the maternity suite: those crookedly-hanging formica cupboard doors, the hoover-like gas-and-air pipe, that picture on the wall: a cheery vase of chrysanthemums.

'You're not going to die, Poppet,' the midwife soothed (her name, I recall, was Wendy Bridges). 'You are going to have a beautiful baby.'

I gave birth on my own, at the age of fifteen and ten months. I did not die. Wendy Bridges was right.

'Good girl,' Wendy Bridges told me. 'You're doing brilliantly. One more big push now.'

And I pushed and then I lay there, still alive. Somebody handed me a thin, warm, oddly heavy baby.

'Is it supposed to look like that?' I asked.

Outside the window I could see pink cherry blossom, and a blackbird sitting on a twig. I looked into my baby's peculiar eyes.

And in that instant, I forgave them:

I forgave my baby.

I forgave Mark Malone.

I forgave my mother.

But the person I never quite forgave was Sally Tuttle.

At a quarter to ten a small gang of waitresses enters the breakfast room and begins, noisily, to tidy up. One of them clears the tables, another goes round with a highly fragranced spray, a third, her young face set in a world-weary expression, wheels the enormous, stainless-steel egg-poacher back into the kitchens. Sometimes it seems extraordinary to me, that such things as wheeled egg-poachers exist.

'Shall we go?' I say to Kenneth.

'Yes,' he replies, and we get up.

Kenneth has eaten six French toasts with chocolate spread.

I have eaten a third of a boiled egg.

Arrowhead

She sleeps badly, waking up three times in the night to stare at the dull drape of the curtains. She falls asleep at 5.30 with a headache. The noise of seagulls wakes her again at seven.

She pushes back the duvet and regards the sticking-out bone of her left big toe: an inheritance from her mother. She has feet just like her mother's. *Probably,* she thinks, *Pearl will end up with feet like mine too.* It does not seem fair. She feels obscurely guilty about her feet.

Her feet. Her hair. Her mannerisms.

Today is the day when she will have to describe her love of satin stitch, needle-weaving and overcast bars. People will expect her to know things. She doesn't know how she is going to get through it.

While waiting for her *Out of Eden*-scented bath to run, she gets Martha and Mary out of their portfolio, opens the little plastic box of sequins and stitches four silver ones into the grass – dewdrops in the lawn.

'But of course, your use of sequins . . .' she imagines someone saying, some Interested Party, after her talk. 'I read about it in *Embroidery Times.* Is that something you've always done? Applied sequins to your work?'

'When I'm in the mood,' she will reply, grumpily. 'I don't know why everyone is making such a fuss about the damned sequins.'

Nora and Jeremy will be in the background somewhere, gazing at each other. Sally's voice, which she will hope to give a light, laughing inflection, will sound flat and accusing. And the Interested Party will look at her. 'I was only asking,' they will say, and shortly after this they will wander away.

Her heart is jumping now. She needs to talk to someone who knows her.

She presses the little 'On' button on her phone and dials John's number. But there is no answer. He is probably sleeping or welding. So she phones Pearl's mobile.

A boy's voice answers.

'Good morning. World of Leather customer services. How may I help you?'

His voice is falsely nasal, irritatingly adolescent.

'Who's that?' Sally says. 'Is this – ?'

Then she hears Pearl's voice in the distance. Something that sounds like 'Oh my God.'

There is a scuffling noise, giggling, then Pearl's voice on the line.

'Who was that?' Sally asks, astonished.

'Oh. Just . . . a friend.'

'A friend?'

In the background, Sally can hear the boy speaking in his annoying voice again, trying to put Pearl off her conversation. A male tactic as old as the hills. *Don't fall for it, don't fall for it.*

Pearl sounds flustered. 'He's just a bloke from school,' she says, her voice bright and strained. 'We, like, walked in together? From the station?'

'But it's nearly half past nine. Hasn't school started?'

'Yes. But it's just . . . We're just in a café for a bit. We're sitting in a café. It's just . . .'

And there is, now she listens, a clink of cutlery in the background, the murmur of people in calm conversation.

'I see,' Sally says, breathing in, because she suddenly feels short of breath. She wonders which café they are in. The Deep Sea? The Me-n-U? Who is this boy?

'So. Are you on your way in now? If I phoned in say, twenty minutes, would you be at school? Or would you still just be sitting in a café?'

There is a pause. 'Yes. We should be there by then.'

How admirable, in retrospect, her mother's maternal skills were. How intuitive. 'I'll give you a ring tonight then, at Dad's,' Sally says, 'and we can have a proper chat.'

'Yes,' says Pearl.

'Fine.'

The boy continues to drone on unimpressively. Sally imagines someone angular, shoving French fries into his mouth.

'I'll phone you later then.'

'OK.'

'Pearl?'

'Yes?'

'Is he . . . your age? He's not –'

Pearl sighs. Sally has never told her anything about Colin Rafferty, nothing at all, but she detects a note of accusation in her voice. 'Yes, mother,' Pearl says.

'Well,' she replies, and she finds herself blushing at her own double-standards. 'Good.'

The boy's voice chunters on, and before Pearl can say goodbye the phone is switched off.

She sits on the bed with the little phone in her hand. She feels as if she has just lost some complicated argument. She finds that she is shivering slightly, and wraps her dressing gown more closely around her. She senses the passing of time, gathering momentum like machine-worked running-stitch.

She thinks: *I shouldn't have left her.*

How would it be, she wonders, if she left the conference, got on a plane and flew back home to her daughter, to face whatever she is up to. But it is the kind of over-reaction she always makes.

'I will go downstairs,' she thinks, closing her eyes. 'I will go downstairs and eat croissants with the other embroiderers.'

The green numbers on the radio clock say 9.28.

Sally has her bath, changes into her *embroidery expert* attire (a blouse with smocking detail, a long, flared skirt, hoop earrings), regrets her choice (*I look like bloody Gypsy Rose Lee*), picks up her yellow conference folder, her embroidery and her handbag and leaves the room. She stalks along the dimly-lit corridors, enters the lift, presses the button that says Press to Travel. She imagines the lift doors opening and herself emerging miraculously in Helsinki or the Dominican Republic.

'Good morning,' says the man with slicked-back hair at reception.

'Good morning.'

She gives him one of her smiles and makes her way to the Conference Suite, and the provision of breakfast.

But she has missed breakfast! She can hardly believe it: it is only nine forty-five but the embroiderers have descended upon the croissants and the cereal like the wolf on the fold. There are just baskets full of crumbs and smeared plates. Still, there may be time for coffee and a couple of biscuits, she is not too – but no, there go the waitresses, carrying away the coffee urns and the little biscuit trays. Sally's stomach rumbles sadly as she watches it all disappear through the swing doors. And now that feeling returns: that incomprehension as to why she is there. She continues towards the back of the conference room, which is beginning to fill now with Embroiderers' Guild people, amateur needleworkers and French historians. What a curious combination. The majority are women, but there are a few men in suits, dotted about like needles in a haystack. She notices Jeremy Bowes, entrancing a new woman by the water dispenser, and feels a sudden rush of panic.

Green canvas-backed chairs are lined up in rows in front of the speakers' desk. And there is her desk, with her name pinned to it. MS SALLY TUTTLE, SPEAKER. Oh Jesus, a *speaker*! With her nervy accent! Her nothing-to-say! Her exemplary bundle of threads! And there is the microphone, and the vase of flowers and the upended water glasses. It reminds her of end-of-term assemblies at St Hilary's, thirty years ago, with all its dull dignitaries behind the chrysanthemums, handing out prizes. She thinks of Miss Gordon, the deputy head. She wants to run.

'Hello!' says a young woman, approaching her. She has a sort of Alice band in her hair, and a wide, amiable face. A name-badge pinned to her jumper says AMBER. It seems that only the guest speakers are allowed surnames.

'Can I help you?' says Amber.

'I was just . . . I'm speaking later on. If I can summon up the –'

'Are you Sally Tuttle?'

'Yes, I –'

'Sally! Excellent! We were worrying that you might have got lost.'

'Yes, sorry I missed the registration. And the breakfast. I actually –'

'It doesn't matter. You're here now.'

'Yes, I –'

'Did you arrive late?'

'No, I –'

'Anyway, here's your name badge,' Amber says, locating a white laminated label on a bench and handing it to Sally. The pin pricks her finger. 'Ouch, ouch,' she says, automatically, the way she does when she is sewing with the girls in the shop.

'Oops. Sorry.' Amber pauses. 'Occupational hazard, isn't it? We're all Sleeping Beauties, aren't we?'

'I suppose we –'

'So. Come and meet some people.'

'Right,' Sally replies, wondering if it is Amber's mission in life to stick pins in people and interrupt.

'We were just having an interesting chat,' Amber says over her shoulder as she hurries forth, 'about sequins. I'm mad on sequins. How about you?'

Sally says 'Pretty much everything I do is covered in sequins.'

'Ha ha ha,' Amber says, as if she has made a tremendous joke. 'I can see we're going to be entertained this morning.'

That was not meant to be funny, Sally thinks. She looks out through the big shiny window of the hotel. The sky is immense, a huge, Scottish sky, a kind of luminous grey, with seagulls gliding around it. She thinks of her daughter in East Grinstead. She looks at the clock above the reception desk.

'So. This is Sally Tuttle,' Amber is telling a small group of Embroiderers' Guild women who have all stopped talking and are smiling at Sally: polite, mature, interested, expectant. They all look as if they have been embroidering for most of their lives. They probably all know the precise difference between a French knot and a four-legged knot. *And they expect me to say something wise!*

'Sally's a sequin fan,' says Amber.

But I'm not a professional, Sally wants to shout. *I just embroider because I like embroidering.*

And she is about to say something about sequins, something, anything, to stop them staring at her, when there is a sudden, abrupt, tap on her shoulder. *How rude!* She turns.

'Well hello there, Sally Tuttle!,' a woman booms. A middle-aged woman, glamorous in cashmere, her brown hair expensively styled and coloured. There is a scent emanating from her, a warm, rather wistful scent akin to Chanel No. 5. Instantly Sally recognises her – her eyes and her voice and her stance – but she cannot comprehend why.

'You don't remember me, do you?' the woman asks, delighted.

'I do,' Sally says, 'but I'm sorry, I can't quite –'

'Mary Button!' the woman beams. 'Although, of course, you used to know me as Miss Button. Actually, I'm not a Miss or a Button any more . . .' And now she is turning, smiling, at the little group of Embroiderers' Guild members, assuming her teacher's role.

'I was the famous Sally Tuttle's Needlework teacher,' she says.

Sally stands, transfixed. Miss Button.

'Hardly famous . . .' she begins, her heart blanching.

But Miss Button interrupts. 'I was wondering if you might be here actually, Sally. Having read about you in the papers.'

Sally feels herself blushing. She feels she might as well be standing there in her school uniform. The best part of three decades stretches and breaks, like a dividing cell.

Miss Button says, 'Sally used to be my star pupil.'

'Really?' someone replies.

'Yes. There was this sort of Damascene conversion, wasn't there, Sally? That winter. Do you remember? You'd been making a pig's breakfast of that blouse all autumn, and then you suddenly took off!'

'Hmm,' Sally replies, hot-faced, thinking of that blouson (*very easy / très facile*) and watching Miss Button's lipsticked mouth. *She is still pretty,* she is thinking. *Lines on her forehead and around her eyes now, of course, but still she has that neat nose and lipsticked mouth . . .*

Miss Button still favours shades of caramel: a caramel roll-neck sweater and a caramel checked skirt. And her clothes still seem to resist evidence of normal life: cat hairs, creases, small marks on the cuffs. Some people have that ability. There always *did* seem to be an impenetrable shield around her, protecting her from grottiness . . .

'. . . and of course I was only twenty-four myself at the time,' Miss Button is saying, 'and embroiled in this *terribly earnest* relationship with a quite inappropriate young copy-writer . . .'

And she pauses slightly, to glance at Sally. Sally looks back at her. Miss Button smiles. And Sally is aware of something, some intangible thing, some transgression made years ago – insubstantial, untouchable, like a fine fabric floating just out of reach.

'Oh yes, I was quite the floozy – isn't it funny how teenage girls always think their teachers are *desperately ancient* and respectable?' Miss Button beams. She holds Sally's gaze for a moment, infinitesimally pleased.

'And, anyway,' she continues, 'just as I was *really* beginning to despair that Sally would ever finish this *awful blouson* . . .'

Sally stands and listens, time suddenly truncated, like a folding telescope. A *'quite inappropriate young copy-writer.'* Miss Button's eyes are still a deep, treacherous brown.

'But those blousons I made you all sew!' she is saying now. 'Those blousons, Sally! Weren't they just awful?'

Sally opens her mouth but no word emerges. She thinks of that blouson (*very easy / très facile*), that ridiculous blouson of Rowena's at the foot of Colin Rafferty's bed.

Miss Button is standing very close. 'Do you know,' she half-whispers, 'I actually used to take some of them home with me in the evenings to unpick! When I first started at that awful school. I used to try and sort out the ones that had gone completely pear-shaped. Wasn't that self-sacrificing of me!'

The other embroiderers have gone quiet, watching Sally and Miss Button. They stand, clutching their bags and empty coffee cups.

'I used to macramé things,' one woman says eventually into the silence. 'I had all these macraméd owls . . .'

Sally thinks of her best friend Rowena Cresswell, twenty-eight years ago, sitting in the Me-n-U café with her mother and the new, pink, crying baby. And something pulls tight in her heart. Something pulls and hurts.

Wave

What would the collective noun be for embroiderers? A skein? A reel? A knot?

'A hassock?' suggests Kenneth.

The embroidery conference is gathering momentum. People in tasselled waistcoats, in knitted tops with too many bobbles, are putting together their presentation tables. People are appearing with rolls of canvas under their arms, wooden frames, baskets of cotton reels, tapestry sewing bags. Waitresses are bringing in jugs of orange juice and coffee flasks. And an earlier conference is departing, dismantling: something to do with plastics, something entitled *We Get There First.*

'Suits and hand-knits,' Kenneth observes from the doorway.

It is not unlike one of the Jollies we attend, apart from the style of clothing. The academics we usually mingle with favour fawn corduroys, Marks & Spencers' turtle-necks, suede shoes. Here, the plastics men are wearing pale grey suits. They are taking down huge, unstable-looking boards bearing logos and pictures of plastic tubing. They are winding up pieces of electrical cable. I look around at the arriving embroiderers, darting about like tailors' mice, in their bright colours.

Kenneth is paying our bill at the reception desk when who should stride past but Jeremy Bowes. And I almost applaud. I *knew* I would bump into him here, just as I always do, in cities all over the world. *Spotted you!* I knew it! I feel like a birdwatcher, jotting down another sighting in her notebook.

Jeremy has not noticed me. He is striding in a *noli me tangere* way towards the doors. He appears to be wearing the same bargello waistcoat I first saw him in all those years ago in the Musée de Cluny. He has aged but he is still wearing that waistcoat. And this makes me feel oddly fond of him. Maybe he is not the person he seems to be. Maybe he does not have wardrobes full of clothes. Or perhaps he is more nostalgic about old things than he might seem. I think of the number of times we have endured canapés and small talk over the years, in dingy university suites across Europe. He is, I suppose, one of my oldest acquaintances.

I step forward.

'Jeremy!' I exclaim. 'Hello!' And he stops, slightly alarmed. He looks blankly at me for a moment. Then he smiles.

'Rowena! How lovely to see you!'

'I noticed you were in town! I saw your name on the posters.'

'Ah, yes. The embroidery conference.'

'It looks interesting. We nearly saw some of it. What's it about?'

Jeremy does not look happy. He purses his lips and considers. 'Well,' he says, 'It's a glorified women's sewing circle really.'

My fondness for him erodes a little. 'Well,' I say. 'You've spent your life being adored by women. I'd have thought a women's sewing circle would be right up your street.'

Jeremy frowns. 'But my lecture is about courtly love,' he says.

'Surely love and sewing aren't mutually exclusive?'

'No, of course not. Far from it. It's just, it's not an academic conference. Not quite my usual environment.'

He looks white-faced and tired.

'Oh well,' Kenneth says, walking over from the reception desk. 'Can't win 'em all, Jeremy.'

Jeremy looks at Kenneth.

'Apparently not. I think this lot are more interested in the techniques of embroidery.'

'Well. The techniques of embroidery are important. There'd be nothing to talk about if nobody actually embroidered.'

'True,' Jeremy says. 'But there's this one woman,' he begins, frowning – but he seems to think better of it, and stops talking. Some kind of jockeying for position has gone on, I think, and he has lost, like a battle-weary knight.

'Well, I think it sounds interesting,' I say.

Jeremy looks wan.

'Are you going back to Paris afterwards?'

'Yes. I'll be at Charles de Gaulle by eight tonight. Hooray!'

And I have a vision of Jeremy in some apartment in the thirteenth arrondissement. I imagine he is the sort of man who lives an unexpectedly cluttered life, full of academic papers and divorce papers and books and shoes. Not enough people; too many journeys, pieces of fluff, small buttons, paper clips, collecting around the skirting boards of his home.

'Well,' I say. 'See you at the next event. Over the finger food.'

'No doubt. No doubt. Oh well, I'd better go and do this. Bye, Rowena. Bye Kenneth.' (*Sleep!* his face says. *A glass of warm milk and an early night!*) And he turns to face the collective noun of embroiderers.

Tête de Boeuf

The keynote speaker is a few minutes late but this is probably to be expected. Just as the volume of murmured conversations begins to rise he appears in the doorway, walks across the room and hops on to the small chipboard stage. There is a hush. People end their conversations and fold their programmes in their laps. Jeremy Bowes smiles a rather tight smile and snaps on the overhead projector. It makes a humming noise and projects a too-light image on to the wall behind him.

Medieval man offering medieval woman a rose.

Jeremy Bowes turns to his audience and begins. 'Medieval tapestries,' he states, and then he pauses.

'Works of elegance,' he continues. 'Works of fidelity. Works ... of love.'

He is one of those people who can speak in short, ungrammatical bursts and still sound impressive. His confidence is almost too much for Sally to bear. She can feel her palms begin to sweat.

Jeremy smiles down at his audience and his audience smiles up at him. 'Family tapestries,' he goes on, 'were symbols as much as things of practicality ...'

The woman sitting beside Sally fans her face with her programme. Sally feels as if she might be sick. Now a kind of singing has set up in her head. She looks up at the tapestry projected on to the screen – the lord offering his lady a rose – and it makes her think of all the mistakes she has made. All her assumptions, misconceptions, wrong conclusions. The next image – a scene from the Bayeux Tapestry – is not particularly comforting. It reminds her of the first time she saw it, in France, on canvas.

The audience peers up at poor Harold trying to pull the arrow out of his eye; at the casualties of war amongst the pretty flowers. Jeremy tells them there are over 626 human figures in the tapestry, 190 horses, 35 dogs, 506 other birds and animals, 33 buildings, 37 ships and 37 trees or groups of trees. Sally thinks of all the women who embroidered it, their hearts full of love and fear.

'The imagery in this particular scene . . .' Jeremy is saying, pointing out a piece of crewelwork with something that looks like a magician's wand. And quickly, Sally glances across at Miss Button. She is sitting diagonally across the aisle from her. She has sheer tights on. Her varnished-nailed hands rest elegantly in her lap.

Jeremy Bowes is now handing round courtly love printouts detailing points of interest. Sally looks down at her copy.

France, around 1340. Linen with gold silk embroidery.

This is an 'aumoniere' or alms bag. These were popular presents from lords to the ladies they courted, which explains why scenes of courtly love were the most common decorative motif. A young couple flirts here, while on the reverse a more mature couple are exchanging love tokens.

Oh, nothing has changed. Nearly seven hundred years later, people are still flirting and giving each other love tokens. People are still attempting to entrance with fashion: a scarf, a bag, a dress. It means no more than it ever has done.

Her pulse is thudding like a horse. She looks at her watch. It is ten thirty-eight. She wants to be anywhere but here. She wants to be with Pearl, with her mother, with Sue, with John. Her hands are cold and she thinks she really may be sick. But she can't run away now: it is too late. Jeremy Bowes is finishing with a last, professional flourish – some joke about the pretty tote bags carried by women at today's parties – and, oh God, he is walking off the stage. He is walking down the steps to the accompaniment of laughter and applause. And here she is, Sally Tuttle, getting to her feet! Here she is, standing up, an amateur in home-made clothes, a non-academic, about to give a talk on what she does in her spare time.

Jeremy Bowes looks a little flushed as Sally walks past. But he manages a small nod as they cross in the aisle. Sally cranks a kind of smile on her face. She can smell his aftershave, like an animal picking up the scent of fear. And she continues, continues towards the stage. She looks down at her feet as they move her along the rows. Plod, plod, plod. Here are the steps. Here is the microphone. Here is the overhead projector which she is not sure how to operate. Plod, plod, plod. And now she has gone into a different state. Suddenly there is nothing at all in her head. No fear, no words, no thoughts. Something has taken over. She moves across to the stand where Mary and Martha are waiting for her. They look as terrified as Sally. She opens her mouth.

'Well,' says a voice – and extraordinarily it is quite a clear voice, with comprehensible speech coming from it. 'When I first began to embroider I never thought I'd be standing here nearly three decades later . . .'

It doesn't even *sound* like her voice – it sounds like another woman's – *Needlewoman's voice!* – composed, measured. Needlewoman starts to talk about her reasons for embroidering: appalling marks at school in everything except Needlework (*ha ha ha*, responds the audience); time on her hands; a general lack of anything else to do. 'And,' says Needlewoman, 'now look at me! Look what it has led to! Fame! Riches! Awards!'

She feels as if she is in a hot air balloon rising gently skywards. There is a rustle of laughter and she looks down at people in the audience. She tries to focus. Women are smiling at her, acknowledging their own peculiar obsession for needle and thread. And Miss Button, sitting in the second row, is smiling at her too. She has a small, perky, sad smile on her face.

We have loved the same man, Sally thinks, as if she is observing some natural phenomenon. *Me and Miss Button. Once. Nearly thirty years ago. And it doesn't matter any more.*

Afterwards, she almost runs to the Ladies. She pushes open the heavy door, scuttles past the chrome paper-towel dispensers and the thoughtful display of winter greenery. All the cubicles are occupied. She stands by the wall, avoiding her reflection in the mirror. She stares instead at an advert for hosiery. *If you've got the legs we've got the tights.* After a while there is the noise of a bolt being pushed back and – *Oh, fantastic!* – Nora Wheeler emerges from one of the cubicles.

'Hi,' Sally says.

'Hi.'

There is hardly any room for them to manoeuvre around each other. *I will have to say something.*

'Were you at Jeremy's talk? I didn't –'

'No. No. I didn't make it I'm afraid.'

Nora smiles and tucks her handbag tighter beneath her arm. She is wearing her fabricky suit again. The fabric is noticeable before the cut: the old-fashioned, flecky tweed. And above it, her face is teenager pink. Her eyes are a little bloodshot. Her mascara is blobby and spiderish on the tips of her lashes.

'Are you OK?' Sally asks.

'Oh, fine. Just got contact lens problems.'

'Oh.'

'I missed *your* talk too, I'm afraid.'

'Did you? Oh, well. I didn't really know what I was saying anyway,' Sally replies, her words coming out now in a big, unprofessional rush. 'It all seemed to go so fast and there I was going on about stranded cottons and I just –'

'Oh no, I'm sure people were really interested.'

'Right. Well.'

And Sally makes her way into the nearest cubicle, closes the door and hovers over the toilet. She gazes at a small, framed sunset advertising weekend breaks for the over-fifties and listens to the whoosh of the electric hand-dryer outside.

After a short silence she rearranges herself and unlocks the door. She wants very much to be alone. But Nora is *still there*. Damn it. She is standing at the basins now, motionless, as if she is playing Statues. Sally smiles vaguely, steps forward and stands beside her, glancing cautiously at her reflection in the mirror. She doesn't want to look too closely. But she can't help having a quick glance. She sees a whitish blur, her hair untidy, her eyes ringed by dark circles.

'Oh dear,' she says, out loud. She leans her handbag against the counter to take out her hairbrush. Beside her, Nora is attempting to turn on the tap, first pressing it then trying to twist it. Nothing happens.

'I think it's one of those automatic ones,' Sally says. 'I think it's got one of those –'

'Oh yes,' Nora replies waving her hands in front of the tap. 'So,' she says. 'Have you got much more to do of Martha and Mary?'

'Mainly the sequins, I suppose.'

'Mmm. I love sequins. The sparkle.'

'Me too. I . . .'

But something curious is happening. Sally watches as Nora Wheeler's mouth suddenly twists and a sob emerges from it. She puts her wet hands up to her eyes.

Sally stands at the basin, the water running over her hands. She doesn't know what to do.

'Sorry,' Nora says. 'Sorry. How embarrassing.'

The tap stops running. And Nora bends to look for something in her handbag. Sally watches her pull out a packet of Handy Andies.

I should say something, she thinks. *I should do something.*

But she is no good at comforting. She has never been sure if other people want to be touched.

'Can you tell me about it?' she asks eventually, like Mrs Bonniface, her old counsellor.

'You must think I'm insane,' Nora replies. 'I'm forty-seven, for God's sake. It's just Jeremy, you know . . . How stupid of me! I thought we were getting on so well, and he cut me absolutely dead at breakfast this morning. Didn't want to know. It's just so . . .'

And Sally thinks of Jeremy Bowes, with his charm and his lovely eyes and his shoes and his anecdote about the horse.

'Well, you know . . .' she begins, and Nora looks at her hopefully, as if she is about to say something very wise about men.

'Some men . . .' she says slowly.

Nora sniffs.

' . . . should not be taken too seriously.'

'Yes, well, I know that,' Nora snaps.

'They will always,' Sally continues, 'take themselves seriously. So we shouldn't have to bother. It is ultimately,' she adds, 'a big waste of time.'

Nora looks disappointed. She sighs and looks close to crying again. She says, 'I suppose I thought he was different.'

'That's a common mistake,' Sally replies, glancing up at a sign above the basin that reads 'Now Please Wash Your Hands'.

'Some of them are very nice of course,' she says, 'but some of them aren't. The same,' she adds hurriedly, 'could be said about women.'

And she pulls a paper towel from the dispenser, dries her hands and dabs her eyes, realising that there are tears in them too. Then, before leaving, she *does* put her arms around Nora Wheeler and gives her a hug. You never know when a hug might be helpful. Or when something – anything – might be the right thing to say.

*

When she gets back to her room she folds Mary and Martha up and puts them gently in their carrier. She takes off her presentation clothes and packs them away too: her blouse and her skirt, her over-heavy earrings. She pulls on her trousers and shirt and coat and sits on the bed to wait until it is time to leave. She has just under half an hour. There is nowhere to visit in this time, nothing to do.

She opens her bedside cabinet and takes out an inevitable small maroon Bible. She turns to Luke – to a passage she already knows and has always struggled to understand. Her comprehension always falls slightly short.

'*. . . Martha, Martha, thou art careful and troubled about many things: but one thing is needful: and Mary hath chosen that good part, which shall not be taken away from her.*'

What is *that good part*? She has never understood that. Ignoramus. She fails to comprehend again, and puts the Bible back in the cabinet.

Now she sees that she has overlooked something. She has forgotten to pack her little box of sequins. It is sitting forlornly on the window sill where she left it the night before. She goes to pick it up and is just putting it into her coat pocket when there is a loud knock at the door. It makes her jump. She wonders if it is Nora Wheeler, come to say goodbye. Or, God, could it be Miss Button? Miss Button, come to talk about old times?

She edges around the end of her candlewicked bed to open the door.

There is a short man holding a large bunch of flowers. 'Miss Tuttle?'

'Yes?'

And he pushes the flowers towards her. 'Oh,' says Sally. She reaches out to take them, as if she does this every week: receives bouquets, like an opera singer. The flowers are predominantly yellow and white – gerbera, chrysanthemums, marguerites, punctuated by skeins of greenery. And a balloon! There is a balloon – a silver one, bobbing theatrically and bearing the words *Well Done.*

'How . . . lovely,' Sally says to the man. She feels she should sound more jubilant. She has never in her life received a congratulatory helium balloon. And unfortunately, now she has, she does not feel she deserves it.

'There could be a card somewhere, like,' the man says.

'Thanks.'

'Enjoy them, like,' the man says, walking away and beginning to whistle.

She shuts the door and looks at the flowers. They have a slight scent – a kind of mild, jungly fragrance. Attached to the cellophane is a little cream-coloured envelope. She thinks of John, who once presented her with a bunch of hand-picked daffodils stolen from Wandsworth Common. And she thinks of Pearl, who used to run in from their tiny garden with flowers from the lawn – buttercups, daisies, chickweed – for her to put in an egg-cup filled with water.

But the flowers are not from John or Pearl. There is a note that says: 'Congratulations, Big Shot! With love from the Needlepoint Sisters – xx'.

My friends. The balloon bobs like a speech bubble above her head.

Sitting on the bed again, she gets the phone out of her handbag, switches it on and dials directory enquiries.

A girl answers. 'Which town please?'

She holds the phone close to her ear and reaches for the courtesy notebook from the bedside table. She lowers her voice. 'East Grinstead,' she says. 'I'm looking for a Second Glance in East Grinstead.'

'A second glance?'

'It's a dress agency.'

'An estate agency?'

'No. A dress agency'

'A dress agency? What's that?'

'It's like an estate agent's, except it deals with dresses.'

There is a small silence at the other end of the line.

'I've got a Second Glance on the High Street, East Grinstead. Will that do? Shall I put you straight through?'

'Yes, that's the –'

There is already an automated voice telling her what the number is. She jots it down in the notebook, hesitates, then dials.

'Yes,' the agency woman in the polo-neck jumper informs her, 'yes, I was going to phone you later. Because we've just sold your dress. We sold it yesterday in fact. I thought it would go quickly, because it was a pretty dress. Such a pretty colour. Would you like me to send you a cheque or will you come in to collect it?'

'If you could send me a cheque,' Sally replies.

How easy, how easy it is, sometimes, to let things go. Material things. Bye bye, dress. She wonders what she will spend the money on. A pet-hair de-fluffer? A bra organiser? Or, no: something Rowena would have liked. It is the only way she can apologise.

Before phoning Pearl she sits for a few minutes beneath the bobbing balloon. It has a little sandbag tied to the end of its string, to weigh it down.

'So how did your talk thingy go?' Pearl asks.

'It went pretty well.' She leans against the bed's headboard and flicks over the hem of a pillowcase to examine the stitches: a habit formed years ago.

'So. It was funny,' she says, not wanting to broach the subject of the young man in the café. 'My old Needlework teacher was at the conference.'

'How bizarre.'

'Yeah. It was. It was . . .' She tries to think of the best word to describe their encounter. But thinking about its implications is a little terrifying.

' . . . revealing,' she says to Pearl. 'A blast from the past.'

'A what?'

'It was just quite strange.'

She doesn't know what on earth to say to Pearl about the young man in the café. Where would she start, without feeling hypocritical? She imagines her daughter standing in John's kitchen, fiddling with the little piles of domestic jetsam and flotsam that always end up there. Biros. Rubber bands. Bits of flux. Corners of envelopes with unfranked stamps. Maybe she is in love with this boy. Maybe everything she sees is altered because she is in love.

'Guess what?' Pearl says.

'What?'

'*Embroidery Times* came today.'

'Did it?'

'Guess what they've got in the "makes" section?'

'I can't imagine.'

'"Embroider your own cafetière cover."'

'No!'

'And,' Pearl adds, "Embroider a sleeping bag for your pet hamster."'

'You made that one up!'

'No I didn't!'

There is the sound of a door opening in the corridor outside, two voices speaking, a man's and a woman's. The rumble of a wheeled suitcase. Then the door closes again.

'Mum?'

'Yes?'

'You know that vase I broke?'

She thinks for a moment. 'Yes.'

'Well, it's OK. It's just, it was . . .'

Sally looks up at the balloon moving in the breeze from the open window.

'Sweetheart,' she says, 'It's not a disaster. People break things. Things can be mended. That's the beauty of inanimate objects.'

She clears her throat and feels motherish. She pictures herself progressing into her future – walking, wisely, motherishly, on to the plane.

'It's just, I broke your sewing machine too,' says Pearl.

'Oh.'

'It kind of fell off your table. I was looking for your pinking shears in those little drawers and it kind of –'

'My pinking shears?'

Still with the phone at her ear, Sally bends and attempts to pick up her portfolio and her handbag. She nudges her rucksack with her left foot. She looks at the flowers and the balloon. *Do they allow balloons on planes?*

'What did you want my pinking shears for?' she asks.

'To cut someone's hair.'

'Someone's hair? With pinking shears? Whose hair?'

'Liam's,' Pearl replies, almost inaudibly. 'You know, that guy you spoke to yesterday? He's kind of . . . I was going to tell you before but you went up to Scotland and everything . . .'

Sally gives up on the balloon and lets it rise in front of her again, tugging at its own weight.

'It was for a fancy dress party,' Pearl is saying. 'He went as a tetrahedron. I went as a circle. He's going to get it cut out. It's, like . . .'

Well done, says the balloon.

'Sweetheart, I've got to go now or I'll miss the plane,' Sally says. 'I'll have a look at the sewing machine when I get back. It's pretty resilient. And it doesn't really matter. It . . . You know, the main thing is . . .'

And she looks up at the balloon and wants to say something to her daughter about the young man. About being with people who make you happy. That is really all she wanted to say.

Into her head comes a picture of two girls, best friends, roaming around some basement shoe shop full of teenage footwear. Laughing, one of them picks up a tasselled platform boot.

Long and Short

The words on the badge Sally Tuttle once gave me were *so* tiny that you had to get really close to read them.

'*What are you staring at?*'

An example of irony.

I pinned it to my school scarf the day Sally gave it to me. Then I lost the scarf, with the badge on it, a few weeks later. And I always felt strangely guilty about it. It seemed a bigger thing to have lost than it was. Sometimes, in the later stages of my pregnancy, I thought about that scarf and that badge. I wished I could have pinned the badge to my jumper, right over the bump.

Sally used to stare at me too, then; I could sense her staring in disbelief across the playground. She appeared to have formed some alarmingly hostile opinion about me. Maybe she'd had some attack of morality. Or some strange kind of jealousy. Whatever, she no longer spoke to me. And I didn't know what to do. I didn't know how to tell her how it had happened. A teenage kiss that had progressed, altered, turned into something else. Very quick, very easy. It had not even been the romantic event I had been led to believe. But I had still ended up pregnant.

Pregnancy had been something Sally and I *joked about*. 'Never say *Ich bin satt* to a German person,' Sally once informed me after one of her swiftly abandoned German lessons. 'It doesn't mean I'm full, it means I'm pregnant!'

Our conversations had been like the ones in bubbles in *Jackie* magazines. (*'D'you think he loves me, Rowena? I'm not sure if he loves me . . .'*)

Neither of us had talked about the practicalities of love. We had not considered that love was bound up with practicalities.

Kenneth and I are late arriving at the airport and have to hurry to the check-in desk. We trot, pulling our suitcases behind us. We jog past other travellers, all looking tired and wide-eyed, as if they have just been jolted awake in the middle of the night. And we have nearly made it – there is the British Airways sign and the queue – when my ankle suddenly twists and I find I am falling, all my belongings clattering about me.

There is a tiny pause, a snag in the smooth fabric of our airport surroundings.

Kenneth says, 'What are you doing?'

'Well, I've just fallen over,' I retort. The floor tiles are hard and glittery. All around us there is the sound of trundling luggage and clicking shoes. People walking past stare; some even look back over their shoulders at this floored woman, who appears to have knocked over a yellow plastic cone which says 'Caution! Wet Surface! Trailing Cables!'

'You OK?'

'Oh yes. Absolutely. I'm absolutely fine.'

Kenneth gathers my things and hangs on to them. I pull myself up and hobble on. My ankle hurts quite a lot, actually. I imagine it swelling overnight, puffing up taut and pale.

'You're tired and emotional,' Kenneth says, offering his hand as we walk past the whisky boutique.

'I know I'm tired and emotional,' I snap. Something too big is taking up the space in my chest.

The queue is full of people with the *We Get There First* bags. Instantly I am annoyed. Who are these people who get there first? And *why* do they want to get there? What are they trying to prove with these canvas bags? With these suits? These enormous suitcases on wheels?

I think of asking Kenneth but he is looking absent now, crunching a fruit sherbet, and I don't bother him. I am, actually, very pleased to have Kenneth about. I don't know how I would have got through this without him. We are three people away from the front now and he is watching all the despondent-looking suitcases as they are labelled with orange tags, placed on to the rungs of the conveyor belt and parted from their owners.

'That one looks as if it belongs in an Inspector Clouseau film,' he says, indicating an overstuffed red-and-blue tartan hold-all. I don't reply. I'm thinking that even the brand new suitcases look over-hopeful.

When we get to the desk we ask for a window seat and a middle seat and watch our own blue and orange suitcases disappear miraculously through the theatrical little curtain. There they go. I can't help wondering if we are to be reunited at the other end.

Now we have to look for Gate 34. Kenneth picks up his briefcase and my shoulder-bag and reaches for my hand. 'Good,' he says.

'Yeah.'

He doesn't say 'Cheer up.' He doesn't find me a handkerchief. He knows when not to offer a handkerchief. And I love him for that. You don't love that in a man when you are young. But later you do.

It was something about the suitcases, I want to say. But I suppose, having grown-up daughters, he knows.

'OK?'

'Yes.'

'Shall we go then?'

'Yes.'

I allow myself to be lulled by the synthetic comforts of Edinburgh Airport: overheated WCs, fluffy toys, magazines, sock and scarf displays, all helping to alleviate the trauma of parting. A kind of anaesthetic of blandness: the mild scent of coffee, the pink liquid soap, the over-large choc-chip muffins.

We have half an hour to wait for the plane. We skulk around for a while, in the environs of Gate 34. In the magazine shop we buy a copy of the *Guardian* and a copy of *Le Monde*, then go across to Costa Coffee and order two cappuccinos.

'To go?' the girl enquires.

'Well, I suppose so,' Kenneth says, looking at his watch. An aeroplane's engines roar above our heads, and I wonder whether Jeremy Bowes is in it. 'Seeing as we're not staying,' says Kenneth to the girl.

The girl takes a marker pen and writes something on to a large polystyrene beaker. Kenneth clears his throat.

'We *are* going to sit down though,' he says. 'Briefly.'

'Not to go, then.' The girl sighs tetchily. 'To sit in.' And she crosses out what she wrote on the polystyrene beaker.

We don't really sit in, there being no 'in'. We sit up, our legs dangling from the high, uncomfortable silver stools.

A few feet away from me a young mother is attempting to feed her baby. She is sitting on one of the preposterously elevated stools, struggling to get him into the right position. And I remember that too: how difficult it was, fumbling with the bra strap, with the swollen, over-large nipple and the too-small baby-mouth. How were you supposed to hold your baby and keep him there? There had been nobody to show me what to do. This was in the privacy of my own bedroom, my discarded Cindy dolls staring crossly down at me from the top of the wardrobe. *You can breastfeed your baby anywhere: nobody need know!* commented the helpful baby books. The 1980s were so enlightened! But I never fed my baby in public.

The cappuccino is strong and rather bitter. I dunk my courtesy ginger biscuit into it and add a spoonful of sugar. Kenneth opens the *Guardian* and begins to read. Lives falling apart, lives reconnected.

Beside us a woman is addressing her husband. 'I told her I've got pastry hands,' she is saying, taking a sip of tea, the label hanging down the side of her cup, 'because they're cold, see?'

She pauses, and then reaches forwards and puts one of her hands on top of his.

'I know you've got cold hands, Sheila,' her husband sighs.

His wife gazes out through the big window.

'I told her I've always had pastry hands,' she says, 'and Rita's got bread hands.'

Kenneth sits and smiles at me, imagining, I suppose, a woman with ten bread rolls for fingers.

I stir my coffee.

'Warm hands, cold heart,' the woman says.

When our flight number appears I spring to my feet. Kenneth continues to sit, not seeing the need to hurry. There *is* no need, but I still do. Most people do.

'The plane's not going to go without us,' says Kenneth.

'Yes, I know that,' I reply, picking up all my possessions. I seem to have accrued a lot more, even in the departure lounge. A bagful of newspapers and books. A packet of Simmers biscuits. Then there is my coat, my cardigan, my handbag.

Getting up a few seats away is a woman about my age who appears to have even more stuff than me. Impossible amounts of stuff. Propped against the side of her chair is a large black portfolio, and she stoops to pick it up. She is also carrying a plastic bag, a handbag with an inordinate number of buckles and straps, and a small rucksack. Swung across her left arm is her coat, a bright green thing – green as a privet hedge. And tucked beneath her right arm is a large, slightly battered-looking bunch of flowers. Gerbera, chrysanthemums, marguerites, more greenery. I wonder if the flowers were given to her by a lover or a husband. I wonder if her portfolio denotes that she was an embroiderer at the conference. A needlewoman of some kind, anyway. Or a designer, perhaps. Or a painter. And I feel obscurely jealous of her – of her artistic career, her brightness, her style. Maybe she has made more sensible choices in her life.

Now there is an altercation at Gate 34. A man with a *We Get There First* bag has lost his boarding pass. He raises his voice. An airport employee responds with a raised voice. I can't hear the actual words.

Out of the corner of my eye I continue to spy on the woman with the portfolio. She is standing there in a slight dream, edging slowly forwards in the queue to Gate 34. With her flowers and her green coat and her silver-stranded hair she looks like a middle-aged water nymph.

As passengers begin to disappear through the departure gate, Kenneth finally gets up from the uncomfortable, metal-legged banquette. He walks over to me, smiles and looks at his watch. 'How's the ankle?'

'Swelling up nicely. It'll probably swell up even more on the plane.'

'Well,' he says. 'We'll be back in time for supper. Supper and a nice warm bath.'

'Hmm.'

Why, I am thinking, *am I drawn to this over-burdened woman?*

'Home in time to phone Joe.'

'Mm-hmm.'

I am still watching her as she nears the gate. She says 'Oops, sorry' to an elderly man she has just whacked in the ribs with her portfolio. Then she makes a little movement: she tucks her flowers higher beneath her arm and twists slightly to reach into her pocket for her boarding pass – and it is the way she moves, leaning her portfolio against her leg, it is the way she knocks something from her pocket on to the floor – a small, rattling, transparent box – that makes my heart jump.

I know who she is.

I know who she is.

And I don't know what to say.

I put my hand on Kenneth's arm. 'Shush,' I say.

'What?' he replies, 'I didn't say anything.'

'Shush.'

'What do you mean? What's the matter?'

I look at her again – at the woman with the flowers who is scattering sequins all over the floor now, the lid having flown off the box, causing a tinselly, iridescent clatter of gold and silver and ruby and turquoise against the airport's floor tiles.

'Oh God, sorry,' I hear her say to the fixed-face gate attendant.

'Can you stand to one side please?' the attendant says. 'To let others past.'

'Yes, sorry, I . . .'

'I'm surprised those things didn't show up in the X-ray machines.'

'Yes, but they're not metal,' the woman says, looking up from her hunt. 'They look metal but they're actually . . .'

And she is hardly any different from the way she was when I knew her. She really isn't. Even the way she pronounces 'metal' and the expression she has on her face. Serious. A little cross. It was never intentional, but there it still is. And the same flopping hair. And that billow of determination around her: something close to a cloud or a shadow.

I don't know where to look. So I stare through the window. A man walks along the edge of a runway holding two round red boards which look like table-tennis racquets. A white plane rumbles past before heaving itself miraculously up into the air. And all the people at Departure Gate 34 look up at the aeroplane, and tut.

I turn my gaze back to the woman with the flowers and the scattered sequins. She has scooped up about half of them now and is looking around, a little pink-faced, at the irritated crowds.

I push my coat and bag into Kenneth's arms and walk forwards a few paces.

'This kind of thing always happens in the *worst possible place*,' Sally whispers to me.

'I know,' I say, as I kneel to help her.

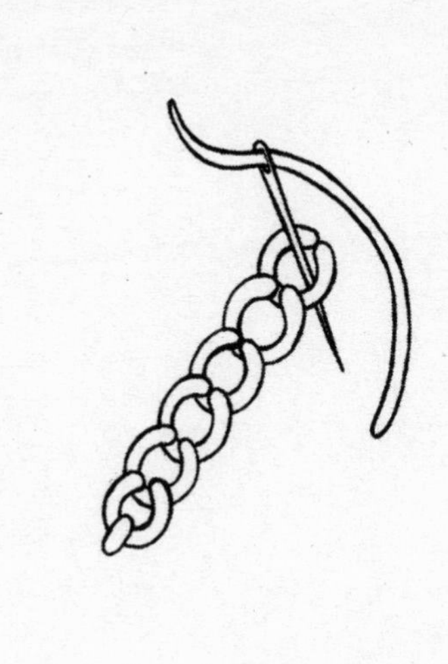

Renaissance

She has the house to herself all morning and stays indoors. It is January, the sky as white and cold as Egyptian cotton. She is wearing three layers including a thermolactyl vest and her Aztec slipper-socks.

Her mother phones at nine to ask her to pick up some dry-cleaning, an eiderdown and their living-room curtains – the ones she made for them, with the pelmet and the swags.

Sue phones to arrange a meeting in Starbucks. They will eat Granola bars and drink too much coffee.

Her bank phones to ask if she wants to change her account to something called a Gold Reward. She thinks of gold bars in suit-cases, nuggets, bullion. Her bank is very pleased with her.

The Reverends Avery, Hope and Beanie are not, unfortunately. She *knew* it. She knew, as soon as she mentioned the vibrant animals all those weeks ago, that they were rattled.

It seems that Mary and Martha are not, after all, quite what they had been looking for. A little too cartoonish, the Reverend Avery's voice had suggested soothingly over her mobile phone. The concern, the Reverend Avery said, is that they may appear a little too, well, comical. Almost irreverent. Because the story of Mary and Martha is, in fact, quite serious. It makes a serious point about people's place in society. And about Jesus. And we do not wish to offend.

'You knew what my work was like,' Sally replied stonily. 'I thought that's why you commissioned me. You wanted some-thing naive.'

'Yes, yes, it's just in this particular instance . . . Martha in particular looks quite . . . cross-eyed. It was not quite what we had in mind.'

She never trusted him. Even before she met him, there had been something about that little sign in the lobby: 'Please D'ont Leave Your Cups Here'. There had just been something about it.

'I can unpick it if you like,' she said, 'and start again.'

'Oh no no no no,' the Reverend Avery said, startled. 'We like it, we like it. We really do. It's just . . . We just thought, perhaps next time a different subject matter? It is charming, absolutely. The colours . . . We just thought perhaps you might like to use a less – a more – a better-known story next time. With Jesus in it. We thought perhaps Jesus feeding the Five Thousand.'

Sally considered for a moment. She imagined embroidering five thousand fish and loaves of bread.

'Well,' the Reverend Avery said, 'why don't I give you a few days to think about it? The offer's there. Just something a little more . . . accessible. We like your work very much indeed.'

'Just not so many sequins or funny faces.'

There was a small intake of breath, and in the background, the sound of a barking dog.

'Absolutely,' said the Reverend Avery.

(' . . . *and Mary hath chosen that good part, which shall not be taken away from her . . .*')

'OK. I'll think about it.'

And Sally Tuttle, Needlewoman, put down the phone.

She spends some time tidying her workroom, rearranging the embroidery silks in her little chest of drawers. She lines them up in subtly shifting colours. Yellow, ochre, tawny, orange, red. Indigo, midnight, navy, air force. Having finished Mary and Martha she doesn't have enough to occupy her hands. She misses embroidering them, and her hands seem to shake a lot.

She wonders if there is something wrong with them. Sticking stray needles back into her needle case, she keeps pricking her fingers. She should have started her new commission by now – a big picture of Amber's cat lying in a washing basket (taken from a photo). This is her career now and she has to be pragmatic: she has to not bite the hand that feeds her.

When her alarm clock goes off at eleven, she jumps.

Time to go into the kitchen.

She has decided to make a quiche for lunch. It is in memory of a cookery lesson they had once, when the contents of Rowena's quiche had risen up like something Biblical and leaked through the bottom of the oven door.

'Look at Rowena's oven!' somebody exclaimed, and they had all stood and watched this yellow, milky puddle creeping slowly across the linoleum. It was extraordinary. Miss Andrews, jowelly and aghast, said she had never seen anything like it. 'And I have seen some disasters in my time,' pronounced Miss Andrews.

Her own quiche had actually turned out quite well, she recalls: the pastry light, the filling golden and symmetrically decorated with bacon strips. She had been planning to take it home on the bus, to eat with her parents that evening. But, walking with it to the display table at the end of the lesson, she had tripped and neatly upended it into the bin. Flip: there it goes! It happened so deftly that it seemed right. A sacrificial quiche. But what a waste of ingredients! The exact opposite of what was meant by Home Economics. It was the only time she ever heard Miss Andrews swear.

The bell rings ten minutes later than arranged and she is in such a state of nerves that she almost mentions the quiche incident as soon as she has opened the door.

'Hello,' Rowena says. She is alarmingly composed. Glamorous, her hair expensively cut. She has on smart leather gloves and a beautifully sweeping woollen coat.

'Hello,' says Sally. She has changed out of her slipper-socks and put on a nicer top. But still. *Plus ça change*. She is still hard-up and living in East Grinstead. She is still too tall and awkward, the words still spin garishly out of her mouth. She glances down and sees that she has left three needles pinned to her jumper, high, near her right shoulder. One of them has a piece of silver thread attached to it. She notices Rowena looking at it too. She nearly says 'the ties that bind', but then she doesn't.

'Well,' she says, standing aside to let Rowena in. And then they kiss – Sally veering to the wrong side – and in she comes, on a trail of perfume.

'I'm in the kitchen,' Sally says.

'No you're not, you're in the hall,' replies Rowena.

'Ha.'

And now she can't think what to say at all. She doesn't know what Rowena expects, after all these years. She just feels terribly domestic, a pastry-baking needlewoman, particularly skilled at blowing her chances. Terribly awkward and Big Birdish and ashamed. And here is this old acquaintance of hers, this professional person, this translator, this jet-setter who has turned up at her house for an hour or so. It is not going to work. They have pulled apart, the distance between them stretching like worn elastic. Rowena has a mature Canadian husband; Sally has an ex-boyfriend who lives in Chingford. Rowena has a designer coat; Sally takes up hems for a living. She thinks of how long she held on to that dress she gave her. She betrayed her. And she feels the sadness of decades.

'Well,' she says, leading her from the hall into the small, condensation-filled kitchen. Her spider plants hang like sinister pets from her hand-made pot-holders. Her elephant picture looks childish. Her camel place-mats just look weird.

Rowena smiles.

'Did you do that?' she asks, pointing to the embroidery of Mary and Martha which Sally has hung loomingly, a redundant thing, over the cooker. Martha really is cross-eyed, now she comes to look at her. She can see what the Reverend Avery means.

'Those sequins must have taken you for ever!' Rowena exclaims.

'They did.'

Rowena regards the picture. 'Well, wow,' she says, and is quiet for a moment. 'And did you do that one?' she asks, indicating the sunflower. 'And the peacock? And the owl?'

'I did all of them.'

'Wow. You're prolific.'

She peers more closely at the peacock, at the big sequins in its tail. 'Where do you get your ideas from?'

'I don't know. They just occur to me.'

'But you never used to like Needlework, Sally,' Rowena says. 'You were never even any good at it.'

'Something happened. I just became . . . I just turned into Needlewoman.'

They smile at each other, words refusing to leave their mouths. *Oh God, she has changed. She is polite, urbane, normal. She doesn't know me any more.* And it occurs to her that they really should have said goodbye at the airport. So long, Sally! So long, Rowena! They should have left them behind, those girls of 1979 – they are still there somewhere, she supposes – they should have left them to their records and their fashions and their conversations about words and God and hairstyles. But this thought panics her too, almost as much as the reality of Rowena standing there, in her kitchen.

'So. Have a seat,' Sally says, pulling out a chair with an embroidered cushion on it, and Rowena says thanks and sits down.

Forty-three-year-old Rowena Cresswell. She has lines around her eyes, and strands of silver in her hair.

'Just going to wash the salad,' Sally mumbles, turning to the sink, 'and then we can eat.'

She wonders how long Rowena will stay. She thinks of her dates with Graham the estate agent. At least with Graham she knew she had nothing to lose.

At the taps she makes a big fuss with the salad spinner, turning it round so quickly that if she let it go it would spin like a flying saucer across the room. She is aware of Rowena's calm presence at the table behind her.

'I like your kitchen,' Rowena says. It is something anyone would say.

'Thanks.'

Sally shakes the lettuce leaves – over-priced rocket and cos – into her best wooden salad bowl, pours on oil and vinegar and takes it to the table.

'So,' Rowena says. 'Are your parents well?'

'Oh yes, both fine really. Both enjoying their garden.'

Some expression close to sadness moves across Rowena's face. 'I liked your mum and dad,' she says.

'Yes, well. They, you know . . . Nothing's . . .'

'And how's your daughter? What's she up to today?'

She has removed her coat now – something Sally forgot to suggest when she arrived – and is sitting there wearing a silk blouse. Blue, with a small floral pattern.

'Pearl?' Sally replies airily. 'Oh, she's meeting her new man.'

The thought of Pearl roaming around the hinterland of East Grinstead with an adolescent called Liam Cruikshank does nothing to calm her. She turns the salad leaves about with the overlarge wooden servers. They make an un-salad-like clonking noise. Rowena regards the spoons, and Sally finds herself blushing. *Say something, say something.*

'Do you remember –' she begins.

'That bloke you were in love with?'

She can feel the blush increasing. 'Well, no, I wasn't going to . . .'

Rowena leans back in her chair and smiles. 'The thing I remember most about Colin Rafferty,' she says, 'is that time you went to London and recited poetry at him.'

'Do you? Do you? I'd forgotten all about that. I don't remember even telling you that.'

Rowena looks at her. 'Well,' she says, 'you did. *I wonder, by my troth, what thou and I did till we loved? Were we not weaned till then . . .*'

'I'd forgotten.'

'Anyway. I always thought it was very sweet.'

Her heart is thumping. *Here is Rowena, here is Rowena Cresswell, in my house!*

'Right,' she says, moving away from the table. 'Anyway. He wasn't the romantic proposition I imagined.'

'No.'

And remembering what Colin once said to her about embroidering cushion covers, Sally flits domestically about. Maybe that *is* all she is good for. Domesticity. She thinks of what Rowena has told her since they met. The countries she has visited, the things she has done. The boy she slept with in 1979.

Lifting the quiche from the sideboard, she slides it on to a dish and nudges it straight with the edge of her thumb. She turns back to the table and places it on to one of her embroidered place mats, the one with poppies (burden stitch) and dandelions (half chevron). Then she picks up a serving knife and starts to cut into it. But the pastry is stubborn, tougher than she had hoped. It looks like baked earth. The slice finally breaks into two, the knife slipping and clanking against the dish.

‘Oh,’ she says, and she wants to cry. ‘Well, anyway. Help yourself to salad.’

And she hands Rowena the enormous salad servers.

‘Thank you,’ Rowena says. She looks at her plate and the place mat beneath it. She glances up at her, as if waiting for some social nicety that Sally is unaware of.

‘Pastry was never my forte . . .’ Sally begins.

But Rowena does not reply. She picks up her fork and smiles, a little wistfully, her glance sliding from her plate to Sally’s face, to the embroidery on the wall. Then she looks back at her plate and the salad upon it. She puts her fork down. She looks at Sally again. And she laughs. It is a laugh Sally has not heard for twenty-eight years.

‘What?’ Sally says. ‘What is it?’

‘Those women, Sally, those women! Look at their faces! God, they’ve been through the mill, haven’t they?’

Sally looks up at Martha and Mary and then sits down. She thinks of that song they used to sing: ‘I am a wee weaver confined to my loom . . .’

‘Who are they meant to be?’ Rowena asks.

‘They’re just two women.’

‘Just two women? Honestly, Sal! Do you think you could embroider *me* two women like that?’

Sally picks up her napkin and places it on her lap.

‘I could,’ she says.

Stranded cotton has been used for this embroidery in the following colours:
0213, 0214, 0215, 0216, 0217, 0968, 0337, 0881, 08, 09 and 010.

Acknowledgements

Thank you to the Scottish Arts Council for a bursary which helped me begin this novel.

I owe a great deal of thanks to my husband Mike Norman for his support, technical and emotional, over the years, and to my parents Liz and Eric Thomas for their encouragement always; also to many friends for keeping me cheerful, in particular Jennie Renton, Cherise Saywell, Elizabeth Ezra, Sonja Henrici, Margaret Burnett, Kirsteen Davidson-Kelly, Anne Hay, Jane McKie, Steve Renals and Jane Rourke, Alice Taylor, the 'Clambers Mothers' and my sister Ann Jones. The support and insight of Hannah Griffiths and the rest of the team at Faber and Deborah Rogers and Hannah Westland at Rogers, Coleridge and White have been wonderful, as has the encouragement of Halla Beloff, Shena Mackay, Cynthia Rogerson, Marion Sinclair, Sue Wilson, David Jackson Young and the Digger's Writers. I would like to thank the memory of the late Sandie Craigie, a wonderful writer and friend.

Thank you to the Coats Sewing Group and David & Charles, publishers of *The Anchor Books of Embroidery Stitches*; to Sharon B's *Dictionary of Stitches for Embroidery*; to www.bayeux-tapestry.org; and to Alain Erlande-Brandenburg, editor of the guide to the Musée Nationale du Moyen Age, Thermes de Cluny (Paris). Thanks again to Elizabeth Ezra for the French translations, and to Lucie Ewin for the proofreading.

All my love to M.G.N., C.M.N., G.B.N. and A.W.N.